Edward Hogan was born in Derby in 1980 and now lives in Brighton. He is a graduate of the MA creative writing course at UEA and a recipient of the David Higham Award. *Blackmoor* is his first novel.

'A debut novel of ambitious substance and style . . . charged with a bite and passion harking back to his Northern forebears: DH Lawrence, most obviously, with a passing touch, perhaps, of Charlotte Brontë . . . Hogan is clearly a writer to watch'
Independent

'Outstanding . . . Hogan's writing is so forceful that the extraordinary elements of his plot are made utterly convincing, and more mundane aspects sparkle under his acute observation . . . In this powerful and sensitive novel, twenty-eight-year-old Hogan has achieved a striking debut'
Times Literary Supplement

'While the delivery is graceful, the sense of understated, growing menace is what really holds this book together . . . As everything else crumbles, the elements of [Vincent's] teenage world start to slot into place, bringing warmth to an already deeply felt novel'
New Statesman

'There's a subtle magic to Hogan's prose, and a passionate concern for the part of the world where this novel is based, which invites comparison with D H Lawrence . . . [This novel] has confidence, mystery and an entrancing sense of itself'
Independent on Sunday

D0302155

'[A] memorable debut novel . . . Blackmoor becomes a haunting study of losses which, like the firedamp accumulating in the pits, still threaten the lives of those who seem to have survived them'
Sunday Times

'The novel seeps into your mind . . . It's hard to shake'
Nottingham Evening Post

'It's a long time since I've read such a powerful and confident first novel. Edward Hogan's voice is utterly distinctive: strong, emotive, haunting. His powers of observation seem almost supernatural . . . A major new talent'
Hilary Mantel

'Dead smart and heartbreaking . . . Offbeat and incredibly compelling. I love the way Edward Hogan writes'
Miriam Toews, author of *A Complicated Kindness*

blackmoor
edward hogan

**POCKET
BOOKS**

LONDON • SYDNEY • NEW YORK • TORONTO

First published in Great Britain by Simon & Schuster UK Ltd, 2008
This edition published by Pocket Books UK, 2009
An imprint of Simon & Schuster UK Ltd
A CBS COMPANY

3 5 7 9 10 8 6 4

Simon & Schuster UK Ltd
1st Floor
222 Gray's Inn Road
London WC1X 8HB

www.simonandschuster.co.uk

Simon & Schuster Australia
Sydney

A CIP catalogue record for this book
is available from the British Library

ISBN 978-1-84739-126-1

Typeset in Palatino by M Rules
Printed by CPI Cox & Wyman, Reading, Berkshire RG1 8EX

To Ma.

ACKNOWLEDGEMENTS

I would like to thank my mother, Julie Redfern, for her endless help and love. She's a great reader and an inspiring person.

Thanks also to Big Eddie Hogan for his touchline support in all things Little Eddie; thanks to brilliant Blake too.

This book has led me to meet some great folk:
Sarah Flax, a fantastic friend, who gave me sharp daily readings, a room, and larks. Daniel Jeffreys offered many excellent suggestions and generous friendship. Thanks to my mate Emma Sweeney, for another address.

Veronique Baxter was in it from the start – she is a tenacious and astute agent, and a good friend. Rochelle Venables did a wonderful job editing the book. I've enjoyed working and boozing with both of them.

David Higham Associates gave me a lovely award, which got me out of strimming gardens – thank you DHA. Thanks to all at Simon & Schuster.

blackmoor

ONE

Church Eaton, April 2003.

George Cartwright's Ford Mondeo cuts through the pleasant Derbyshire village of Church Eaton, far away from Blackmoor. George drives aggressively. His son, Vincent, sits in the back, holding the seat belt away from his body because the sun-cooked nylon burns his bare teenage chest. Vincent watches his father's short brown hair stiffly lifted by the warm breeze coming through the open window. This one-week spring heatwave will bring out bumblebees and daffodils just to drown them with sudden showers.

George curses. Up ahead, a group of cyclists hog the road like wasps in the neck of a bottle. Their bright jerseys look melted to their bodies. 'Two abreast,' George says under his breath. After several attempts, he makes his pass and leans out of the window. 'You're supposed to be two abreast, not bloody four,' he shouts.

One of the cyclists thumps the boot as they go by. Vincent yelps and George nearly swerves off the road. 'Townie bastards,' he says, and puts his foot down. As they drive the half-mile to the Anchor pub, Vincent listens to his father justify what he is about to do. 'There are rules, okay? So everyone can get by. When you're on your bike, it's two abreast, not four. Do you see? Do you see how that helps people?'

'Yep,' says Vincent.

They pull into the pub car park. George winds up the window, gets out, locks the car, and crouches behind the dwarf wall by the entrance. He looks down the road, waiting. Vincent watches him, the lines of the rear-window heater in shadow on the boy's face. After a few moments, George jumps over the wall and throws himself into a blur of colour. His punch seems to knock the cyclist clean into existence. The injured man is suddenly there, crawling on the pavement. He keeps bending his knee in an attempt to stand, a cruel parody of his cycling action. His mouth is bleeding, and his bike lies upside down, squeaking as the buckled rim catches the brake pad.

Vincent frowns and licks the salty residue forming on his dry lips. His father returns to the car, gets in and starts the engine. One of the other cyclists runs after them as they pull away. Vincent thinks he looks strange without his bike, in his redundant helmet and padded shorts. The man swears at them but George just smiles. 'Two abreast,' he says. 'So folk can get by.'

If they were to hear of such an event, the few Church Eaton residents who know George Cartwright would say that the cyclist episode is perfectly characteristic of his behaviour. Mrs Rogers on

Vicarage Road would refer to the time when George clipped one of her decorative garden rocks with his car and then proceeded to hurl the stone down the street. He used bad language in front of the children. Even Vincent would agree that aggression is his father's dominant trait, for he never knew the Blackmoor George, and a lot has happened since those days.

In fact, not too many people hear of George's attack on the cyclist. Unlike Blackmoor, Church Eaton is not a place for rumours. For better or worse, people are not so interested in each other's business.

George and Vincent have lived in Church Eaton for a long time now, in a house built into a hill. It seems like a bungalow from the front, the bottom floor revealing itself as the land drops away behind. George bought the house because of this unusual design. Most of the windows, even on the top floor, open on to the ground. That is how he likes it. The place is furnished with a magpie mix of cut-price flat-packed chairs and expensive pine wardrobes, an ugly leather sofa in the living room; everything bought as required, for convenience.

Vincent cannot remember living anywhere else. At thirteen, he is growing rapidly in an awkward, lanky way. His hair is curling – blond, but not that blond. He does not have the antisocial paleness of his mother. His face is breaking out in spots and his upper back is already covered. Father and son sleep in the same room on the bottom floor because the upstairs bedroom opens on to a drop. Vincent does not find this strange, for it has always been this way.

The slugs arrive with the spring rain. The damp from winter temporarily revisits the lower floor of the Cartwright house and the slick creatures quickly seek out these dark continents. Vincent is fascinated by them, especially their ability to appear so suddenly, while seeming so slow. He measures how long it takes a slug to move eight centimetres along his shatterproof ruler (on which the other kids have scratched 'Birdman is a twat'), and then calculates the time it would take one to get to his room from any conceivable opening. He estimates a journey time of eighteen hours from the front door, yet one night he waits up until 3 a.m. and there is not even one in the hall. Each morning he watches their slow surge along the skirting boards, or else he opens the door to those stragglers who flop, semi-erect against the milk bottles.

He pulls everything on slugs from the school library and finds they are hermaphrodites that breathe through a hole in their backs. Not only can they climb trees, it transpires, they can also abseil back down along 'thin wires of their own mucus'. He pictures slugs swinging from the shade of their bedroom light.

His father does not share his enthusiasm. One morning over breakfast, George confesses to finding one on the windowsill as though it is some embarrassing disease. 'Have you seen any over your side?' he asks.

Vincent thinks about the right answer, about the blind affection of the slug by his bedside cabinet that dawn. The searching of its beaded horns across his finger. 'No,' he says.

'Well, I shouldn't worry. I know how to get rid of the buggers.'

'I don't mind them.'

'I mind them. They eat the hosta and the lupins. Besides, there isn't a living creature on this earth carries more bacteria than a slug.'

'Hosta?' says Vincent. 'Slugs can abseil.'

George holds his toast by his lips. 'You need to stop talking like that. Funny talk. I've told you, it can get you into trouble.'

'I'm just trying to tell you that it might not be so easy to get rid of them.'

'It'll be easy. Slugs have the same vices as men, that's what your granddad used to say.'

That night George declares war on the slugs by pouring flat Pedigree bitter into old vases. Vincent watches him kneel on the doorstep like a fanatic. He watches the streetlight bend through the syrupy dregs and cut glass to make thistles on his father's face. Vincent stares at the trap. 'They're living beings,' he says.

'Not in the morning they aren't.'

The next day, Vincent wakes with optimism, convinced that the slugs have won. You don't use your own phlegm as a zipwire and then fall for the old hustler's booze trick. It is early, still dark. Vincent gets out of bed and sways curiously. He often loses his balance these days, since a boy at school pulled his arm behind his back. Sometimes at night he reaches for the door handle and it takes him a few attempts to grasp it. He goes into the bathroom and finds no slugs. There are no slugs in the hall either. Outside, the vase has clouded slightly but Vincent can already see what has happened. A fat slug curls into the beer, its drunken head pressed against the base. Another one is half-submerged, sliding slowly along the inside of the glass like a disarranged joke shop moustache. Vincent scoops it out and places it on the handrail of the steps leading down to the garden. It slips off and makes a wet kiss on the concrete.

This goes on for several weeks. Whenever Vincent finds a sozzled corpse, he wishes some accident upon his father. The thoughts, which are almost spontaneous, frighten him. His schoolteachers criticize his 'overactive imagination' and he takes this literally: he almost believes that if he imagines something with enough quality, it will take place. Lying in bed across from his father, he fantasizes about car crashes and policemen at the door. ('Are you Vincent Cartwright?' 'Yes.' 'There's been an accident. Your dad.' 'What's his condition?' Vincent asks, and they are surprised by his maturity.)

Vincent begins to sneak outside and throw the dregs on to the grass when his father has gone to bed. It works for a few days. He feels a great sense of glee when the moonlight catches the beer and burns a mauve wormcast on to the sky above the garden. But within a week, his father counters by waking early and sprinkling salt on the slugs outside the door. They foam gruesomely, dry out to brittle sticks. So now Vincent takes them down to the bird table to lend their deaths some meaning.

The garden is large, on three levels. George leaves it wild. Vincent spends his mornings on the top level, looking out over the Amber Valley with a dead slug in his hand. He watches the birds living out their parallel lives over the oblivious villagers just 130 feet below in Church Eaton. Vincent believes he has more chance of deciphering the coded movements of the magpies and jackdaws than he does of understanding the rituals of the living room or school corridor. The silver badge of the Young Ornithologists Club shines upon the detachable arm of his jacket/body warmer. He cannot count the number of times that arm has been forcibly detached by his classmates.

'Birdman,' they say.

'Yes?' says Vincent, and they laugh.

'What's so good about birds anyway?'

'Apart from insects, birds are the only animals that can fly. I think that's pretty good.'

'Flamingos can fly.'

'Flamingos are birds.'

'So? Twat.'

A field borders the Church Eaton garden on the east side. It slopes down towards the Cartwrights, and the farmer keeps his Friesians on the hill. Vincent knows that in summer he will be able to lie on his back and – if he gets the angle right – it will appear that the cows are floating above the fence. For some reason this bovine flight heartens him.

George often wakes before dawn, to the sound of his son singing in his sleep. Vincent belts out songs from George's era: James Taylor, early Michael Jackson, right up to Kate Bush and The Smiths. His voice is on the edge of breaking so he can hit the high notes and the low. George creeps across the room, shakes his son until he stops singing.

When this eerie crooning interrupts his sleep, George goes up to the kitchen and tinkers with various broken appliances. Clock radios or toasters. It soothes him.

Hours later he looks through the blind slats at his son walking to school. The other children cross the road to avoid Vincent. George has been watching him a lot lately, watching him bend backwards with his binoculars in the garden, watching his hand expand in the green water of his makeshift Tupperware marina, tadpoles swimming through the fingers like dark thoughts growing.

Vincent does not know what happened in Blackmoor. George told him that his mother became ill and died. Nothing to do with anyone else. It is hardly a lie, and George knows that if you tell a child something when they are young enough, they will never challenge it. Like sleeping in the same room as their father.

Whether he means to or not – whether consciously or otherwise – George blames his son. But blaming someone is only satisfying and simple when you can *tell* them what they did. When you cannot voice the accusation, it becomes your own burden. George has come to resent his son's ignorance, his freedom from guilt.

Sometimes George *wants* to tell him, he wants to say, 'It was your fault. You killed her.' But if he told him that, he would have to tell him everything.

In the evenings George descends to the living room and stares out of the French doors – the 'patio windows' as he calls them. In the valley, the lights blink behind the silhouettes of gently shivering trees. Sometimes as night falls, he believes he can see the other village, although this is impossible – Blackmoor is twelve miles away. Nevertheless, a thick black space the size of a postage stamp seems to appear against the pimply illuminations of the other towns and villages. He does not seek it but sometimes it transfixes him, that tiny hole. Then he shuts it out and shakes the memories from his head, like a wet dog ridding itself of water.

A Blackmoor woman jumped to her death from the second-floor window of her house last Thursday.

Witnesses believe that Elizabeth Cartwright, 36, of Slack Lane, had watched her young son fall from the same window moments before. The boy, a toddler, had landed safely in a flower basin below the house.

A report in the *North Derbyshire Herald*, 26 June 1992

TWO

Blackmoor, May 1994.

Take a look at the place, before it is smashed to the ground.

From above, it looks almost normal. Blackmoor is a tumour of grey roof tiles in the muscular hills of Derbyshire, its isolation exaggerated by the disused loop track that encircles it. The village consists of seven terraced rows, a pub, a church, a school, the Miners' Welfare Club, a recreational ground and a few slack heaps where the old pit works used to be.

It is only as you swoop down that the irregularities become apparent. There are few vehicles, and almost no people. A team of security guards patrols the streets in shifts. Most of the inhabitants have left for their new homes, so the guards protect the remaining villagers, many of whom are elderly and accustomed to the safety of numbers. The guards usually work as doormen at the busy nightclubs in the nearest cities, and they are bored here. Indeed, the only thieves in Blackmoor are the foxes, who come for the soupy guts of abandoned rubbish bins. They gain in boldness as the human population decreases. Even by daylight, a red flash sometimes startles a security guard from his walking hibernation.

Behold the forsaken appearance of the place. You have heard that the mining villages have degenerated in the post-industrial age, but really, you have to ask, what has *happened* here?

Pebble dash lies in crushed chunks on the pavement. Residential doors have warped and cracked. Most of the windows are covered with black chipboard, and the lawns between the houses (once communal, in the good old days) sprout wildly, and hiss in the wind. Unwanted goods lie buried in the long grass, the things they could not sell to their neighbours as bric-a-brac before they left: seconds from the china factory, action figures, and an ornate clock which appears to be ten minutes fast, but in fact stopped five years ago.

A simple plaque marks the capped shaft at the disused colliery. Dropping below ground, the tunnels remain, like one infinitely recurring mouth with herringboning for teeth, the tool-chipped ripples of the strata so similar to the veins and ridges of the human palate. These burrows are filling slowly with water and other, more sinister elements. No more the tock of hooves, or the shouting, or the guttural rumble of machines. Just the hysterical emptiness of the flumed earth.

And no coal, of course. At least, not right here.

The coal lies less than a mile away, under the muddy field beyond Slack Lane, in a shining black stripe worth £600 million. Slack Lane is the final row of homes. It seems like an architectural irony: a terrace of tall thin, three-storey houses cramped together like too many men in a lift, yet with miles of open land behind. But there is life here – just about.

Behind the fifth door of Slack Lane, its only remaining inhabitant, George Cartwright, has transferred the belongings of his dead wife from the attic to the front room, ready to go into storage. George is waiting for the van. He half-smiles at his work, and rubs at the swooping pouches beneath each eye. He keeps his receding hair cropped to a brown graze now, and hunches to hide his height.

George has spent a long time planning the removal of her possessions. He knew he could not burn Beth's things, because open fires are now banned in Blackmoor. The distinctiveness of her clothes prevented him from giving them to charity, for he could not entertain the thought of some woman walking past him in the street wearing the green cloak, or a shop assistant handing him his change with Beth's artfully distressed cuffs at her wrist. So he picked a storage company at random from the phone book (trying not to take too much notice of the name), and arranged the collection.

As he surveys the meagre pile, he realizes that it does indeed consist mainly of her handmade or hand-altered clothing: cheap blouses with deftly embroidered cotton tattoos, her old basket-weave slippers with the pink paint flaking, and the velvet cloak with its fur-trimmed hood. If George looks for too long, the garments begin to assume animated forms, scrambling from the suffocating jumble.

At first glance, little else remains. It is the journals, however, that cause George the most consternation. Four shoeboxes filled with twenty-one exercise books. The dates on their sea-green covers stretch from May 1990 to shortly before her death two years later. He has not opened any of them, for he knows what that time contains – the accusations, the illusions, the truths. Curses and fires. He can hardly bear the slanted handwriting on the covers, and has wrapped several thick elastic bands around each shoebox.

Although it is mid-afternoon, and bright, George draws the curtains, and turns on the lamp by the sofa. He will be damned if some security guard is going to peer in at her leftovers. He runs his hand along the ecru canvas lampshade, and finds that his fingers are covered in a fine dust. George studies his fingertips with discomfort, knowing what that dust contains. Five luminous paths of clean fabric have appeared on the shade. He remembers her standing before the mirror with the clippers raised to her half-shaved head in a strange salute. George unplugs the lamp and throws it hard on to the pile for storage.

He must wash this colourless pelt from his hands. As he walks through the front room, however, he notices her indentations in the corduroy sofa on which he no longer sits, the wear from her heels on the armrest. It has got to go. He scans the room, and discerns her possible fingerprints on the mirror. He takes this down too.

He strides through the house now, assaulted by her trace at every turn. In the kitchen he sees her blood in the grain of the chopping board, her brushstrokes on the varnished chairs. Her destruction, her repairs, her matter, everywhere. George tears it all down, drags it into the front room with the rest. Lastly he rips the curtains from their pole and drapes them over the pile, shielding his eyes against the light.

The men from the storage company protest when they see the

load. They are nervous, take shallow breaths and refrain from smoking. Nobody wants to hang around in Blackmoor.

'You said it were only—'

'I'm not interested,' says George. 'I'm paying for it, aren't I? That's what's got to go.'

'Well, it's more than one carton-worth. We'll have to call for backup.'

George makes sure they get everything. He tries not to look at the name on the side of the van, but he cannot quite ignore the distinctive company emblem: an orange sphere bound by yellow rings studded with three or four smaller black spheres. An atom, or solar system.

He remembers when he last saw her alive, lying on the roof. The drain caught the June sun and underscored the length of her. And he remembers turning the corner on to Slack Lane hours later.

He continues to stand on the street when the van has left. George will not move to the new village with the others. Instead, he will take his son away from this place and its proximal replacement. Tomorrow they will set up home in Church Eaton.

In front of every third house on Slack Lane stands a concrete flower basin, six-by-three feet. An unusual adornment in a plain village. George stares at the basin in front of his own door. It is the only one on the street empty of soil and weeds. George asked the council time and again to remove the thing. He does not want it there, reminding him. One day in December 1992, a man in overalls shovelled the soil and flowers on to the back of a tipper, but he did not remove the basin itself.

It makes no difference. Soon, like everything else here, it will be destroyed.

THREE

Blackmoor, 1990. Before they made the connections. Before the talk of curses and witches.

Beth waddled into the garden, a comic pregnant ghost, draped in wet bedsheets with clothes pegs clipped to her arms like stegosaurus fins, blanching the pale skin still further. Her belly dented the linen. She sniffed the air, must have caught that off-season treacly whiff of bonfires. 'Somebody's always burning,' she said, pulling the sheets off her face.

George emerged from the shed on to the grass, which he found to be curiously hot.

'When you say that, I always imagine some poor bleeder running around on fire,' he said.

'And all I can think about is my whites.'

The hem of a sopping bedsheet trailed against the lawn, and a faint steamy hiss could be heard.

*

Late that night, he came downstairs to see her kneeling, her swollen belly hanging down and her head thrust into the cold fireplace. She used a piece of folded card to dislodge and gather deposits of soot from the back of the chimney. When she had scraped a sufficient amount, she carefully transported the card out from the fireplace and sat on the rug with her legs apart, studying the soot. George watched her bring the black powder to her nose and sniff, still unaware of him on the threshold of the front room. Then, her eyes flickering, she extended her tongue down into the soot, and brought it back into her mouth.

'Evening, Beth,' said George.

She did not startle as he had expected, and was careful not to disturb the remains of her meal. 'Hiya, Georgie.'

He got down on all fours and crawled towards her. 'You know, if you're hungry, there's stuff in the fridge. Just 'cos no bugger else in this village works for a living, it doesn't mean *we* have to go without.'

She gave him a sly grin, licked the blackness from her lips, and moved the card with the soot towards his face. He held a hand up, demurred. 'I couldn't,' he said. 'Not last thing at night.'

'Don't knock it till you've tried it,' she said, and winked. A hollow rumble came from below, and George could not tell if it was her stomach or the foundations of the house.

'Come back to bed, duck,' he said.

They were raised two streets apart, and in their separate ways, both were outcasts, wilful or otherwise. Beth always said, in her dry understated manner, that her birth was the most interesting thing that ever happened to her. She was born a long-shot on the leap year day of 1956, and the doctor noticed her extreme pallor and that strange movement of the eyes. The pupils swayed slowly from side to side, or else trembled like a clenched fist.

'She's not quite blind. That . . . wobble is caused by a minuscule disconnection between the eye and the brain. Nystagmus. It's not uncommon in babies like Elizabeth.'

'Babies like Elizabeth?' said her mother.

'It's attendant to albinism.'

Beth was only ocular albino, 'near normal' to quote the specialist. You would not have picked her out on the street, but she was more than albino enough for her father, with his beetle-black short back and sides. The anomaly did not go unnoticed in Blackmoor either. He was gone by her second birthday.

George was also a mystery to his father. Harry Cartwright was a sullen, quick-tempered miner, tethered to the minerals and mercy of the earth. In his youngest son he saw a smart-mouth obsessed with numbers, who uttered feminine phrases like 'ever-such-a-lot-of-trouble'. He feared a sweet-boy future for the lad.

He need not have worried. In his teens, George was drawn to the scarcity of Beth Fisher, whose distinctions had made a recluse of her. She was an exotic sight – that scythe-slash of long white hair flashing past the window as she walked the right of way between the houses. At school she tilted her head down and to the left and looked at him out of the corner of her eyes, nervous, yet appraising. He liked that. He liked the way you could see the network of veins through her skin.

Such glimpses across a classroom were not enough for George, and he surely did not have the skills to approach her, so he began to follow Beth around the village. The pursuit soothed him,

focussed his hazy ambition. He learned the details of her life –
where she went and why. He could calculate how much money
she had earned from her shifts cleaning the kitchen of the Miners'
Welfare Club and work out when she had enough to go to Derby
to buy fabrics. He was the firefly fag end in the dark of the lychgate
when she stepped off the bus at night. Mostly, he wished he could
go up to the hills north of Blackmoor and look down on her from
there, to seek some pattern in her movements through the slim
grid of terraces.

Beth knew George Cartwright, and at first the idea of him
being predatory or infatuated amused her. He was outspoken
and a little arrogant, much less taciturn than the usual Blackmoor
boy. She laughed when he appeared behind the Miners' Welfare
Club where she sat on a metal beer barrel, drinking soda water.
'Break-time?' he asked, looking smug. She did not flinch, just
pulled out another barrel for him. He told her what she had done
that day, told her he felt like a magician, that he could pretty
much put himself in her path anytime he wanted to. She told
him he was a very powerful man, and that night, as he waited for
her to pass the lychgate, she sneaked around the back of the
church, trod through the graveyard and scared the living shit
out of him.

At first, his surveillance gave her vague comfort. As she left the
house, she would seek George, confirm his lingering presence.
Sometimes, if he did not follow, an obscure emptiness possessed
her. Without his offbeat footsteps behind, she felt like a character
in an unread book.

But she was a girl of varying moods, and eventually George's
stalking began to exert a darker influence upon her. As she looked

at the notices in the newsagent's window she saw his reflection appear. 'You sniff your armpits before you go into a house,' he said, and walked away. Without replying, Beth dismissed the remark but later froze on her aunt's doorstep as she felt herself lean towards the thin pectoral bow, seeking that spicy scent. She began to find her own actions sinister, almost predetermined by *him*. She grew conscious of her tendency to flick at her hair or stretch her arms behind her back like a swimmer, and then she became unnerved by her awareness. And she developed a brand new affliction, of course: looking over her shoulder.

Beth was even more anxious when talking to her few friends now, aware of the burden of her pursuer. What once seemed homely to her became dangerous. It was like an antisocial illness. Her eye-flicker worsened. Once, as she walked past the Co-op, she heard the trolleys clang by the delivery entrance and gasped with anger. 'Just leave me alone will you, for God's sake. I'm so bloody tired of this. Sick and bloody tired of being frightened to even go out my door. If you want to say something, then say it, but stop following me.'

It was not George, but Mrs Gretorix who emerged from the delivery entrance in her Co-op uniform, carrying a crate of tinned pineapple chunks and staring icily at foul-mouthed Beth. Such episodes did little for the girl's reputation.

It came to a head that winter. As she walked back from the Miners' Welfare Club in the frosted midnight, the road suddenly ignited with a pale light that caused Beth to drop her apron. She looked across the road to see George sitting on a bench with one of the new Polaroid cameras. She strode furiously towards him, caught twice more in the flash. 'It's got to stop. Right now.

Tonight. Give me that,' she said, eyes trembling through the sinews of her frosted, lamp-ambered breath.

'What?' said George.

'You know what. Camera and film. Give it.'

'Doesn't have a film. Pictures come straight out bottom. Look.'

She tore the picture from him and watched it bloom. 'Oh,' she said, seeing herself trapped before the houses, her apron floating in front of her in mid-air. 'It's beautiful.'

'Aye. Even if you say so yourself.'

'Can I see others? You do have others, don't you?'

'Aye.'

In the nettles and long grass behind the Rec, he talked about leaving Blackmoor, said he couldn't stand the staleness of the place. The same surnames on the cricket teamsheet since 1901, only the initials changing. Beth was attracted to his idea of a life in the city, but George's ambition fell short of it. When his school-mates signed up for the pit, however, George saw Heath's government flexing for a fight and he moved sideways into sewage, taking a job with a water treatment company. 'Good pay, shit conditions,' as he liked to say. With his new wife beside him he quickly climbed out of the sewers and into the office, making steady money while the miners' strike gripped the region. But they stayed in Blackmoor. They moved into number five Slack Lane, with its flower basin full of lobelia and nasturtiums, a back garden fenced off from the communal path and the fields beyond.

He held her in bed, the streetlight blasting amber like a noise through their top-floor window. As she fell towards sleep she told him that they were tiny figurines in their tall thin house. Us against the world. George felt slightly saddened by this closeted image, and the resignation in his wife's voice. He put his hand on her belly, and thought he detected a subtle change therein. He drifted off to sleep without a word.

The hours went by, bringing them closer to 18 April. When they began to reorder the events of the year, the people of Blackmoor would return again and again to that date. And they would find one woman at its centre.

At dawn, Beth woke, starving. She climbed out of bed, heavy and naked, and pulled on a flimsy home-made Indian maternity dress, swirled with saffron and maroon. She descended to the kitchen, took a wooden spoon from the drawer and walked out of the front door into the clean, steely air.

The puffy sleeves of the dress filled with the breeze and a flap of material fell away from the unhooked buttons to reveal part of her left breast. Her hair was one unblemished mass, like an immaculate sheet of yolk-varnished dough. She stared up and down the quiet lane. Toasted, tawny daffodils stood in the flower basin now, but Beth ignored the flowers. The sun had touched the soil for half an hour or so, drying the top layer, enriching it. Beth slid her finger along this crust until her skin was barnacled with dirt. She screwed the finger inside her lips and across her teeth. Her eyes trembled and she made slow circles with her tongue, pressing against the thin skin of her filtrum.

Half a mile away, fellow Blackmoor resident Polly Grimshaw stepped out of her supervisor's car and began the short walk home. She worked the night shift at the chocolate factory just off the motorway. The dark roots and orangey ends of her hair looked spidery, while her good figure was hidden beneath her brown work bib. She did not wave as the car pulled away. She was grateful for the lift – it saved her money – but she was ashamed of the alternative currency her supervisor took for his trouble.

Polly had taken the job because her husband, Steve, had been unable to find work after the pit closed. They had tried for a while to synchronize their waking hours, live their days in negative. More and more, however, he slept when she was awake.

The heating had not yet come on when she arrived back at their end terrace house, and the place was colder than the outdoors. She left two champagne truffles in the kitchen for her sons, and washed the stink of her supervisor from her hands. Still nowhere near godliness.

Upstairs she found her husband, his hair cropped and red, snoring into the pillow. She climbed in beside him, her hands still wet, and fell quickly asleep.

Polly confused the initial suck of the blast – that brief inhalation of energy – with the falling sensation that sometimes invades a dream. The noise that followed pierced her eardrum, and the force threw her across the room, so that she lay looking back at her empty bed. 'Jesus. Jesus. I'm sorry. Steve?' she shouted.

Through the pink dust clouding the room she saw her husband roll over by the window, which had shattered. Blood covered his hands and arms, glass sparkled in his skin. 'Fuck me. Pol? Shit, the kids.' And he was gone in the direction of the crying. After a few seconds, he shouted back. 'They're right. Everybody's all right.'

Polly shook and then screamed as her wardrobe collapsed. When the atmosphere had cleared somewhat, she found herself standing in the middle of the bedroom, looking out on the dawn through the space where her wall used to be. Blackmoor grew light in a peaceful, sober way, but she could hear the voices of her neighbours in the street, whining, circling, feline. Bricks and plaster were scattered among the overgrown bushes next to her house. A picture of her mother sat in the upper branches of a tree, together with her long mirror, which now reflected the soft sky. A melting, chemical smell rose from below, and her husband shouted up, 'Pol, duck, we need to get gone. It's going to catch light.'

Polly's dressing table still stood on the edge of the room, miraculously stoic against the clouds. Some of the bottles had broken on the floor, and as the dust drifted into the day, there was an overpowering smell of her cheap perfume.

On Slack Lane, just a few seconds before, Beth had scooped some soil on to the wooden spoon with the help of her little finger, and put the spoon in her mouth. She smiled to herself, relishing the gritty noise between her teeth. She spat out a tiny stone. Looking down at her bulging stomach, she asked, 'What buttons are you pressing, eh?'

Beth thought she perceived an answer in the shuddering ground beneath her bare feet. Instead this quake was followed soon after by a squeal and bang two streets away which lit the windows of the village. A dark object made a high, silent arc towards Beth from behind the house across the road. This projectile hit the pavement, crumbled, and rolled to a smoking stop by the flower basin. Half a housebrick.

George came to the door, in his dressing gown.

'Somebody's been throwing stones at me, George,' Beth said.

'Eh? Did you hear that noise?'

'Aye.'

'At this time in the bloody morning. Alls we can hope is that Martin Wagstaff's exploded. Bloody derelict.'

'George.'

'Well. I says to him in the pub last night, I says, "Folk like you are neither use nor bloody ornament."'

'George.'

'What, woman?'

'Get your shoes on. I think I'm about to give it up.'

Doors began to open. People stumbled backwards into the street, their bed-hair mimicking shock. The metal bounce of shouts echoed off the houses, unnatural in the early light. As her husband laughed and struggled with his laces, Beth caught the eye of a neighbour and hid the muddy wooden spoon behind her back, but in the first grip of pain her reactions were not fast enough. She had been seen.

Vincent G. Cartwright was born just after midday, and weighed in a little heavy at 9lbs 1oz. The midwife commented that Beth had obviously been eating the right things. In the 'Baby's Scrapbook' they made Beth produce when she returned to hospital there was a picture of the boy, moist and oven-red, during his first few hours. The caption, in a spiky version of Beth's hand, read 'Healthy and Happy'. Mother, however, was out of shot.

FOUR

Through her adolescence Beth had made her own clothes primarily because she could not afford to buy new ones, but she soon found she had a talent for it. Even as she fingered the materials on the industrial rolls at the market, possible garments abruptly suggested themselves, as if transmitted through her hands. Frayed grey wool held in its loose mesh the possibility of her difference.

She tampered with and ciphered her existing clothes too. These distinctions began discreetly, with a renegade line of golden thread along the hem and cuffs of her navy school pullover. But soon her boldness grew, and she painted bright pink the basket-weave slippers bought from Skegness. She sewed sheer web-like pleats between the arm and trunk of a black blouse. When young George saw this creation, he asked her if it was a dig at the legendary Blackmoor tendency towards inbreeding. 'My old man's got webbed feet you know. I seen them in the bath.'

When they first fell in love, Beth would watch George's reactions to how she looked, and she learned to manipulate her unusual appearance. She found a strange wool-blend in Nottingham, creamy white and furry with lint. It was beautifully soft but going cheap because of its tendency to moult. She fashioned it into a tight cowl-necked sweater and read the results in George's face.

He saw her coming over the hump of the play tunnel as the sun moved out from behind a cloud, and her body turned tadpole black within the haze of the glowing wool. In minutes his clothes were covered in white fluff, and the next morning he coughed some into the sink. The lint reminded him of her hair then, and years later, when she was dead, he would run his fingers along the lampshade and the dust would remind him of the fine fibres from that sweater.

When they were married she made the green velvet cloak, the hood trimmed with grey synthetic fur. In an August thunderstorm, George watched from the top window as she crossed the field behind their Slack Lane house, her hair spilling from the hood. How had she known it would rain? The ploughed peaks of the field had hardened in a month of sun, and were slippery, treacherous, in the deluge. Beth looked as though she might fall, and once she slipped on to a knee. George was furiously aroused, and they made love immediately in that room, the metallic scent of the storm on her skin, the animal vulgarity of wet velvet, George looking at the field where she had just been.

Now, as he sat by that same high window, George wondered if that had been the time of Vincent's conception. Already, a week after the boy's birth, that moment seemed to George like a bullet hole in glass, spreading its fissures like a web. Something had happened to her mind in that hospital and George could not fathom it. His wife was suddenly outside of his experience, beyond his imagination.

Downstairs the stampeding foot of the sewing machine continued, as it had done for the last five hours. He had closed every door behind him, drank every can of bitter in the fridge, and he could still hear it. He could still smell the bleach too. She was talking to the child above the din, swearing, laughing too loudly. Perhaps the neighbours might hear.

George thought of his father, drunk, saying, 'It all changes after first kid, youth.' Such a prosaic thing to say; how disdainful George had been. But he knew there was only before and after now. He knew this because he was sitting in his house, twenty feet above his wife, and he was *remembering* her.

Take a look at Beth through the eyes of her neighbours. See how the rumours were set in motion, and then set in stone when she returned with the child.

The curse caught up with Tom Betts next, made him dance to a scorching tune. Like the others, Betts, slicked-up quiff and gas-burner blue eyes, had spent some time on the dole when they capped the shaft of the drift mine, but a wish for a woman had driven him into private enterprise. He bought a van and a lawn-mower on hire purchase, and started 'Hedge Your Betts'.

One spring morning in 1990, he let himself in around the back of the tall Cartwright house and rested for a moment, watching Beth's clothes turning slowly on the washing tree. He stood close to one of the dresses, a thin silky one printed with a swirling Indian pattern in saffron and maroon. From its size, Tom identified it as one of the maternity dresses she must have worn when she was pregnant. The top two buttons were undone.

A heavy knock on the glass startled him into a guilty step away from the garment. Her face was at the kitchen window, squinting. 'Hiya, Tom. Do you want me to take them down? Are they in the way?'

'These? No. I wasn't. I can work round 'em.'

He realized after a few silent seconds that his face was locked into an expression of terror. Beth's skin was blotchy, as though it had been pawed at by a dog, but she was still smiling zealously.

'It's dark over Bill's mother's,' she said, referring to the mucky clouds stumbling drunk towards them. He nodded and turned to his equipment. When he looked again she had vacated the kitchen. He crept to the window and peered in. The kitchen was so clean as to look unused. A photograph of George and Beth hung by the telephone. It was a strange picture because it seemed like they had just argued, Beth walking away, looking down, and George behind her, holding her coat like some kind of deposit. Tom felt jealous. The photograph showed more unknowable intimacy than a posed wedding snap; it was everything Tom did not have. There was a chalkboard too, on which someone had written, *I've Got You*, and Tom turned away, thinking for a moment that the message was meant for him, that he had been caught peeking.

He got to work, took the secateurs to the borders, pulled a few weeds. He lingered by the washing tree and occasionally a dress brushed against his arm. After about ten minutes his face began to sweat and his knees felt hot. This seemed at odds with the chilly temperature and thin Tom's reputation for being nesh. He assured himself that the heat was simply proof of his toil. He was a rational man these days. He did not even salute the single magpie.

He began to mow the lawn, and the drone of the small two-stroke engine flattened his suspicions for a while. It started to rain slightly, big, irregular drops, and yet his feet were insistently hot. He had worked on coalfaces at ninety degrees in these boots and he had never fucking . . . Eventually the worry and discomfort became too much and he flicked the mower off and unlaced his boots, cursing himself, cursing his secret voodoo heart, his lingering belief in his mother's tales of lakes of fire. *Shouldn't have touched the dresses.*

Tom did not wear socks, so he stood now with his feet on the grass, the toes square, the nails tilted inward like Virgin faces, a brush of black hair on the chafed insteps, scaly yellow calluses on the heels. He waited for the synapses to fire, and fire they did. His soles swelled and stung with the heat. Meanwhile, the shower became a downpour and as the rain hit home, steam rose up between his toes. And all around him, slow-dancing drifts of steam. 'Bloody hell, fucking place is on fire,' he said aloud. He dropped back down to his knees and cautiously, in jerking feints, put his face to the hot ground. A deep growl came from beneath, like thunder. It was all too much. He jumped to his feet and skipped across the steaming lawn like a smooth pebble, through the back door, past Beth, who was on her way to make tea, and into the front room.

Beth, focussed, unperturbed by eccentric behaviour, just continued through to the sink and filled the kettle. Afterwards she went back to the front room where Betts was swearing.

'It's not right,' he said, looking past her, over her.

'What's not right?'

'Sommat's wrong with your garden and it's not right. I don't want paying but you'll have to do rest yoursen. I'm not going back out there, not for any money.'

He put his hands on his hips as though expecting an argument. Then, as the adrenalin faded, the appearance and smell of the room knocked the words out of his lungs. It was *clinically* clean and reeked of bleach. The furniture had been rearranged around a sewing table in the centre. Eight piles of tiny T-shirts in five colours sat by the table; a green T-shirt, half-made, was trapped in the jaws of the sewing machine. The boy was in the pram, quiet, by the window. When Tom looked back to Beth she was struggling to control her breathing, just staring at his feet, which were stained green, flecked with grass cuttings, cuttings strewn around them on her impeccable carpet. 'Eh up,' she said with a strained calmness. 'Feet.'

'Right. Sorry. I'm gooin', anyway. I'm gooin'.'

He unlocked the front door and stepped out into the rain. 'I'll come back for me stuff later,' he shouted back, halfway down the street.

Tom walked directly to the Red Lion, paying no heed to the piercing grit, letting the wet pavement cool his bare feet. The landlord squinted at him as he walked in. 'Fuck off,' said Tom. 'Pint.'

As he sat with his drink, Tom thought of Beth's skin, the chemical stink in her front room and her smoking lawn. 'S'up with you?' said the landlord.

And Tom began to talk.

*

In the month following Vincent's birth, sightings of the Cartwrights were rare. Tom Betts quietly returned to the house that evening, after spending most of the day at the pub, and watched Beth continue to sew through her front-room window. The room was completely black but for a patch of light the size of a face flannel – the underlight on the sewing machine – which illuminated the metal foot, the stomping needle, a piece of red fabric, and the familiar white hand that slid through the light into darkness and back. Despite a residual fear of the uncanny, Tom returned each night for a week. In the light, her thin bones fanned out to the fingers, showing through the skin like the scaffold of a corset, and each time her hand veered off to the side with the cloth, her lower arm was revealed, like a leg from a slowly hitched skirt. Tom was mesmerized.

He was, perhaps, one of the few people who could have saved her; it would only have taken a few kind, rational words to the right people. Indeed, he noticed wounds on her hands: trenches of broken skin next to the fingernails, growing night by night, and then, on the sixth night, bright abrasions at the knuckles. However, Tom did not wish to complicate his pleasure; he was resigned to taking what he could get from a safe distance and therefore continued merely to watch her injured fingers, pressed together, gliding over cotton as if through the resistance of water.

Mrs Hargreaves, who lived directly opposite the Cartwrights on Slack Lane, had seen Beth hide the wooden spoon on the day Polly Grimshaw's boiler exploded. As the former leader of the Women's Action Group, she had taken it upon herself, in these calmer, defeated days, to perform more regular social functions, such as welcoming new arrivals to the village. Her visit to baby

Vincent had yielded unexpected news, as she reported to the women outside the Miners' Welfare Club on bingo night.

'Wouldn't even let me in at first,' Mrs Hargreaves said, her tight bronze perm shuddering. She wore a large black and white checked jacket that had arrived in a parcel sent by their comrades in Eastern Europe during the strike. She called it her Jackie Kennedy coat. 'Kept saying the place was a pigsty, but when she finally opened the door it were spotless clean. Big smell a paint and all. 'Mulsion, you know. I opened the window, because I thought it had to be bad for the little un.'

'Where were she at time? Beth?' asked Polly Grimshaw.

'Kitchen. Scrubbing some poor frying pan to within an inch on its life. I don't know what liquid she were using but suds were pink. Anyway, I had a little play with the kid. Ever such a bright thing, it is.'

'Has it got them wobbly eyes like what she's got?' asked Polly Grimshaw, and the other ladies sniggered.

'Eyes are fine. She starts on about his *feet*. How he's got this dry skin and she's been rubbing cream on it every ten minutes, but it won't go. Well there's hardly oat there, for me, but she shouts through that it looks *serpentine*.'

'You what?'

'That's what I said, and in just that fashion. "Aye," she says. "Serpentine. Like a snake." She were in the room now, hands behind her back, eyes going like they do. But she's gabbing on a mile a minute about this scaly skin, and you know how quiet she is, normally.'

'How's her figure?' asked Polly.

'Top drawer. Tits up here, not like my knee-shooters.'

The other women looked disappointed and Mrs Hargreaves returned to her story, telling how a drip of paint had fallen from the ceiling on to the elm coffee table and spread like a star. Mrs Hargreaves had looked up to see the ceiling shining with paint, little humps ready to turn into drops and fall on to the clean, deep, green carpet.

'What did she say?' asked Polly Grimshaw.

'Not much. "Been painting." Stating the bloody obvious. Anyway, speaking a home repairs, how's your kitchen coming along, Polly?' asked Mrs Hargreaves, moving smoothly from talk of an eccentric woman to a sinister accident.

When Polly Grimshaw heard a car slowing down behind her in the early morning dark, she assumed it to be her supervisor, back to give her more grief. Thus she was relieved to see George Cartwright leaning over in his Orion to wind down the window. She thought him good-looking, his short hair receding in a satisfying 'M', his skin dark; the bags forming beneath his eyes gave him an appealing, hunted appearance. 'Eh up, George,' she said, as though it was perfectly normal to converse on the street at this time of day.

'Yes. I don't suppose you've seen my wife, have you? She's about your height, but with blonde hair—'

'I know what Beth looks like. No, I haven't seen her. She doesn't work, does she? What's she doing out and about at this hour?'

'Nothing. She walks around. Because she has trouble sleeping and that; she walks around. It's fine.'

'Oh right. No, same as I say, I haven't seen her. I'll keep a look out though.'

George Cartwright pulled away. Trouble at mill, thought Polly with a grin, barely remembering the conversation with Mrs Hargreaves before bingo the week before. They had all worked together during the strike, and Polly had disliked Beth at first. They were supposed to be the '*Miners'* Wives' group after all, and George had his tidy little desk job at the water treatment plant. Beth had this askance look too, out the corner of the eyes, like a bull ready to charge. Eventually, though, they all came to accept her; she turned up on time, and seemed genuinely disturbed by the lies and the doctored TV footage. Almost as soon as the strike was over and the pit closed, however, the old resentments had returned – Beth went back to her big house while Polly took work at the factory. Polly had even blanked Beth once, in the Co-op.

Since the explosion, Polly and her family had moved in with her mother, who lived by the Rec. As she approached the house, Polly saw the Orion pull up on the far side of the Rec, by the gates. In the brief moment before George turned off his head-lights, Polly thought she saw a figure running around the outside of the cricket boundary. Clouds covered the moon, and there were no streetlights nearby, so the place was very dark when George cut the engine. She heard him get out of the car. 'Beth?' he shouted.

An urgent female voice came out of the black. Polly walked carefully by the rough-cut sandstone wall of the Rec. She could not make out what the woman had said, and neither, it seemed, could George. 'What?' he said.

'*On*. Turn them fucking *on*.'

The voice was breathless, a laugh of angry exhilaration behind it. A few moments passed. Polly knew she would have to walk past George's car to get home, and she approached cautiously. She was afraid. A cough and a little whoop of joy came from the Rec and made her jump.

George got back into the car, started the engine and turned on the headlights. Silver knotted oaks popped up around the perimeter, and the voice was revealed as Beth Cartwright's. To Polly's astonishment, Beth was running towards her on the other side of the wall, her eyes closed, oblivious to Polly's presence. The light behind gave a silver edging to Beth's limbs. She wore small red shorts, basket-weave slippers covered with sea-green sequins, and a red T-shirt with the arms torn off. She ran so fast that her face shuddered with the impact of her feet on the ground.

When Beth had passed, Polly turned to look after her. In the light from the car, Beth's white hair swung in a high ponytail, and the back of her T-shirt held a sweat print in the shape of a hammerhead shark. The arc of the beam gave out just past the cricket pitch, and Beth soon outran its reach, became a faint white flicker, like a moth recoiling from a hot lamp.

Polly's eyes hurt from straining to see Beth, so she stopped trying and continued to walk home. Under the steady hum of the car engine she could hear Beth's footfalls getting louder as she came back around.

As she walked past the Orion, George Cartwright refused to make eye contact. He watched his wife jogging laps. The baby looked to be asleep, and they were both pond-coloured in the green light coming from the dashboard dials.

People enjoyed these stories, and retold them with relish. The rumours circulated and multiplied, with cruel embellishments. It was said that Beth had asked the man at the Post Office if he could feel two 'lumps' on baby Vincent's head.

Beth also had a bad habit of talking to herself in the vicinity of inanimate objects, so that she seemed to be addressing them. Mick Chambers, the landlord of the Red Lion, had seen her apparently speaking to a flower basin near her house.

'Well she's blind, int she? Probably thought it were a kid,' said old Martin Wagstaff, a veteran of the mines. 'Eh up, Chambers, change the fucking barrel, will you, I've been waiting for a pint for twenty minutes, youth.'

Mick Chambers went down to the cellar, but did not return. Wagstaff sought him a while later, and found his friend bent over a barrel, not a scratch on him, blue-lipped and quite dead. The doctor said it was asphyxiation, but all of Blackmoor knew Chambers as a man who drank half of his own stock, and – at the time – they assumed that the booze had killed him.

The inertia kicked in abruptly. In the Co-op one day, Beth left a basket of yet-to-be-purchased goods on the floor by the cleaning products, walked out of the shop, and out of public view for a considerable time. Tom Betts found the Cartwright curtains closed that evening, and they stayed closed the next day.

But what of George?

George was on the inside, and when her energy began to diminish he noticed it in the things around him. Take a look at the crooked crease in his trousers as he steps out of his car after work. The powdery yellow ridges on the inside of his shirt collar.

In early May he walked down the alley which used to lead to the communal lawn but now gave on to his private patch. He hesitated when he saw the baby's buggy in the garden. Beth was not there. George had to walk a few more steps before he saw Vincent wrapped up and lodged between two folded towels, with sunblock across his cheeks like Indian war-paint. The child looked so small against the hills that stretched up over the small fence. A tiny pebble.

Seeing him like that, finally away from his mother, George was struck by the invincible tethers lashing him to the boy. George raised his hands to his skull and squeezed. It was not supposed to be like this. For years, George had defiantly sat in the Red Lion with men he hated, in a state of exquisite bitterness, but it was *fine* because he always had that feeling of privilege, something superior to return to after the silent stand-offs with his father's friends and the closed circle of working (or not-working) men. Yes, he was stuck – despite his wife's wide-armed proclamations that they could 'just leave', he insisted he was *stuck* – in this backward pit village with these morons, but he could always go back to his tall house and his exceptional wife. His son – this child before him – was supposed to be the final deal breaker, the very thing that tipped the scales in George's favour.

What in God's name had happened? And what, more to the point, had George done about it?

Above the sunblock, his son squinted, croaked. George could not even resent him. When he tried to enter his house, George found that Beth had barricaded herself in, probably to escape the noise of the crying child. George had to smash the glass in the back door. As he reached inside for the bolt he wondered briefly whom she had really meant to lock out.

FIVE

Vincent began to speak of the past even before Blackmoor was demolished and they left for their new home. This, of course, was something his father had feared since the incident – 'the gradual surfacing of repressed memory', as the doctor had called it. However, the particular periods in history to which Vincent referred were not the ones for which George had prepared.

It started with the typical nonsense of a child new to language, such sentences as, 'When I was a man, I lived in Dracula.' Among the other phrases cobbled together from TV and books ('Bosna hurts the governor', 'Harold be thy name'), this did not concern George greatly. But as the foundations of speech settled, and his vocabulary grew, Vincent continued to start sentences with 'When I was a man . . .' or 'When I was a woman . . .' These introductory phrases often led on to hazy descriptions of Victorian market days or eighteenth-century sea voyages. George listened to the youngster's tales warily. 'You want to be careful about telling folk you used to be a woman, kidder,' he would say.

After these early glimpses of inherited memory, Vincent's first insight into the future – the beginning of his overactive imagination – came when he was ten and found a chalk-drawn cross on the tarmac close to their Church Eaton drive. In all likelihood the marks had been etched by the gas company planning pipe maintenance work, but Vincent (who had been unable to sleep the previous night because of his father's snoring) became convinced that the cross was a sign of his impending death. At first he decided that finding the omen was not necessarily a bad thing, as he could erase it and therefore sidestep mortality for a while longer, but when he tried to rub out the cross with his small hands and some spit, it would not even smudge. His father found him on his knees, screaming and scratching at the ground.

As he grew older, he became preoccupied with these mortal warnings. He asked his father if people saw any indication that their time was at hand. Was the fatal chain of events set off by a sign? Could there be some pattern in death?

'Of course not. If there was a particular sign, then people would spend their whole lives trying to avoid the bloody thing, wouldn't they?'

'What if it was something really normal, so as they didn't even notice it? In the Saxon days, they used to think you were going to die if you saw a crow on your right.'

'If it were something as commonplace as that, then people would be dying all the time.'

'But they are, aren't they?'

'Yes,' said George.

'Dad?'

'Listen. I'll tell you what you see before you die. A big bloody truck about two yards from your head? Do you get it?'

'Yep.'

Despite George's discouragement of these morbid investigations, the inevitable questions eventually came. Where did she go? Where are her things?

'Dad? What was Mum like?'

'Blonde.'

Vincent learned quickly that his father was not to be pressed on such issues.

Vincent now wakes, more often than not, to the sound of his father disassembling the cine-film projector in the kitchen. This is his spring project, the slugs having been soundly defeated.

'Dad, you know what will happen, don't you, when it's finished?' Vincent says as he fastens his school blazer.

'What?'

'It will be fixed.'

George mutters something about funny talk and stating the bloody obvious and Vincent leaves for school.

At the end of the day, they surround him, making bird noises that sound suspiciously like the words 'fuck off'. One of them, David Sulley, sings 'Bill Oddie, Bill Oddie, put your hands all over my body' to the tune of 'Erotica', by Madonna. Vincent finds this amusing and laughs in spite of himself. This annoys David Sulley. 'Fuck off, Birdman,' he says.

Vincent is not immune to violent thoughts, just because he likes animals and gets bullied at school. Let us not forget that he often fantasizes about the death of his father. If he was not so gangly, weak and outnumbered, he would retaliate viciously and without remorse. Instead he sensibly waits for them to pass before turning to walk in the opposite direction.

There is nobody within yards of him when he falls. He gets the pain in his shoulder, wonders briefly why the newsagent's is tilted to forty-five degrees and then he is on his back. He cannot get up because his rucksack is too heavy.

A one-syllable laugh echoes in the street. It is Leila Downing from his English class. This is all he needs. An association, however momentary and helpful, with such an outspoken, swatty, and quite frankly foreign-looking girl is unlikely to abate the bullies.

Leila has browny-blonde hair just a shade lighter than her skin so that they seem to be made of the same material in different states. Black freckles spread across her nose and cheeks. The collar of her white shirt rises with indignant starchiness above the dark blue blazer which she has – just recently – been unable to button across the chest. She bends down to retrieve something that has fallen from Vincent's pocket. It is his Young Ornithologists Club membership card, and for the first time he feels embarrassed by it.

'Can you help me?' he says, trying to roll on to his front.

She holds up a finger to shush him while she reads the card. 'Mister Cartwright then, is it?' she says in her haughty posh voice.

'You know who I am. We're in English class. And it's *Master* Cartwright on that card.'

'Oh I don't like that word.'

'The card's actually out of date. I'm really eligible for adult status now.'

'Woo. Aren't you a big man? You can't fly yet though, can you?'

'What?' says Vincent, annoyed that even Leila Downing can taunt him.

Leila holds out her hand, which he reluctantly takes, and she drags him to his feet. The pain almost sends him blind. 'Ow, God,' he hisses under his breath, clutching his shoulder.

'Your arm, ha? We can sort that out. Walk me home.'

'Why should I?'

'My mum used to be a physiotherapist. She'll take a look at you. Besides, I'll show you some really nice buzzards. Birdman.'

Vincent follows, two steps behind. After the best physical efforts of the boys in his class, it has taken this aloof girl to antagonize him. He is intrigued by the sensation.

An S-bend drive of crackling hard core winds up to a dwelling that Vincent would describe as a 'castle', because of its size and the fact that it has battlements. A plaque above the doors reads 'Wood Edge 1847'. The garden blends into the woods, and is dominated by a colossal cedar of Lebanon. To the west is a large modern annexe called The Stables.

Vincent looks up at the castle. 'Nice house,' he says.

'This is where Mum and I live. Dad stays in The Stables over there.' She pushes open the large wooden doors to Wood Edge with some effort.

They walk through an entrance hall with marble pillars and badly faded red carpet, up the old servants' stairs and into a room which curves to a bow window. It is dusty, with boards on the floor and rotten window frames plugged with putty, yet the furniture is plush and expensive, gathered in the middle of the room as if to protect it from the coal-tainted woodchip walls. The place is like a rich man's pantry – cold and dark, with sofas like soft cheese and rugs like slabs of raw meat. A woman with Arab features stokes a failing fire.

'Mum, this is my friend Vincent. We're going to do our project together in English.'

It suddenly clicks for Vincent. This is why she wants him.

'A guest!' says Mrs Downing, in a posh voice similar to her daughter's, but with more of a foreign tinge. 'What a wonderful excuse for the halogen heater.'

She abandons the fire and turns on a standing heater that gives out a rich orange glow. Vincent realizes that this is also the only light in the room; its heat is certainly welcome.

'Vincent has hurt his arm,' says Leila, with a flatness that suggests she is embarrassed about what is coming.

Mrs Downing approaches him, looks him over. She has very large dark eyes, which take on a professional glaze now. She is quite old, although all mothers must seem so to Vincent. The smell of the coal on her fingers turns on lights in the dark chambers of his memory. She wipes her hands on her jeans. 'Did you fall over, Vincent?' she asks.

'I fall over all the time.'

'Ah. It's your right shoulder?'

'It started when someone pulled my arm behind my back.'

Mrs Downing looks indignant. 'They did what?'

'We were just messing around,' says Vincent.

'Vincent is bullied at school, Mum,' says Leila.

'Really? Is this true?' asks Mrs Downing.

'I don't get bullied.'

'Could have fooled me, Birdman,' says Leila.

'Leila!' says Mrs Downing. 'Now *you're* bullying him. Let's look at this shoulder, ha?'

Mrs Downing half bends, then kneels, then stands. 'We are of incompatible height, Vincent.'

She presses his shoulder. 'When the boy pulled your arm—'

'I'm not bullied. They don't bother me.'

'Okay. Did you feel your arm pop out of the socket?'

'Kind of. And then it—'

'Popped back in?'

'Yep.'

'Do you feel dizzy?'

'Sometimes.'

Vincent glances over at Leila, who stares at him, obstructs his exposure to the heater. The orange light curls around her grey skirt. He remembers her one moment of school popularity, when they had a dozy supply teacher in year seven science. Leila had climbed out of the big lab windows, walked around and knocked on the classroom door, introduced herself as a new member of the class. Then ten minutes later she had repeated the trick and apologized for her lateness. She has grown since then. Vincent cannot imagine those obscurely stirring wide hips sliding so easily through the window now.

'Leila, come here please, and stand in front of Vincent.'

Leila obeys with her hands behind her back. She has taken off her shoes, and Vincent sees that he is taller than her. Her lips are a lighter shade of the same brown. She is *monochrome*. Vincent knows the word, can spell it, which may account for his lack of friends.

'Put your arms out in front of you, Leila,' says Mrs Downing.

She does so, with her palms out, as if protecting herself from an oncoming vehicle.

'Okay, Vincent. Close your eyes.'

He stumbles, and feels Mrs Downing's hands steady him. 'Right. Do you remember what Leila looked like?'

'Mum, he isn't a retard. He's only just closed his eyes,' says Leila.

'Leila, quiet. You remember how she had her hands out, Vincent?'

'Yep.'

'I want you to keep your eyes closed and place your hands over hers.'

'*Point*? You need my permission for this, Mum,' says Leila.

'Oh give it a rest, girl, in the name of medical science.'

Vincent reaches out slowly. His left hand soon hits Leila's right palm, but he feels nothing with his right. He waits, pushes a little further, and feels skin.

'Open your eyes.'

Vincent sees that his right hand is spread across the base of Leila's neck, just above her collar. Her chin is lifted in distaste, her eyelids lowered. She waggles the fingers of her free left hand, a yard away. 'Missed.'

'What's wrong with me?' says Vincent, quietly.

'You're a pervert,' answers Leila.

'Don't panic, Vincent,' says Mrs Downing. 'It actually feels like an old wound. You've got reduced proprioception. It's not serious.'

'Appropriate what?' Vincent turns his head to look at Mrs

Downing, but keeps the rest of his body locked in position. Leila takes his hand away from her neck.

'Basically, you have all these little nerves in your arm joint. Golgi organs and such. They tell your brain where your limbs are. They are constantly adjusting to keep you upright and balanced,' says Mrs Downing.

'Mine aren't working.'

'No. Sometimes, with a dislocation, they get confused and give out bogus information. They might tell you that your arm is up when it's really down.'

'So his brain doesn't know what his arm is doing?' says Leila with a smirk.

'Full marks, madam. It has a mind of its own at the moment. But there are some exercises you can do to help.'

'Will they involve molesting me?' says Leila. Vincent and Mrs Downing both turn to look at her, frowning and half-hot from the halogen. 'Be nice, Leila,' says Mrs Downing softly.

Leila takes him into the garden. 'Mum's Egyptian in case you were wondering. Dad's English.'

'Oh.'

'You don't say much.'

Vincent is unaccustomed to such sustained and varied company. In truth he is exhausted. She leads him past the cedar, which has, over the years, spread a springy iris of brown, bird-worried old needles around its base. They pass a red tent before reaching the gate that gives out on to the woods. 'Where are we going?' asks Vincent.

'The quarry. To see the buzzards.'

'And we're doing our English project together?'

'Yes. It's the least you can do,' she says, but smiling now. 'Everyone knows you're the best at English. It's my worst subject.'

'But you're in the top group.'

She looks at him as if she does not comprehend. 'I should have gone to a proper school, but the money ran out. Remember that you can't do birds this time, and I can't do science. It's got to be about people.'

'I thought maybe Houdini.'

Leila stops suddenly. 'That's a terrible idea.'

The sun is dropping as they reach the quarry. JEM – the concrete company that extracts the sandstone – exhausted the west side of the woodland many years ago and left several scoops in the bank, forty feet at the deepest but with easy access on the open side, at the base of the slope. Leila's quarry, long abandoned, has ruddy brown or yellow walls, depending on the time of year. Today the sandstone mass of the high ridge looks like the muscular hindquarters of a bay mare.

Vincent, a fellow hermit, recognizes the benefits of the location. A line of conifers on the top ledge hides it from dog-walkers, and the quarry can only be traversed by a dangerous sandstone bridge, some of the bricks from which have dropped into the basin below. A fallen tree guards the entrance on the low side, its excised roots appearing like the head of Medusa to curious mutts and passers-by. Vincent nods his appreciation at these measures of concealment, and strokes Medusa's ringlets.

'People dump their shameful and melodramatic rubbish here,' says Leila, picking up a pile of soggy pornographic magazines, the curling pages of which had caused Vincent to believe they were a sort of fungus. 'Cum on my wet tits,' reads Leila, and absently drops the magazines. She lists the humiliating waste she has found, counts the items off on her fingers. 'The bottom jaw of a dog, the blades from a lawnmower, a pair of high-heeled shoes wrapped in cellophane . . .'

So, thinks Vincent, she is just one weird thing amongst lots of weird things. Leila spins around, and for a moment Vincent worries that he has been thinking aloud. 'Listen,' she says. 'They're here.'

Despite the pleasant spring sunset, rain has begun to fall, and all Vincent can hear is the oak and beech leaves describing the acceleration of the shower. It is a comforting sound. The shards of a torn magazine flip in the rain, as if spontaneously exploding, and reveal girl-on-girl action on the underside. Medusa's locks become studded with snake eyes of unabsorbed water.

Leila taps Vincent on the shoulder and points up through the canopy. Vincent sees the bird. She has lost some of the feathers from her left wing, which gives her a haggard appearance countervailed by the stubborn grace of her soaring. Her body and wings are absolutely still as she circles.

'I call her Piano. On account of the missing keys. She's the mum.'

Vincent's mouth has dropped open from looking up. 'She's huge.'

'Watch this. Here come the kids.'

Two smaller birds emerge from the sun and dive at the mother, who lithely evades them with subtle movements.

'What's going on?' says Vincent, concerned that this serene picture is about to go the way of the slug war.

'Hunting practice I reckon. They're useless at the moment but it's only spring.'

Vincent and Leila climb to the bridge for a better view. The Parish Council have condemned the bridge as unusable, but Leila shifts the bollards and hazard signs. 'You'd better sit down considering your dodgy balance.'

Vincent sits in the rain-speckled ochre dirt and Leila joins him among the broken teeth of the bridge. The indigo rain clouds have tinted the sun and improved visibility. With the enduring drift of rain, the light has taken on a strange sourceless clarity, and from this height Vincent can see the brown whorls on the underside of Piano's light wings. Her colours make it seem like she has been peeled from the rock of the quarry. She does not move those long straight wings, or the elegant 'fingers' at their ends. Instead, she dips and tilts as her two charges swoop clumsily down on her like pieces of tumbling flint.

Vincent is entranced by the show, and his preoccupation, coupled with the rhythm of the rain, almost causes him to forget that he is not alone. In fact, there is something about Leila which makes him feel that he *is* alone, that he can act in ways that bring him censure at home and at school. He looks at her, the sharpness of her chin. 'Thanks,' he says, and then turns shy, 'you know, for the arm and stuff. I mean, say thanks to your mum.'

'Shut up,' she says and then does her one-syllable laugh.

That night, George watches his son from the top level of the split living room. Vincent stands before the mirror with his eyes closed, one arm out to the side, the other pointing to the ceiling. When the boy opens his eyes he looks disappointed. Closing them again, he touches his nose with his left index finger and then pokes himself in the eye with his right. George watches him massage the right shoulder, that same shoulder he injured in Blackmoor all those years ago, when he fell from the window.

'What's wrong with your bloody arm?' says George, startling his son.

'Nothing much.'

'Stop touching it then. You'll get an affliction.'

'It's just a bit of . . . induced perception . . . probably.'

'What? Do you need to go to the doctor's?'

'No. I . . .' He decides not to tell George about Mrs Downing. He has his secrets too.

'Leave it alone then. Touching yourself all the while.'

They silently look at each other, Vincent craning his neck. He smiles generously and shrugs. 'Probably an old injury flaring up,' he says, repeating Mrs Downing's diagnosis.

'No it isn't,' says George.

Six

Beth was admitted to the psychiatric unit in June, at least a month after she should have been. They told George that she had puerperal psychosis, a severe and dangerous form of post-natal depression. George had no trouble remembering the name of the condition. *Pure peril.* It resonated with the acute and specific terror he felt when he saw her knuckles scraped to raw flesh by the wire wool and the pink tinge of the suds in the basin, or when he woke at 3 a.m. to find the bed empty. How could he describe that fear? Encountering his wife in this state gave him the same plunging gut sensation as when he found his own corpse in a dream.

During what doctors retrospectively identified as Beth's manic phase, George had felt weak. Beth had wielded a new power – the power to destroy him with fear. But when her energy drained away and the depression reared, it became unbearable in a different way. The bizarrely spruced house sank back to normal and then beyond. George tried to keep the conversation lighthearted, domestic. 'Sommat smells good,' he said when he came home from work. 'I'm bloody famished. Haven't eaten since eleven.'

'I haven't eaten since Wednesday,' she said.

In this way she regularly defeated him. The things she said about herself now seemed childish, attention-seeking and repetitive. Quite frankly, it was *boring*.

An hour after he found Vincent in the garden, he had called the hospital. George himself could barely survive with Beth in this condition, so the baby had no chance. She offered a beleaguered resistance to his suggestion. It was just a bit of baby blues, she said. The nurses had told her it was normal, and if she was struggling to cope it was *okay* to wrap him up tight and get three closed doors between her and the noise.

'Baby blues' sounded like a jazz song that George's parents might have danced to, so he knew it wasn't that. No, pure peril was right.

Vincent stayed at the hospital with Beth for much of the time, as part of her rehabilitation. George, unable to deal with his house – the punctured double glazing, stained bedsheets, the carpet of tiny flies in the cupboard under the sink – went back to live with his mother for a while. He spent his evenings at the Red Lion, hiding in the corner and listening to men talk about his wife.

'She's like a witch,' said Wagstaff, leaning down to the pool table with arthritic discomfort. 'I know Bettsy's soft as shit, but I'm starting to believe him about that lawn catching fire. She's doolally, youth.'

'*You*'d g' mad if you were married to that limp-dick. He's not worth a light. What she needs is a bloody good seeing-to,' said Steve Grimshaw.

'They're all tapped though, aren't they? Them aborigines.'

'Aborigines?' said Grimshaw. 'You mean albinos?'

'Aye. There were a programme on telly. Cannibals they are.'

'She can eat me, youth,' said Grimshaw, pointing to his pool cue.

'Another bitter. No nozzle,' said George to the barman. The two pool players swung around on hearing his voice, but he did not meet their gaze.

Somewhere in the midst of the loose talk in the pub and at the allotments, at the tea mornings and bridge nights, the boundaries between 'Beth Cartwright's Prolonged Stay in Hospital' and 'The Impending Damnation of Blackmoor' became blurred. Exploding boilers, women running through the night, men dropping dead, lawns on fire – the subjects just seemed to flow together, and when Beth returned she found herself a firm outsider.

She was discharged at the end of summer. When George collected her, the nurse told him that puerperal psychosis does not clear up like a cold, never to return. It takes a long time to get back to normal and even then, relapse is always possible.

'There are things you need to understand about how Beth feels at the moment,' she said.

'Right.'

'You see when you're depressed, you become the centre of the universe. Everything that happens in the world seems to be directly related to you.'

As an example of the depressive state of mind, the nurse told the story of a woman who had made good progress on the ward. A few days before her release, the patient had seen footage of the Heysel stadium disaster on the news and had a severe second breakdown. The nurses found her huddled in a corner, shouting that it was her fault, that she was responsible.

'Right, I see,' said George, looking away. They turned the corner on to the ward, and Beth gave him that sly, knowing grin, this time tinged with an apology. Her hair was tied back, and looked a little duller than usual. George stood about ten feet away from her, and stared. He turned to the nurse. 'It was the fault of the police of course,' he said.

'Pardon me, Mr Cartwright?' said the nurse.

'Heysel. They were totally unprepared.'

'I'm sorry,' she said, often.

'For *what*?' said George. She always took that as a rhetorical question but George wanted to hear a detailed confession of her wrongdoings. She did not remember everything and that seemed unfair to him. Most of the time, the drugs coated her like a cormorant in an oil slick. She did little, said little. When she spoke it was to say that she had made a mess of everything, that she had ruined her life. Again, George was surprised by the banality of it all.

After two or three mornings, he found that he could no longer eat breakfast with her. Eating seemed to be one of the only things she enjoyed now, although she wasn't excessive, would never gain weight. She swallowed gulps of cereal with slow blinks of pleasure, mopping up the trickle of milk from her chin with the spoon. The cattle grind of her jaw through the toast was more than he could take, especially when she slurped tea at the same time.

He sat on the sofa while she ate at the table. He drank instant coffee, timing his sips to coincide with the pauses in her munching. Later, he realized he could not stand food waste either. A rotting apple core inside a banana skin made him gag, and he couldn't even drink with that in sight. The drift of toast crumbs down the inside of the teacup disgusted him. This physical reaction against mess frightened George, because that was how Beth had started. Was this thing contagious? Fortunately Vincent was a clean baby, refusing the irritation of a bib around his neck, and spilling hardly anything. He screamed when his face got dirty.

Several weeks after their reunion, Beth gently ran her hand along the side of his body, over his leg. She pressed her breasts into his back, and pushed her thighs against his hamstrings. She slid herself into the grooves of him, like water filling a jug.

What she did not know was that her breathing alerted George. Her body, its warmth and comfort could probably have fooled him, but the breathing gave everything away. It contained her calculations, her motives. His dry eyes opened in the dark. He felt the intentional lightness of her breath. She was trying to keep him in that state where his body responded without his mind, trying to trick him into arousal. Unbeknown to Beth, the heat from her breath caused a patch of moisture to form on the back of George's neck, and this patch cooled uncomfortably when she inhaled. He rolled away to the other side of the bed, congratulated himself on avoiding this nightly hazard. For how could he even touch her again if this madness was the result? He knew he had – in the most evident of ways – caused the illness, and he could not risk a repeat. Abstaining from sex was an easy decision, and George was a man who could shut himself down.

Apart from eating, she liked to bathe. She bathed every day, and for hours. The first time he noticed the length of her bathing time, he went up to the middle floor to confront her. Through the locked door he could hear that the tap was still running, and he froze, fearing the worst. As he opened his mouth to call her, the tap stopped. After a few seconds a rhythmic tinkle ensued – fingers moving through the water. George stood still and listened. He assumed the posture of one who is walking past a door, one leg in front of the other, and he listened, with his mouth open, until his wife's rapid breathing defeated the splashing water, and stopped abruptly with the sharp familiar intake of her orgasm.

George was paralysed, aroused. He continued to wait outside the door, although he did not know why. When Beth eventually emerged from the bathroom she was trailed by a gush of steam. Her skin had pinked, and her hair was soaked into several thick tendrils. He had forgotten all about the rich wheat colour of her hair when it was wet. She hitched up the small towel at her chest, revealing for a second a wisp of ashen pubic hair. George perceived the trace of a cooking smell beneath the various cosmetic scents. He could not move.

'George!' she said. 'Did you need the toilet? You should have knocked. Did you knock? I wouldn't have heard you because I was underwater.'

'Didn't knock.'

'Oh.'

He walked past her into the bathroom, where her vaporous ghosts surrounded him. He shut and locked the door. The water continued to drain from the bath. It was speckled with golden globs of vegetable oil. He could feel her heat all over him, and began to sweat. George sat down by her moist footprints, closed his eyes and waited for his desire to pass.

She had been back for five weeks now, but every evening when he came home from work, he held his breath. If he predicted another breakdown – if he thought about it – then surely it could not happen. From the pavement he noticed that the downstairs window was open. As he walked past he could hear a bee or a wasp in the front room. The wasps were a nuisance at this time of the year, lashing out because they knew they were done for. Again he entered the covered corridor down the side of his house. The acoustic change of his footsteps always made him feel like he was entering a hollow skull. Snails crawled impossibly above his head, unperturbed by the tinny squeak of his shoes. A small iron tap, unused for years, had left an orange trail of rust over a flaking scab of white paint.

When he came through the back door, he realized that the buzzing was not an insect. Beth stood in the middle of the front room, with George's electric razor three inches above her right ear, and half of her white hair settled in a fluffy pile on a piece of newspaper laid across the carpet. He said nothing, just stared. He could see her face in the mirror, and he could see her back with his naked eyes. George felt sick. It seemed wrong to behold so much of someone in one go.

The baby lolled in his buggy. George bent down and wiped some fine hair from Vincent's face, then stood up again. Beth switched off the razor and the teeth slowed to a stop with an obedient little shuffle. 'S'all right, George, it's no big deal. Unless I stop now, of course, in which case I'd look a right plonk.'

'What are you doing, Beth? You gave me a fright.' George noticed how vapid his own voice sounded.

'I've been talking it over with Polly Grimshaw in the Post Office, and we thought this might be a good look for me.'

'Polly Grimshaw?'

George took Vincent upstairs to the bedroom and sat quietly until the buzzing stopped and Beth went for her bath. Even then he could not rest easy in the front room, for the hair remained on the carpet, disrupted now, like the site of a peregrine kill. In the dusky, net-strained September light, George saw the tiny haloed shavings peel away from the pile and float upwards, against gravity.

Seven

Vincent continues to stand on the top level of the garden, but his posture has changed. He now spreads his arms like Christ the Redeemer over Rio, as part of his exercise routine. When he closes his eyes he hears sheep coughing like humans, beer barrels rumbling off trucks on to dusty landing mats, the gasp of cars on the bypass and the glassy tinkle of telephones.

After a few moments, he begins to feel that insuperable movement, and he knows not to fight it. As he hits the ground, however, he realizes that he has been pushed. The memory of hands on his back. This is encouraging because it means he did not fall. When he looks up, his father is blacked out against the sky. 'What were you doing?'

'Nothing.'

'Look. Stop it. Whatever it is. The neighbours'll think we're odd.'

Vincent looks over the fence, and a Friesian briefly glances back. His father walks towards the house, stooped against the incline.

Vincent is unperturbed by his father's abruptness, because a powdery green stain already marks the crease of his school trousers and he knows it has come from the bark of the dead tree in the quarry. And when they call him 'duckfucker' or 'bird-bollocks' at school he can look down at the shard of pornography caught under his shoelaces, he can see the photographer's light pooling in the channels of the model's back and it reminds him that there is a place of solace which exists simultaneously, just two miles away. He is always aware of the quarry, if only by the sandstone scuff on his shoe, and he is always aware of Leila too. He sees her occasionally at school, in their English lessons, but she is part of the woodland to him now, an intricate, awkward and beautiful root.

Her manner is frosty, but he likes this because he knows he can thaw her out. The 'funny talk' he has been carrying around with him like a burdensome anchor suddenly has a purpose.

If they are not at the quarry they are in the sizeable red tent in her garden. She sleeps here during summer. It is warmer than the house, she says. He visits her before school and they lie on their stomachs and watch the young fox yawn and scratch his ear behind the cedar while rabbits sit obliviously, yards away. 'My dad says foxes are just orange dogs,' says Vincent.

'Yeah *right*. House dogs are so dense. I like foxes because it looks like they're wearing eye make-up. My mum always says she'd die for the eyelashes of a fox.'

'But they've got a moustache too. That black bit around the mouth.'

'Can't have everything,' Leila says stroppily, licking at the hairs above her top lip.

Other animals they see together, from the tent and the quarry:

Grey squirrels (too many).
A noisy field vole.
The three buzzards, of course.
Nuthatches climbing up the battlements, and treecreepers
walking down.
A lasso of racing pigeons.
The badgers, which they observe after dark, the tent lit by
Leila's battery-operated globe lamp so that from the
porous windows of Wood Edge it looks like a throbbing
pancreas in the undergrowth.

'Never corner a badger,' Vincent says earnestly. 'They're the most vicious animals in Britain.'

Leila studies him with a frown, so that he does not know whether she will slap him or smile. 'When am I going to corner a badger?' she asks.

Leila Downing's family history is complicated. Vincent is unable to imagine the life of his *own* mother and father in Blackmoor, so he would be unlikely to comprehend the international adventures and cross-cultural rule-breaking of his friend's parents.

Robert Downing, a telecommunications entrepreneur, first saw his future wife at a racetrack in Egypt. She was fifteen, he twenty-seven. Leila's paternal and maternal grandfathers owned racehorses. Robert Downing approached Mohammed Al-Sharif and said, 'I'm going to marry your daughter.'

She had been promised to one of her cousins and, as a non-Muslim, Downing's proposal was highly irregular, but he had a way of getting what he wanted. He brought her back to England on her sixteenth birthday – Mrs Downing often jokes that she was sold for two fillies. She quickly adapted to western life, trained and worked as a physiotherapist and gave birth to two boys while Robert Downing funded the speculative development of mobile phone technology.

They were happy with Timothy and James. If you look at the magnolia trees close to Leila's tent, you can see the weather-beaten hi-fi speaker which Downing rigged up outside. It used to emit pre-recorded owl noises and ghostly murmurs to amuse the boys. Robert and his sons would hide under the covers in 'the haunted castle' while Mrs Downing played 'Tubular Bells' on the grand piano in the hallway. The Downings tried to instil a sense of adventure in their children and that, Mrs Downing sometimes reflects, is probably what made them leave.

The marriage soured when the boys left, one for New Zealand, the other for London. The Downings had planned to make a modern home of the old stables and fund the project by converting Wood Edge into eight 'quirky apartments in the Derbyshire countryside'. But The Stables swallowed money, and when Mrs Downing found out that her husband was having an affair she petitioned for divorce and won the right to stay in Wood Edge. They both used their considerable resources and connections during the separation, running down their accounts so as to appear destitute, cutting off each other's electricity.

Downing pulled his money out of telecommunications and invested it in surveillance. He had his wife followed but she led the dazed private investigator through JEM woods and full circle into their own garden, where she hid in the rhododendrons. Downing watched from the window of his half-finished conversion, with a BB gun and a large prototype of a mobile phone.

One evening in the middle of it all, Downing went down to the hole where the swimming pool used to be, and saw his wife smoking a cigarette, which she quickly hid behind her back. 'What are you doing here?' she said.

'It's *my* swampy redundant former swimming pool. I can stand in it if I like. Why are you hiding that fag?'

'I told you I had quit smoking.'

'Did you?'

They laughed. During the conversation that followed, they both realized that the divorce had made them more passionate, inventive and invigorated than anything they had done for years. They fucked one last time on the lawn, had another row and went back to their solicitors. Mrs Downing had thought that her husband's tendency to carry one of those stupid walkie-talkies in each pocket might be as good a contraception as any. She told her friends that she could sometimes see his bollocks glowing in the dark from Wood Edge. Nevertheless, it seemed that the Downing testicles were still fully operational. Leila was born, and they bounced her, as amicably as possible, between the two failed houses.

Leila knows little of this, and would think it was a 'total melodrama' if she did. In fact, it was her schoolmates who (humiliatingly) taught her that most people's parents did *not* live in separate gigantic houses partitioned by a neatly coiffed lawn and a cluster of evergreens. In any case, she finds her parents boring, because she knows them. Coming from such different back-grounds as they do, and being such a strange pair of teenaged philosophers, Leila and Vincent are both interested in each other's origins in an unconscious way. Vincent's parents lived within a street of each other, and so he is bewildered by Leila's mongrel heritage, how she has *come to be.* He picks up the warm globe lamp and spins it, puts his finger on Cairo. 'So your mum came from here?'

Leila, her hair tugged into a spray on top of her head, shuffles across the groundsheet. 'Yes.'

Vincent traces a line over the hump to Britain, most of which he can cover with his thumb. 'And your Dad was from here.'

'*Point?*'

'Well, it seems pretty unlikely.'

'What?'

'That you got born. I mean that's a lot of distance. What are the odds? A gazillion to one? A googol maybe.'

'It was obvious. It's the only thing that could have happened.'

'As if it is.'

'Listen, I don't want to think about my mum and dad doing *that*. It's gross.'

'It definitely explains why you look so weird.'

'Oh thanks.'

'I didn't mean it in a bad way,' he says, unable to look at her now.

'Shut up. Anyway, what about your family? You don't talk about them much. Are they from around here?'

'No. We used to live in an old mining place called Blackmoor but they knocked it down.'

'They knocked down your house?'

'The whole village.'

'Wow. So everyone had to move?'

'Yep. Except Mum. She died before.'

'Oh. I didn't know.'

'See. You don't know everything.'

Vincent revels for a moment in the sudden switch of power, but Leila has already stopped feeling guilty. Her mind plays the apocalyptic scene of an old village booming with detonated buildings, and diggers munching through playgrounds and pubs. She has a romanticized idea of coalmining towns, informed mainly by the funny parts of the film *Kes* and repeats of Ridley Scott's Hovis advertisement on *The Best One Hundred Adverts of All Time*. In fairness, Vincent knows little more.

'So why did they knock the place down? This . . . Blackmoor?'

'I don't know, do I? I was only about four.'

'Ask your dad.'

'Yeah right.'

'It's so interesting.'

'Eh?'

'Well, imagine wiping out a whole village. This is going to be perfect for our English project.'

And so it is decided. A little later that night, she makes him write down everything he remembers about Blackmoor, to see if they can get a starting point for the project. Vincent writes:

Holes in the field (this might not be real)
Sheds at the backs of the houses
Foxes

Not many shops, some of them shut down
Nobody wearing suits except for Dad
Foggy

Leila sighs. 'It's not much of a help, *Vince*. We can't write about foxes because they're wildlife and I think we have fog in Church Eaton.'

'I was young, same as I say.'

'You don't remember much about your mum, then?'

'Bits. But I don't know what bits are real, and what bits Dad's told me about. I don't want to milk it anyway.'

They listen to the woods moving outside, knowing that somewhere up there, Piano is perched, on a church tower or a phone mast, with an upturned view of things, where the red tent is the pupil of a black eye. 'Ask your dad about Blackmoor, that's your next task.'

'Ooo it gets dark, it gets lonely, on the other side from you,' sings Vincent, before dawn, in his sleep.

Across the room, George wakes, wondering at the cruel inventions of grief, its sheer variety. He goes upstairs to the kitchen, makes a pot of tea and sits before the projector. See him there, at the table, his short receding hair sticking up around his bald patch like a cockatoo's crown, his baggy T-shirt marked by the rusty amber of an old nosebleed, the impression of his knees in his jogging bottoms.

He could have fixed the projector days ago, but he deferred completion in order to savour the last moments. Now he switches off the kitchen light, whistles disparate phrases of the Twentieth

Century Fox fanfare, and turns on the machine. The mosquito clicks of the reel begin, smooth as new, and the colour spews out on to the ceiling, the door and part of the wall. In many ways, this does not concern George, because the mechanism obviously works. He has not fixed the projector in order to watch the films. Being such a thorough engineer, however, he decides to check the quality of the picture. So he pulls back the projector and resizes the image on the kitchen door. It seeps over the edges, but the colour is vivid, the focus clear and sharp.

George always finds the lack of audio to be the most pleasing aspect of cine films. The silence buffers him against the realities of the distant moment. The film itself shows Vincent as a baby, on a hot day. He is lying in his buggy, wearing scratch mittens knitted by his mother.

Sitting in his Church Eaton kitchen, George recognizes the sad daytime shadows of the north-facing Blackmoor garden. He sips his tea, unable to imagine having filmed the scene.

At first, only the shadows of her long hands, thumbs crossed to make a flapping falcon, appear on baby Vincent's chest. Then her fingers descend into view, the white flecks on the nails, the trenches healing, the digits hardly shaking at all. Vincent reaches up for his mother's hands, but she evades him and tugs away the mittens. The infant's face changes to stunned wonder. He has worn those mittens most of the day for months, at a time when he is just beginning to recognize his own body, and he has learned a fair degree of control over the blunt pads. Now he has two magnificent five-pronged instruments at the end of his fat bracelets. A considerable upgrade. He looks from one hand to the other and then brings the two together in a lattice above his head. Delighted by this, he begins to clap. Sometimes he connects and sometimes he misses.

George cannot hear anyway. He can see his wife's hands clapping above, the shadows rapidly passing across Vincent's T-shirt. The picture shakes. Had the younger George neglected his camerawork to become involved in the excitement of the new hands? All George knows is that as the cine camera shook in that old garden, the image shakes in his current kitchen, and this causes the central focus of the picture to overlap the grooves in the door design, thus distorting the edges of the buggy. As he goes to adjust the projector, the shot pans around. George holds his breath. The camera is still unstable when it reaches her. She raises a weak smile. The short spikes of her white hair (just growing back) have taken on the shade and look almost blue. Her eyes swing quickly, as they always did when she was tired. George grips his mug. Her light quivers on his face.

Beholding this image, time collapses for George. He tries to imagine pointing the camera at her. Had he felt uneasy, in the garden that day? No. There had been no premonition, no sign that his finger on that button would one morning – in an unknown future kitchen – revive for him the features of his dead wife, the memory of which he has purposefully neglected and allowed to crumble. Yet that, now, seems like the only reason this film could ever have been made.

The cine camera shakes some more, casting Beth's face downwards so it shatters on the edges of the door and her trembling eye rests on the doorknob. The pupil expands and reaches across the kitchen towards George. He tries to turn the projector off, but the switch snaps between his fingers. He is trapped in his kitchen, for how can he put his hand over her giant eye and turn the knob? After a few seconds, Vincent comes to the rescue, opening the door and shielding his eyes against the bright light. He immediately recognizes his father's distress. 'Dad? Are you okay?'

'What? What the bloody hell do you want? Get out of the way.'

Vincent glances down at the melting mess of colour on his school blazer. He frowns, unable to make sense of the image.

'Don't you look. Don't look. Go on. Piss off,' says George.

Vincent stares at his father, who turns away and desperately beholds the projector. 'I can't turn it off. I can't turn the fucking thing off.'

Vincent watches him panic for a while then he calmly walks over to the socket and pulls out the plug. The kitchen darkens a degree and the boy leaves, shutting the door quietly behind him.

George closes his eyes on the emerging daylight, but even then her purple shape floats on his eyelids. How long since she has existed like that, as a figure on his skin? George is afraid, and tries to keep his eyes open. Not long now, before he encounters her simple name.

'What do you remember about Blackmoor, Dad?'

'What kind of a question is that? I lived there me whole life. Why?'

'I remember some things about it, you know.'

'Forget them. They demolished that place for a reason.'

'Right. Right. Why?'

'Because it was useless and dangerous, that's why. Although if you were to listen to the bloody remedials that lived there at the time, they'd have told you it was a voodoo curse or some such bleeding garbage.'

'You said once that Blackmoor killed Mum.'

'I never did.'

'Yeah you did. You came back from the pub and said, "Blackmoor did for your mother, not me or anyone else."'

'I've told you. She got ill. End of. I don't want to talk about that place anyway.'

'Why not?'

'Because I worked bloody hard to get you away from it, and I'll be buggered if you're going to spend your life trying to get back.'

'Get back?'

'Which you can't because it's gone.'

They are quiet for a moment. Vincent tries to touch the tip of his nose with his eyes closed.

'I suppose you don't think that a place can kill a person,' says George.

Vincent shrugs. 'I just want to know how.'

'Slowly. That's how.'

EIGHT

Imagine it. You cannot even remember.

When you arrive home, your house is like a cave at the back of an old dream, the uncanny misplacements and omissions. Once familiar household objects are missing. Where is your cut-glass trifle bowl? What happened to the framed sketch the man made of you on your honeymoon? You find your best goblets in the airing cupboard, some of them in pieces wrapped in newspaper like shards of Easter egg, others held together with glue. You hold one of the wine glasses above your son, so that a beam of sunlight turns green and shines on his face, and you roll your eyes at your husband's efforts to keep house in your absence. 'Did you break the good glasses, Georgie?' you ask sympathetically.

'No. You did. I fixed them.'

He seems frightened, and a brief fizz of power possesses you and then subsides, leaving you more aware of your weakness. Hours later you go back to the airing cupboard to study the breakages. You wince at the glued cracks that go right to the lip. Imagine the damage they could do. It hardly matters, you tell yourself, because we never have guests. But then you think, Jesus, if I did this and forgot, what might I have done to my baby? You need to talk to your husband about this, but he's at the Red Lion with men who despise him. You rebuke yourself for the spite present in your thinking, and you mentally thank George for trying to fix what you have broken.

Vincent's face. His granny calls him 'Shock-Eyes' because of the permanent expression of amazement. You wonder if you can be trusted with his life. They told you at the hospital that you can. They said you are – and always have been – a good mother. Just follow these rules, they said. What if you forget the rules? Wasn't 'don't smash everything in your house' a rule of sorts? You stroke Vincent's head and think of shattered glass.

They gave you a pamphlet on the ward, about puerperal psychosis and the symptoms. Case studies featuring Mrs C and Mrs R and Mrs N. Mrs R thought her baby was Satan, and Mrs C thought hers was a wolf. One of them had worked out a complex code in the playlist of her local radio station. Women using hammers on babies they believe to be misshapen, throwing them down the stairs. You laughed incredulously when you read this, because it did not seem to relate to you. Now, however, it is evident that you have done things you do not recall.

As you watch him, little Vincent scratches at his wide eyes, and you begin to panic. There are no witnesses here to prove that you did not cause the little red brackets settling into his face. So you take out some orange wool and the old pattern books and you knit him some scratch mittens. You see your own little counting marks, made years ago, in purple crayon on the pattern book.

As the weeks go on, you realize that people in the village are talking about you. Old Mrs Fitch asks after your health in the Post Office. 'Only our Polly here reckons she saw you on Rec, running round and round real sharpish. It were four in morning and all. Polly thought you'd lost your bloody marbles.'

'Jesus, Mam, shut up will you?' says Polly Grimshaw, pushing the old woman out of the door. She turns to you. 'Sorry about her. She's not all there. I mean from age.'

'That's all right, love,' you say, trying to laugh it off (you call people 'love' or 'duck' much more now, because you feel older). It is a difficult moment because Polly feels obliged to stay and offer some conciliatory conversation. She will not meet your eyes, and you are glad because you know they are flickering wildly (you can barely see). Polly stares instead at your long, white hair. She seems to like you again, but you can never tell. 'You know, I've always really admired your hair. It's so unusual. I have to dye mine and it's still nothing like . . .'

You nod and wait until she leaves. How strange that she should say *admired*. And that word, *unusual*, like a mass of bubblegum in her mouth. You go home, shave your head, and knit yourself a hat with wool left over from the mittens.

Some of the women treat you like an outsider now, not that you have ever really been part of the community. You saw the way they behaved with the girl from Derby who moved into one of the council houses and had a child. They would only speak to the baby. They talked into the pram and ignored the mother.

They do that to *you* now, telling Vincent what a poor little thing he is.

Yes, people have been talking about you for a long time, have they not? And in the recent past, these people have dropped dead in their cellars for no apparent reason. Sometimes their houses have been ripped open by bolts of volatile energy, sending their plates and teacups hurtling towards the old colliery. Tom Betts's boots remain on the lawn, as if he has spontaneously combusted in your garden. It smouldered when he stood there, so you know that he must have been gassing about you too. The grass still hisses in the dewy mornings, and a low mist hangs over it.

A thousand people live in the village, and they have so little to talk about. The subjects currently on offer are your madness, or spontaneous fires. Occasionally the two topics overlap, and you do not know if that is so wrong. In the bath, you secretly try to set the towels on fire by staring at them. A little joke, you tell yourself, when it does not work.

At first you have to stand up in the bath, because of the heat. Steam reaches your thighs and scalding water burns a red sock midway up your calf. You pour vegetable oil into your hands, surrender to its worrying slickness, and lubricate yourself against the water. In the oval mirror you see your misted body: pale, bald, newly hatched. Your muscles have become thin and stringy, and your ribs press through the skin beneath your high, small breasts. Your triceps shake as you lower yourself. You turn on the cold tap and let the water run along your shins. This harsh contrast seems to be the only way to feel anything. You allow your fingers to slide down between your legs.

The bathroom is the only place you can cope with disrepair, because it seems somehow organic. The steam and heat from the bath enliven the place, cause the ceiling to become engorged and the mould to blossom darkly between the tiles. There are two of the old sash windows high above the tap-end of the bath. You keep them closed and watch the clouds drift on outside. Two patches of the cool blue world in the olive green bathroom.

You plunge your head below the hot water, allowing the cold stream to reach your knee and thigh. Here, the world seems gelatinous, stable, silent. You can only just hear your husband climbing the stairs and stopping outside the door as usual, the boards creaking as he adjusts his feet. You prefer things like this: muffled, at one remove.

At night, all you want is appreciation. You *know* about the 'inappropriate advances' you made before (they were in the pamphlet), but you are back to normal now. It is not really the sex you want; it is just that the days are long and full of trying to act like a 'good mother' or a 'recovering patient' . . . at night you just want to feel like a plain old desirable woman again. You almost want your husband to use you, to lose control on you. All day you provoke wary, stilted responses from people. You want to inspire desperation, pleasure, not obligation. And you know you are still attractive, even without the long hair, even with the cold red blotches on your face. You have seen the men look at you in the newsagent's or the Co-op. They are wondering how crazy you really are, what they could get away with. Would anyone believe you any more if it came down to your word against theirs? . . . But at night, when you lean into your husband, he does not wake. He has bathed too, and the soap is bitter to the taste. You graze your tongue on the line of stubble running down his neck. You take his limp hand and place it between your legs, you feel yourself swell through his fingers. 'Fuck me,' you whisper, but he wakes and turns on the light, stares at you wide-eyed, concerned. He sits up and you squint. 'What is it?' you say. 'What's wrong?'

He does not reply, just studies your face, checking to see if you have gone mad again. Of course, it feels demeaning when he regards you in that analytical manner before turning off the light and rolling over. He does not even have the decency to tell you what he is thinking, to explain his objections. Soon, however, you will long for this moment of lamplight, you will pray for him to sit up stiffly in bed and stare at you. In that moment, at least, there is fear in his eyes, and the ever so subtle sense that he might be forced to do what you say. That scared expression, you will remark to yourself, would be better than nothing.

NINE

George's father started work in the mine at the age of fifteen, just after World War II. Harry felt no fear as he squeezed into the cage with the other men, but the bitterness of their bodies surprised him, the constant sharp stench of armpits and the intermittent cheesiness of stale breath. His own father introduced him briefly but he knew every man, of course. They seemed different in here though, angrier. In the minute it took to get to the bottom, the world changed. On the back wall, bore holes leaked silvery water. House bricks and ancient rock hurtled past him as though borne on an ocean's gravity. Halfway down, white spindles began to float above his head. The spindles soon knitted into one mass, and Harry realized this was the collective breath of the men gradually frosting, making its presence visible as if to emphasize its value. Harry had heard that the pit bottom was hot, and indeed some of the men wore old army shorts, carried Dudleys full of water.

On the pit bottom, an older lad, Martin Wagstaff, took him

aside. Wagstaff's jaw prodded meanly out, and his eyes and teeth shone white like those of the blacked-up jazz turns at the Miners' Welfare Club. He passed Harry some chewing tobacco. 'Ay a bit a this, youth. It'll damp down dust,' he said. Then, after a measured pause, he added, 'Steady you dunna swallow fucker though.' But Harry was already retching in vile brown belches.

For the first few years, Harry worked as a pony driver. His father introduced him to Leaf, whose face was mostly obscured by a leather harness with demonic sloping rents for the eyes. 'This is Leaf. She's a stubborn ode mare like your grandmother. You're a fair lad, Harold, and I've note against you, but this hoss is worth more than you'll ever be, so mind how you go.'

Harry did not enjoy pony driving. Leaf was indeed stubborn, not to mention wily. She refused to move if Harry attached more than one tub of coal. 'She can hear you clip second link,' said Wagstaff. 'You've got a hoss what's smarter than you are.'

The two men became friends. They squatted by the wall together at snap-time, clipped back the fasteners on their tins, and watched the bread grey in seconds. They shared a dislike for rats. Wagstaff could not stand the stench of the dead ones, rotting behind the tin walls. 'You canna get smell out your rags. It sticks to you.'

Harry felt that the ability of rats to survive and multiply bordered on the supernatural, and he was a devil-fearing man. In the dark, he sometimes thought he saw rats hatch from bits of broken stone.

Wagstaff told Harry about the next colliery, through the gate, where the men worked a thin seam. Twenty inches. They had to lie on their bellies and scrape the coal back into sacks on their shoulders. 'And what's past their pit?' asked Harry.

'Another one, I'll bet. Me old man reckons you can walk clean out a Derbyshire and rate the way up to Barnsley from here. All underground.'

Harry's eyes widened at this little legend. 'Makes you wonder, dun't it?' he said.

'What's that?'

'Makes you wonder what's holding North of England up.'

Wagstaff roared, his laughter echoing down the pit so that even Harry's cloth-eared father could hear it. 'I reckon it must be us, youth.'

(And how many times, in later years, would Harry tell his youngest, most difficult son about Wagstaff's mythical passage to South Yorkshire. George asked his typical barrage of questions. 'Can you get to Scotland int tunnel, Dad?'

'Aye.'

'Can you goo t'Eastwood?'

'Yes, duck.'

'Can you goo to Russia and all, Dad? Int tunnels?'

'Aye.'

'Can you get to London?'

'No.'

'No?'

'No. It's wrong way. Mr itchy feet. And it's enough bloody rattle out of you. Less talk, more action.')

*

Harry gave up pony driving after his growth spurt, and he and Waggy smashed their way through the decades side by side. Harry got married in 1950 and started a family. He became a tailgate ripper, driving a compressed-air drill into the lip of the rock. Wagstaff trained as a shot-firer. Both received dramatic wage increases, but this was considered compensation for the pulsing, stinking, blinding cloud of dust in which they now worked. The quality of the light from Harry's oil lamp was almost sub-aquatic. Often, he could not even see his drill. When he had finished he would look in the direction of his hands and watch them emerge. His skin seemed to be formed from settling, reintegrating particles. It was nice to hear Wagstaff cough behind him. One man would always cough or whistle to assure the other that they were not alone.

When Harry had drilled fifteen or twenty holes by the scaffold, Wagstaff packed the cavities with dynamite. They walked briskly away, shouting the warning. There were four explosions tapering outwards from the centre of the lip, each slightly quieter than the last. They called them Beethoven explosives because of the quartet of receding notes. When the noise was over, the other miners sang comic versions of that first foreboding bar of the Fifth Symphony.

The two men now had to secure the roof with flimsy corrugated iron, while rocks and water fell through the dust. 'You know,' said Harry, as he swung his pinch bar to strike a rock that rebounded against his knee, 'I can't help thinking we make us own problems down here. Wouldn't have to prop the bloody roof up if we didn't make so many holes.'

Wagstaff shook his head. 'Clever twat.'

*

Hard time passed slowly. Each day, the uphill walk from the cage to the stint took longer. Harry was tall, and his helmet constantly caught the roof of the low tunnels. It never really hurt, but the shock reinvigorated his angry wariness of falling objects. The cuts on his hands from the thin iron sheets seemed to shine again, and the firewater rose in his throat from a rushed breakfast. Another bump on the head. By the time he got set to use his drill, he was so angry he could have cried. His first twenty minutes were his most productive of the day, as he worked off the fury.

Later, when the big machines came in, the noise became such that he could scream his heart out and nobody would hear. Inseam mining machines advanced at one inch per minute and did the work of twelve men.

Sometimes they had to come out of the pit for methane gas, or 'firedamp' as they called it. 'Blackdamp', or CO_2, would just quietly suffocate you, but nobody wanted to encounter the volatile and highly explosive methane. If it was present, the blue flame of the Davy lamp narrowed like a cat's eye. They feared what the deputy called 'incendive sparking', which could ignite the gas. Yet the bell wire by which they communicated gave off sparks, and if their shovels hit the scaffold it sparked, and the cog on the haulage gear was like a Catherine wheel. Fool's gold was the worst for Harry. When he hit it with the drill, the sparks glinted through the dust cloud and he stopped immediately.

'Y'rate?' said Wagstaff.

'Aye. Fool's gold, youth.'

'Don't know what you're worried about a few sparks for. I'm

about to light eight sticks a dynamite and blow fuck out the place.'

'Same as a say: we make us own problems.'

And one day in April 1968, the Fifth Symphony went down a key, and Harry thought they were done for. But Wagstaff's explosion had, in fact, revealed an existing cave that contained a crude rotting shovel, an ancient small shoe and evidence of bowed oak props. 'Look's like someone got here before us,' said Wagstaff.

'How did they get down *here*?' Harry said.

'I don't know, do I? One thing's certain: they had some fucking trouble getting back out.'

'Eh?'

'When were last time you were in such a hurry to leave that you forgot your boot? I've made a dash for the top house before, to get first pint in, but I've always had time to tie me bastard laces. This were a cave-in.'

Harry crouched down, picked up the shoe and nodded. It looked more like a sandal or slipper, with a cleaved heel, and had obviously belonged to a child. A tiny piece of the sole disintegrated as he held it. The two friends cut a deal: Wagstaff kept the shovel, which had eroded to the shape of a dagger, and Harry kept the shoe. The deceased, wherever they were, would stay as they lay, undisturbed by archaeologists.

At home, Harry put the shoe above the fire, despite the protests of his wife, who called it a dirty old thing. He could see the worn bump where the big toe had pressed up through the leather, and this detail, this phantom toe, stirred something in him. He imagined a man and his son, their hands stretched out for each other as the rubble extinguished the candle. Poor bleeders. Harry almost wanted to believe they had escaped, that the boy had pulled off his shoe to free himself from debris. After a while he rebuked himself for being so sentimental. So what if the boy had died? Harry's own grandfather had been a blacksmith's striker, and one day he had slipped in the foundry, plunged his hand into molten metal and then cut his own throat to ease the pain. Death was fast, random, and sometimes a bloody mercy.

Shot-firing finished in Blackmoor in the 1970s, and the last of the ponies were taken to the surface for a breath of fresh air, and to be killed. The seam was pronounced suitable for mechanization. Fortunately, Harry was skilled with machines. After a while he secured a position as a mechanic, taking the giant, jagged rippers and power loaders down in the cage piece by piece, and assembling them on the pit bottom. Timber props were replaced by Dowty five-leg rigid base double telescopic supports: a mechanized corridor of chocks, movable by the flick of a switch. But how much had things really changed? Harry now stood behind a huge boom ripper. Its spinning picks bit the lip, burrowed out new ways, and the dust plumed, still choking him, still blinding him, so that the green and red lights on the dash seemed like the beginnings of a distant city in a valley's fog. The ineffective water sprays designed to dampen the dust just soaked him, and made the floor dangerously wet. The noise was almost intolerable. Despite the machines and the new orange overalls, the work was still hard, accidents still happened, and Harry continued to cough.

*

In the middle of a conversation at the Red Lion, George watched his father's face become docile, almost pitiful. The baggy skin flushed quickly and his eyes filled with water. He quaked like a schoolboy racked with illicit laughter and nodded at whoever was talking to him. Then he turned and marched to the toilets, locked himself in a cubicle. They could still hear him in the bar. The coughing was sometimes deep, drowning, and sometimes rose to the dry pitch of surprised exclamation. The swinging toilet door made the noise come in waves. Some of the younger lads winced, and cursed under their breath. Many of the older men were too deaf to appreciate the full slicing viciousness of it, but they must have felt the tremors through the bar because they held their pints away from their mouths, as though pausing to remember something important.

Harry slouched out, hunched and wheezing. He stopped halfway to the bar, and pretended to read the notices on the board while he caught his breath. George regarded the bilious colour of his father's eye whites, the darkness of the lips.

'It's y'own fault for chewing tobacco,' said George.

'Note to do wi' it,' Harry whispered. 'Baccy keeps the dust out your mouth.'

'Doesn't keep it out your lungs though, obviously.'

A few of the other men shook their heads, annoyed by George's smart mouth. George went to the toilet. In the cubicle, he could not tell the dried-on shit from his father's lung blood.

'Feels like I'm just grinding to a halt,' Harry told the doctor in 1979. 'The only thing I seem to be able to do at any great pace is cough.'

The doctor noticed the colour of his skin. That familiar milk blue. He made a map of Harry's lungs, circled the districts of damage. Twenty per cent black spots: not enough to retire long-term sick.

'What's your advice?' asked Harry.

Shoot yourself, the doctor thought. Travel through time and get born twenty years later, 200 miles from here, and then study hard at school. Never go down a mine. Rob banks, go on the game, work in a sweatshop, give yourself a fucking break.

'Wear a mask,' the doctor said.

Eileen told him to stop. Just stop. He had done so well, she said. From the very start he had been ambitious, going in for ripping when he could have just plodded along with the rest. And by training himself up as a mechanic, he had outstripped everyone's expectations of his earning capacity. 'I'm proud of you, Harry. The kids are proud. No one can take that away from you.'

Harry thought he heard George sniggering in the kitchen. He looked at the shoe above the fire. It was almost grey, growing more and more like the rock he found it in. He thought of the ancient child, thin spine snapping beneath the avalanche. Stone dead.

He looked at his wife, the wisps of white in her curly hair. She had worked hard too. He loved her for it, but where had it got them?

'I'm too tired to feel proud, Eileen. If I had any energy I wouldn't waste it on pride. I'd be angry.'

Eileen held his large head in that way he liked. A clotted strand of slicked-back hair fell errant and hung down to his chin.

And he knew he could not quit now. What made things worse, in the ropey swirls of his conscience, was the fact that the men depended on his skills as a mechanic. If the machines did not work, there would be no productivity bonuses. Harry once stayed down there for eighteen hours fixing a cutter loader, its stubborn teeth grinning at him. The other men passed sandwiches down at intervals. He was the toast of the colliery when he emerged into the light, panting, disoriented, unable to rest. But even then there was talk that a fitter man would have finished the job in an afternoon. Wagstaff told the others that Cartwright coughed more than he worked, that his lungs were so thin they should be using him as a pit canary.

When the strike came, Harry stood on a few picket lines and went to a few galas. It was a hot summer, and the thin air made it difficult to breathe. Often he could not keep up with the motion of the crowds. He knew that if he let his limbs go soft, the people would not bear him, but trample him. So he stayed home and gave money for the strike fund because he knew he had it easier than some of the younger lads who had not had the opportunity or forethought to save their money. The local kids were malnourished, one of their own miners had been hospitalized by a police horse, and unprovoked fights broke out in the Red Lion – strangers in donkey jackets coming out of nowhere to wade in. Maggie's army.

George sometimes paid a visit to his parents with a few extra bits of food, but he was outside of the battle. He came around with his quiet wife one afternoon in July. Eileen set tea on the small round table, with mini UHT milk pots swiped from a motorway café. Harry noticed that George was wearing shorts. His nose, usually a dull brown, had a sun-stung redness. 'On 'oliday are we?'

'Isn't everyone around here? This is the original holiday village. Judging from the queues for food outside the Welfare, it looks like most of them are living half-board an' all. It's like bloody Butlins.'

Eileen nervously scratched her arm. 'Where's our Bob? Have you seen Bob?'

She always spoke loud nonsense when she sensed Harry getting angry. As if she could distract him with noise. 'You know exactly where Bob is, Eileen, don't be stupid. It's a good job he's not in this room right now, I tell you. He'd have sommat to say.'

George, oblivious to his father's warning, leaned back in the worn armchair, once dark green, now faded to peppermint. 'What a fantastic time to have a coal strike. It's 90 degrees out. Who needs a fire? Apparently the parasol salesmen's union went out on strike and got a hundred per cent pay rise.'

George laughed at his own joke with his eyes closed, and Harry was just about to throw him out. That is when he saw it. It was not much – not even a sneer – but when George laughed, Beth winced. The thin lips pursed, one wobbly eye half shut. She recovered her neutral expression quickly when she realized that Harry was looking at her, and tilted her head to meet his gaze. George laughed alone for a few seconds, and then supped his tea.

'George, you need to watch your mouth,' Harry said as they were leaving.

*

When they returned to the pit, defeated, in 1985, they were left in no doubt as to the new status of their profession. The great winding wheel that had dominated the village like a Cyclops for seventy years, and the gantry next to it, had been enclosed, capped off with grey synthetic boxes. The two towers of the head-stock now stared at each other formlessly, like hippos rising from the swamp.

The strike, in the end, had been divisive. John Butcher, an electrician at the colliery, had been revealed as a scab. The Coal Board had given him a huge bonus to put a bag over his head, sit in a bus with barred windows and break the picket at eighty miles per hour, stones and bricks raining down on the roof. In the eyes of the National Union of Mineworkers, Blackmoor went from being a tiny outlying stronghold to a symptom of defeat. The residents did not appreciate this image change, and John Butcher left the village early one morning after finding disparate parts of his beloved Triumph motorcycle (including a very recently purchased brake system) hanging from the high branches of the giant oaks on Blackmoor Rec. Eventually, the men trickled back to work, and the Women's Action Group found themselves picketing at their local pit, barracking men they had been feeding the previous week. The whole thing left a sour taste.

The miners had been back at work for four days when Wagstaff noticed the absentees, shouted his revelation in the cage. 'That's *it*! That's what's missing. That's it!'

The men anxiously turned, fearing an impending accident, looking for the vital missing cable or bolt. 'What, Waggy? What's gone?'

'Rats. Since we've been back I haven't heard, seen or smelt one fucking rat.'

The others groaned. It was one of the first things they had noticed. 'He's fucking sharp, int he?'

'I never thought I'd outlive them boggers,' said Wagstaff.

'Oh aye,' said Tom Betts. 'They've eaten themsens.'

'You what?' said Wagstaff.

'Think on it. Since hosses and hay has gone, they've been living off the snap we chuck away. Crusts and that. Well, we've been out for a year, haven't we?'

'So they've starved?' said Wagstaff.

'More likely they turned cannonball. Eaten each other.'

'Get out of it,' said Wagstaff.

'It's true,' said Steve Grimshaw, winking at the others. 'And it means there's one giant nasty fucker left.'

He grabbed Wagstaff's testicles, and the cage rocked with the struggle and laughter.

The closure followed shortly afterwards. They emerged from the ground for the last time in December 1986 and took their final showers in the pithead baths, which were bulldozed before the tiles had dried. With his pink towel over his head like a shawl, Harry Cartwright coughed for a long time, until most of the other conversations ceased beneath the noise. They saw his waist draw in tight under his ribcage, his body crumpling like a crushed can. He spread his hands against the wall and breathed for a while. Bob Cartwright stepped towards him and just watched. Then Harry turned and looked back in the direction of the pithead. 'Sommat tells me the next time I go underground I shan't be coming back up.'

The works stood for a few more weeks. Everybody turned up to see the detonation: Wagstaff because he could not believe it would happen; Mrs Hargreaves and Polly Grimshaw because they thought it might rouse community spirit; old Enid Alsop because she had seen so many bad things that one more wouldn't hurt; George out of angst hidden by a mask of amusement, and Beth out of the same dark fascination that drove her to look at pictures of her father, secreted within her needle wallet. They stood behind a mesh fence. The tenderised flesh of Harry's face pressed through the gaps, the mesh leaving its white pattern of bloodlessness. He was leaning on the fence for support, his thumbs hooked through, trembling against his weight. His nails had turned dark.

It was a nippy day, and the sky was the faintly bruised colour of an old dishcloth. George laughed when the colliery band began to play, a breeze flinging the sound away and bending it bad. 'Get ready for the competition, boys,' he shouted to the band as the demolition staff made the final safety checks.

The coursing energy of the detonation was palpable. They felt it in their ribs. The loader tower fell first, collapsing as though to its knees, and the boom came just after, reaching them through the ground. A fist of climbing dust shot up from its dark source, and they could hear the faint sad sound of tinkling debris. The event was accompanied by an illumination of that dirty sky: camera flashes, rolling out like bedsheets shaken off the line. The place was a bottled storm, concentrating its light and sound in that small area, trapped or malicious. When the next tower fell, the blast tore off the synthetic cover and the spokes of the winding wheel could be seen one last time. A vulgar revelation.

Harry could not work it out. He had seen those symbols of misery from his gate every day of his working life. They had come to represent an immovable enemy, impervious to weather and men. So often he had wished they would fall, and now they fell. Yet he was not free. Part of him wanted to charge into the rubble, smash it to splinters and grit; part of him wanted to hide, as if he had been exposed, naked. Several of the other miners, he noticed, were looking away. He coughed.

For the rest of his life, Harry's memory of the falling works would be corrupted by the photographs he saw afterwards, the photographs everyone was so keen to show off. Sequences of falling towers, mounted on commemorative sugar paper. One, two, three, four pictures. In Harry's mind, the towers fell with an Instamatic staccato rhythm. Time and space missing in between.

Harry woke from a light doze, his face against the yellow stain made by his Vitalis hair treatment. The fifth of March 1989. The stubble on his chin chafed his neck. As he lay in bed, he could hear Eileen and George arguing in the backyard. 'For God's sake, George, you're a selfish boy. The trouble with you is, nothing bloody matters, does it?'

'Mum, why are you getting upset? I only said—'

'I'm getting upset because your fayther can't walk to the bloody bathroom, because he's got inhalers he dun't know how to use, medicine he's too stubborn to take. He has to have . . . *things* up his backside. My Harold. And you won't even . . .'

Now that his wife was fully occupied, Harry seized his opportunity and struggled to an upright position, using the pillow and duvet for leverage. His arms shook when he lifted himself to his feet. The little sparkly lights drizzled over his vision for a few seconds and then passed. He took the longest strides possible to conquer the barren plains of floor space between stable furnishings, and had made it to the landing by the time she came in the back door. He could hear her sniffing back tears as she walked towards the bottom of the stairs. Harry thought about making a dash back to bed and trying again later but it was no use, he was stranded in plain view. No man's landing, he thought.

His appearance startled Eileen, who was wrapped up in her worries. The fright made her angry. 'What the bloody hell are you doing, Harry? You'll be the death of me.'

He did not respond to her faux pas, just stared, waiting for the breath to catch up with his words. It is like waiting for cistern to fill, he often said to Waggy. These pauses upset Eileen terribly. They seemed like a mocking nightmare of the silent, intent way that he had once looked at her. When they were younger he had stared as though she was beautiful, and even though she knew she was not, it felt good. Now this gaze again, right at the end.

'What have I told you? You need to rest up. What are you *doing*?'

'Ayin' a shave.'

'A shave? Harry, you have to save your energy. That's a waste.'

'Nothing's a waste now, Eileen.'

She watched him walk into the bathroom, which was bright with the midday sun. There was a click at the peak of his inhalation. She knew it would take him a long time to shave, so she followed him into the bathroom and readied the familiar paraphernalia. The shaving cream, the small, porcelain-handled hairy brush, the razor. She removed all the lids, ran a basin full of water, and wet the blade. His blinking had slowed down, and his ankles had swelled. She saw this. When she left the room she heard him lock the door.

The drone of the Hoover prevented her from hearing his final coughing fit. Half an hour later she was washing the kitchen floor, and noticed the skating hiss of the mop, the swill of water in the bucket, all lacking the punctuation of his cough. She ran upstairs, knowing what had happened, and spent a long time wailing and trying to barge the bathroom door open before she called Bob to kick it in. When she saw the blood on his shaving mirror and the blood suspended like a knot of smoke in the water, she thought he had slit his throat. She was taken by the crazy notion that she had nagged him to death, tipped him over the edge. His lips were blue and the blood was burgundy. After his pale decline, she had hardly expected his death to be so vivid.

Bob dragged him away by the armpits, and Eileen began to clear up the mess in the bathroom. She pulled out the plug, rinsed his things and put them into his canvas shaving bag. She scraped away the tidemark of his stubble. He must be half-shaved, she thought. Part way through wiping the surfaces she saw herself, long and bowed in the tap spout. She missed him, suddenly and unbearably.

They buried Harry behind the Parish Church, and the soil settled. He was elementally converted, his every last process feeding the village he had lived in for well over fifty years. A quiet time passed. Blackmoorians were great storytellers, and their tales always had a function: to drive you away or keep you at home, to frighten or justify. Many of the villagers now felt that the story of the coalmine had come to a sad end. They found new stories with other, less benevolent characters. Curses and witches. Harry Cartwright, a subterranean colossus, had died, the shaft was capped and the towers had fallen.

But it was not the end of the pit.

Ten

A life without touch is no life at all, she decided. Her husband spent more time at work, more time in the pub, and Beth could hardly blame him. She turned to her boy, who seemed to float up out of her illness, as if through murky waters. Vincent was happy – he did not seem scarred by her earlier madness, and she was grateful to him for that. But a baby will fill just so much of your life, and no more.

Eventually, in her loneliness, Beth fell in with the rhythms of the tall house. She could tell the time by the shape of light on the wall, and she imitated the hum of the boiler seconds before it kicked in. Cleanliness was still important to her, although she tried to keep her compulsions within the bounds of sanity. Making garments produced dust, and the loose fragments and half-cut cloth cluttered the front-room carpet. She stopped creating, and bought Vincent's clothes from the shops, like the other mothers.

That autumn brought strong winds and she watched with

revulsion as their bin toppled on the pavement, rolled in circles like a drunk and flung the waste of their home into the night. Phlegmy egg white slapped the car. Teabags raced down the street like toads, and a sweetcorn tin hurtled into Mrs Hargreaves's hedge. The shame of it.

Beth could make out a yew tree in the distance, branches pricked back like the teeth of a comb. She watched the wind push it one way and then suddenly wrench it back the other. It seemed like such a deliberate action. It suggested agency. Like when you loosen a milk tooth before pulling it out. Where did the wind come from?

'It's windy, George,' she said.

'Close curtains then.'

The weather had forced him back from the pub early. Or perhaps some wisecrack from one of the men. Now he cranked up the heating and sat in his shorts, silent, watching Vincent sleep. Beth, her head still wrapped gypsy-style in the net curtain, turned and looked at his legs. They were dusty brown and hairy. She stared down at her own: smooth, diaphanous and tainted by the green and blue veins. Like a different species.

She wondered about the structures, the reality of her life. She could never quite believe in the noisy, verbal nature of the world portrayed on television. As long as Vincent slept, silence reigned at number five. Beth wondered, if no one phoned and nobody called round, what proof did she have of her existence? She realized she had thought this before, when she was younger. She had imagined, in the lonely moments of her adolescence, that she only existed when George was spying on her, was only real on his

Polaroid pictures. That shutter blade falling, carving her out. But now she was having that thought again while George was *in the same room*.

On the radio she heard of a French bereavement counsellor who had made a cassette for widowed spouses, which simulated the noises of a 'partner pottering around the house'. But Beth knew that if she bought it, she would forget and become frightened by the footsteps upstairs. The cocky DJ said, 'Wow. Could there be anything sadder on God's green earth than having to turn that tape over at the end of side one? No need to be alone here though, 'cos we've got Joe Jackson on the way, and he's "Steppin' Out".'

Sometimes, she trod a little heavier than she needed to, in the guilty hope that her son might wake, and stare quietly at her, as was his tendency.

She studied the calendar, stared deep into the snowdrift of spare squares at the end of February. She turned the page to March, turned it back again. Her day of birth was swallowed by numerical oblivion. Who made the dates? Who decided on the disposability of the 29th?

Sitting on the edge of the bath, Beth brushed her teeth and looked into the mirror. From that distance, the small details of her white face were lost to her. She spat the foam, turned to George and smiled. 'Sometimes I feel like I'm disappearing,' she said.

George looked her over critically. 'I don't think so. I'd say you've *gained* weight, if anything.'

'I don't mean weight. I look at my reflection, and it's like I'm fading away.'

'Well, you've got bad eyes, haven't you? Stand closer to the mirror,' George said with a laugh.

It snowed in Blackmoor that December, but not everywhere. The Cartwright lawn stayed green, and the flakes refused to settle on the allotments. This latter phenomenon was hailed as a pre-Christmas miracle by the gardeners and vegetable growers. God wants us to have a plentiful table, they said, until every single vegetable wilted and died for no apparent reason. The ways of nature make a mockery of human superstition.

Shortly after Beth returned from hospital, a northern university recorded seismic activity on the site of the old colliery. They hypothesized that this disturbance was a result of 'underground stanchion collapse'. They were wrong. Now that the old water pump had been turned off and the ventilation system shut down, the pit – so often the subject of property disputes – changed owners once again. Just as the microbes and parasites busied themselves with decay in Harry's coffin, so, in the man-made tunnels now free of men, the gases and liquids reclaimed their blind territories. Beneath the feet of every villager in Blackmoor, the place roared. The water levels rose with unobserved patience, forcing the gases towards the surface. Blackdamp had slipped through a crack in the floor of the Red Lion cellar, methane had collected in the boiler closet of Polly Grimshaw's house, courting the ignition of the central heating. In December, there was bad weather, a sudden drop in barometric pressure. Under the Pit Lane bungalow of Blackmoor's oldest widow, methane crept along an abandoned underground shaft, looking for a tiny fissure, looking for a spark.

That Saturday, Enid Alsop had just woken from a fretful early evening sleep and had gone through to the front room to watch Des O'Connor. The room was so cold she could see her breath. She took all the cushions from the sofa, laid them on the rug in front of the fire and lowered herself down. After reducing yesterday's grey embers with the poker, she pulled out the ash pan, tipped the contents into the old brass bucket. She took coal bricks, one by one, and made a little nest for the firelighter. She did not like the smell of these new firelighters, but kindling took ages to get going. She was too weak now for tradition. All this effort made her tired and she rested for a moment. The room was grey and sad-looking. There had been snow. She could see a grimy bow of the stuff against the windowpane. Parts of it were blue from the night, parts of it yellow from the streetlight, and the rest was mucky brown.

She picked up the firelighter and the matches, but as she leaned forward towards the fire, two conical blue flames coursed through the grate and up the chimney, on either side of her little coal nest. The shock knocked Enid off the cushions. From a prostrate position, she looked back at the diamond bright neon twins. They sent mad shadows quaking behind her furniture, gave the room a ferocious submarine luminescence. Enid was so transfixed by the beauty of the two flames that she discarded any thought of evasive action and just stared. They disappeared abruptly, leaving just a firework burst of blue vapour. Enid sat for a moment in her dark front room. It was only now, in their absence, that she noticed the impressive baritone roar of the flames. Her ears rang with it.

Enid called the gas board. Her boiler had been on the blink anyway. A man arrived quickly, fixed the hot water, and confirmed that the flames in the fireplace were absolutely nothing to do with them. 'No idea what it is, duck,' the man said.

'Well, I might be a stupid old bat, but do you reckon it could be firedamp?'

The man raised his eyebrows. 'Methane?'

'Aye. Old pit works are about 'undred yards away.'

The man nodded slowly. 'Bloody hell. Could be. I wouldn't hang around if it is, like. Call British Coal. If anyone knows, it'll be them, and you know how happy they are to help.'

On the evidence of Enid's description, British Coal evacuated Pit Lane and Slack Lane behind it, with immediate effect. Polly Grimshaw, already alert to the reality of explosions, took her golden retriever and her two small children, and jogged down the front of the two streets, knocking on windows and shouting the news.

Beth was bathing Vincent, and heard the first shouts like distorted echoes. She raised her head briefly, and then shook it, unwilling to acknowledge disembodied voices these days. But the footfalls and shouting continued, louder and louder. George was at the pub. Beth plucked the dripping baby from the water, wrapped him in a green towel, and went downstairs to the front room. She could hear the kids outside breaking the snow-piles that had been shoved against the walls of the terrace. When little Liam Grimshaw banged on the window Beth screamed and Liam screamed back. The baby began to cry. When Liam caught his breath he shouted, 'Ever one down Welfeer. There's been a mega gas leak.'

The steps receded, with some haste.

*

In the Miners' Welfare Club, Mrs Hargreaves and the usual village overlords formed an unofficial Emergency Action Group. They were disadvantaged by an almost total lack of knowledge. Enid Alsop reported her conversation with the gas man, which was greeted with muttered expletives.

Polly Grimshaw saw Beth sitting in the corner in her orange hat, rocking the baby. 'Where's her George?'

'Ay a guess,' said Mrs Hargreaves.

'Lion.'

'Are they wellies?' said Polly Grimshaw, wrapping the dog's lead around her fist one more time.

Beth was indeed wearing red wellington boots with a long white skirt. She tapped her feet to the rhythm of her rocking, and little bits of snow tumbled from the rubber on to a patch of darkening carpet. Enid Alsop sighed. 'That's all we need in a situation like this: a nutcase and a box of bloody matches. She's a liability.'

'Just keep an eye out for her,' said Mrs Hargreaves. She sniffed the air. 'Can you smell sommat?'

'Probably my leg ulcers,' said Enid Alsop.

In fact, Polly's frightened retriever had shat on the red carpet. Beth sniggered for a few seconds, and then looked away, hand over mouth.

British Coal kept the 140 residents of the two streets away from their homes for a fortnight. They offered free accommodation at nearby hotels and inns while they carried out 'generous precautionary measures, which are by no means an admission of liability'. Most of the evacuees stayed with relatives or friends in the village, and checked on the progress daily. George Cartwright, however, took his wife, child and mother to a hotel in the centre of Derby, and stayed there for three days after the residents were called back.

Beth enjoyed her time away from the cruel gossips of the village. She and Vincent shared one room, and George and his mother stayed next door. Sleeping apart from her husband, she was freed from her frustrated desires. She liked the smoky anonymity and frosty city mornings, and the great neon cow that stood above the Co-op building, advertising milk. She went late-night shopping with Vincent and Eileen, and they shuffled through the crowds lit red by the Christmas lights. As a teenager, she had come to Derby often, to buy fabrics, and now she took them past the wool shop on the Strand, and to the indoor market. The big hall heaved with remembered feelings. The flapping of the trapped pigeons in the girders high above, the perfect sequence of odours as she walked: raw meat, fish, cotton, liquorice, cabbage. They slotted into place like the lyrics of a forgotten song.

This was where she had come to buy the velvet for her cloak. She had seen a particular roll of British racing green fabric and its purr had cut straight through the swimming bath acoustics of the trading hall. Never before had a fabric made her feel . . . *violent*. It seemed to challenge her with its texture, made her think of tongues and beasts. She had rubbed against the grain first, making a swathe of lighter green from the turned fibres. 'It doesn't feel very nice,' she had said to the stallholder, a haggard woman, yellow from smoking and anxious from not smoking around the fabrics.

'Velvet rubs both ways, duck,' the stallholder had said. Beth had smoothed the ruffled velvet back to its original state and tried not to blush with arousal. In the photograph she had kept of her father he was standing before a racing green Morris Minor.

She tried to stay away from the fabrics now, just glimpsed a new stallholder cutting from the rolls. An old desire gripped her, but she pushed it away, afraid of excitement these days, the instability and risk that comes with wanting something, anything.

Eileen, who had felt dubious about her grandson spending time with someone so 'un'inged', was impressed by her daughter-in-law's knowledge, and thought her worldly. 'How on earth you can find your way around with these great big buildings towering over you, I just don't know.' She had always liked Beth, and realized that she was still the same, just with glitches in certain areas, like the warped tape of a knackered cassette.

They rested in a tiny café. Clouded windows, chintzy wipe-clean tablecloths, tinsel wrapped around the metal dreadlocks separating the kitchen from the dining area. The smell of gravy. Beth rested her chin on her hand. 'I always used to love coming round your house for Sunday dinner.'

'It were chaos with them lot at table. George used to wind our Harry up something chronic with his smart mouth.'

'He was certainly excitable. I remember how Margie used to look after me, and Roy and Bob were always really quiet.'

''Cos they were stuffin' themsens.'

'And Mr Cartwright – Harry – always used to have mushy peas with his roast beef.'

'Aye. It were so's he didn't spill any when he were cutting his meat. He couldn't bloody stand it if a pea rolled off his plate. Bloody chaos.'

'But you were so in control of it, Eileen. You were dead calm, just settling everybody down and sorting them out. I used to think I could never do that. I was right, too, wasn't I?'

Eileen shook her head. She could see that Beth felt weak. 'Don't go black, Beth. You know, I always said that our George thought about things too much. Then I met you.'

Beth smiled, blew on her hot chocolate. Eileen cooed at Vincent, who waved his orange mittens. 'What chance has he got, eh?' said Beth.

'If he gets the best a both a you, he'll be just fine,' said Eileen. Beth pondered the permutations.

Eleven

District councillor Michael Jenkins was born in a rural, bourgeois part of Derbyshire, closer to Church Eaton than Blackmoor. His father was Old Tory, the owner of a commercial timber company. Michael was brought up in a stiff Christian tradition, filled with the fear of his father and the fear of God. He was chastised, beaten and boarded.

Young Michael failed to navigate the institutions in which he often found himself because he had a questioning nature, and saw injustice wherever he looked. His teachers, his father, and the various clergymen with whom he came into contact seemed bent on securing these inequalities. What he remembered most from his childhood was asking his father why he believed in God. While he recovered from his punishment, his mother crept into his room to comfort him. She had in her hand a book, from which she read. 'We do not choose our convictions but they choose us and force us to fight for them to the death.'

For a long time, Michael thought his mother had quoted the passage in defence of his father. Not until he found socialism, in the students' union meeting room, while training to be a teacher, did he see that his mother had laid his future before him with those words.

Of course, it was hardly so mystical. Truly, he was sickened by what happened in 1984, the erosion of civil liberties, the spite, the roadblocks and general ethos of profit before people, but any outsider could see that Michael's beliefs were in very significant opposition to his father's. Ironically, the people with the power to involve him in the struggle considered his family background suspicious. While Michael protested about police brutality against strikers, his father supplied offcuts of firewood to friends in his wealthy village to undermine the coal shortage, and told a local radio programme that the miners were criminals and ought to be treated under criminal law. Despite radical attempts to distance himself from this view, Michael Jenkins had twisted roots, and was frozen out. He would never have admitted it, but he found himself disappointed that his father did not even call him to gloat. They had not spoken since.

Now, as a councillor responsible for environmental health in north Derbyshire, he had a chance to make a difference again. He had decided that working people were diamonds made to cut glass long before he actually met any, but he would soon gain direct experience.

He appeared in a Blackmoor that was trying to mend itself. The residents had returned from the evacuation to find methane monitors in their kitchens and hallways, and a large pumping station above the old colliery to draw excess gas from the flooded pit. More purely precautionary measures from British Coal. Merry Christmas.

The festive period, in fact, was a nervous time in the village. A rumour had circulated that seasonal illuminations were unsafe and could ignite the gases. The vague threat of hellfire was replaced by the imminent and clinical possibilities of suffocation and explosion. The Emergency Action Group talked and complained, but nobody had the boldness to take steps against British Coal. 'They've told us it will be okay,' said Mrs Hargreaves. 'Who am I to argue? I don't really have experience of negotiating at that level.'

'Rubbish,' said her husband. 'It's the same lot, just with a different name. You've challenged them before.'

'Aye. And we all know what happened then.'

The fear did not exactly subside in the New Year, but people learned to live with it in various ways. When Steve Grimshaw was asked to pay his tab in the Miners' Welfare Club, he fell to the ground and pretended to suffocate. 'Am I turning blue yet?' he said as Tom Betts kicked him in the stomach.

Wagstaff told his little audience how he had complained of the 'methane levels' after his wife had used the outhouse. 'I says to her, "Fuck's sake, Joan, strike a match. No wait, don't!"'

Perhaps the worried silence that followed such jokes would have become shorter in time. Maybe the fuss and panic would have died down. Or maybe the place would have exploded into a million pieces. Instead, Michael Jenkins arrived. To begin with, he sat quietly at several Emergency Action Group meetings. After a few weeks of silent observation, he called a meeting of his own on Blackmoor Rec.

As Beth prepared to attend this outdoor gathering, she struggled to remember what Michael Jenkins looked like. To her husband's dismay, she too had been present at the EAG meetings, but Michael had always sat at the opposite end of the long table in the Miners' Welfare Club, so that his features were beyond her visual range.

The brief invigoration of her enforced stay in Derby seemed distant now. Everything had been such a mess when she got back to the village. Beth sensed that her home had been tampered with, in the same way your body feels handled after an operation. The landscape also looked wounded that winter, with the monstrous white pumping station on the old colliery site. Beth had hoped to see more of George's mother when they returned, but Blackmoor had its well-worn slots and grooves that people couldn't help but slide back into.

In a brown duffle coat and her orange hat, she stood at the back window on the top floor of the house with Vincent sleeping against her shoulder. It was one of the only windows in the village that did not overlook someone else's business, and in that way, the view lent itself to meditation. George had, from that window, already witnessed his young wife stumbling erotically in her velvet cloak. The view would eventually transfix Michael Jenkins too. Each person saw a different world, came to their own conclusion.

Objectively, it contained the north-facing garden; the muddy field; the silver birches on the railway bank; the beech copse beyond and the hills rearing in the background, some ragged and forbidding, others just the usual tame, patched humps of farmland. Beth could make out considerably less than this, of course, but she liked to watch the birch trunks turn yellow or pink or that sad autumnal red as the sun moved behind her. She always thought this was the best way to see the sun – vicariously, in the bark. Like the rumour of a better place. At mid-afternoon on that particular cold February day, the birches showed a pretty, weak yellow, like bathroom cleaner fluid.

But in the muddy field Beth also noticed what looked like five large holes. They were deep – she could not see the bottom of them from this angle – more like tunnels, then. The high clay content of the soil gave their insides a smooth finish and a ruddy tincture like a throat. They were about twelve yards in diameter, emphatically regular, clearly man-made. Had they appeared overnight? Were they even real? She feared hallucinations. Vincent reached across lazily and put an orange mitten on her nose, as though Beth were something that could only be comprehended in his dream. Satisfied, his arm dropped.

The wheels of the buggy slid on the mud as Beth approached the small huddle. She noted Wagstaff in his blue overalls and pit boots, glugging from his hip flask, and Sarah Browne, the young mother from Derby who lived in one of the council houses near Tom Betts. Michael Jenkins stood above them on the base of the war memorial, the large stone pillar of which rose up behind him, scorched with the names of the Blackmoor dead along with the inscription: 'FEAR GOD, HONOUR THE KING.'

Beth moved forward so she could see him properly. She felt a rush of amused maternal sympathy for the man – for the grand, collapsed gesture of this poorly attended open-air conference. His curly black hair held disparate patches of premature grey, and he wore a bright red scarf that seemed to irritate his neck. He looked cold, nervous, but quietly passionate, and his goal was clear: to pick a fight with British Coal on behalf of the village. 'Your standard of living has been compromised,' he said, his low strong voice climbing unnaturally from his thin body. A posh accent, she thought. 'And not just your standard of living, your *way of life* too. Think about how you used to feel, here. How do you feel about your village, now? Your homes? Do you feel safe?'

A few rasping coughs from the audience – a consequence of the reluctance of many people to ignite their boilers, just in case. Steam and breath rose from the crowd, and from beneath them came the sound of feet shifting in the tacky mud. Michael Jenkins had obviously expected a more fervent response. He continued, and Beth could tell that the cold had numbed his lips, making it difficult to form the word shapes. 'Of course you don't feel safe. Of course not. Where is Sarah Browne?'

He looked out on the crowd, ran his fingers through the curls, which sprang back into place.

'I'm 'ere.'

The others turned on hearing Sarah Browne's townie voice. She was short, wore an oversized waterproof football jacket. Her face looked scrubbed clean, the eyes and lashes watery and dark. The Blackmoor women rarely spoke to her, and Beth thought Michael Jenkins was making a mistake, teaming up with a girl nobody liked. 'Sarah, hi. Now, you bought your council house, didn't you?'

A gasp from the audience. They did not know this.

'Yep.'

'When did you buy it?'

'About a year ago, wasn't it? When me husband had been working a bit.'

'One year ago. January 1990. You and your husband managed to get jobs, and you've worked hard. And you had a new kitchen fitted at great expense to yourself, did you not?'

'No, it was a bafroom,' Sarah shouted. Some of the women turned around again now, scowling in disbelief.

'A bathroom, I'm sorry,' said Michael. 'A considerable outlay for a young family coming off benefits and trying to fit into a new village. After spending all that money, though, what is Sarah's house going to be worth in a few years?'

Wagstaff laughed and then coughed. Michael scratched his neck beneath the red scarf. He raised his thick voice, rolled it out. 'What are *your* homes worth, *now*? Answer me this: who in their right mind would buy a house with a methane monitor in the kitchen? Nobody. Your houses are worth nothing. Nothing. Who is going to foot the bill for that loss?'

His sudden aggression sparked something in the crowd. He nodded with satisfaction at the noise below, but Beth thought he might be the object of their unrest. She worried that they had mis-understood, and were antagonized by this stranger describing the worthlessness of their homes. In any case, the sound drove Michael on. He flung the scarf over his shoulder. 'Your village might as well have been flattened for all it's worth. And what about the immediate danger that you *live with* every day? You are sitting on a time-bomb, and you *must* be compensated for that.'

The disturbance in the crowd transmitted to Vincent who began to wail into the clear air. Beth pressed down on the buggy, lifting the front wheels, and spun it around on the wet grass. She began to make her way home. Nice ideas, she thought. Pity.

*

112

The next meeting took place in the milder climate of the Blackmoor Miners' Welfare Club, but contained much of the same content. Michael proposed to the growing Emergency Action Group that they launch a legal claim for compensation against British Coal. Afterwards, Beth walked past him in the car park. He recognized her from the first meeting by the hat, and baby. He recalled that she had walked away from the Rec before he had finished. 'Good luck,' she said, as he unlocked his car.

'Thank you,' he replied.

'Won't work, mind,' she added, and pushed the buggy onwards.

Michael stepped away from his car and pursued her, this bird-like, thin woman. He focussed on the back of her neck, beneath the woolly hat. It was so exposed. It almost seemed like a transgression to look at it. 'Excuse me,' he said, and she turned. 'What makes you say it won't work?'

'Well, you've got to get folk together, haven't you?' Beth said.

'I'm *trying* to get people together. That's the whole point.'

'But you've already turned them against Sarah Browne. They didn't talk to her in the first place. None of the women'll even *look* at her now.'

'Why not?'

Beth laughed. "Cos they know she's got a new bathroom. It might sound silly, but you've made her out to be better than all the rest of 'em. People in this place will do anything for you, if they know you're one of them. But they don't like people from Notts or Sheffield or even Derby. And they don't much like you either, at the minute.'

'Listen, madam.'

'Beth.'

'Beth. If you don't like me, I suggest—'

'Never said that. *I* think you're all right. Nice ideas, same as I say.'

Michael needed an ally in Blackmoor. He had thought that Angela Hargreaves, the famous crusader of 1984, would be sympathetic to his cause, but she had been cold so far. Unaware of her low status in the village, Jenkins thought that Beth could help him. She was perceptive and had a tired, half-amused look that made him feel quite boyish. There was something wrong with her eyes and he studied them a little longer than was polite. She looked down and he rebuked himself. He considered the woman's opinions. While the villagers were certainly receptive to the idea of compensation, it was true that arguments had already begun over the criteria for sharing any money.

'Okay, Beth. In your opinion, how do I get everyone pulling in the same direction?'

'Probably asking the wrong girl, there,' she said.

'I'd certainly like to hear your thoughts.'

She paused. 'Okay. First off, it's like my George says: Blackmoor loves an enemy. You've got to drum up some spite. Can't be a team unless you've got someone to play against.'

'Easy enough. British Coal are rather doing that for me.'

'You've got to stop saying *rather*, an' all.'

Michael smiled and rolled his eyes. 'Right.'

'After that, I suppose it's just getting everyone united. You've got to make Polly Grimshaw feel like Sarah Browne's sister, no matter how many bathrooms she's got. It'll not be easy. People have got less in common now the pit's shut. And there's some kids around here with some bad habits.'

'I'd like to pay you a visit, and talk some more. We can go through the issues with your husband,' Michael said.

Beth laughed at the thought of this earnest young man discussing politics with George. 'He doesn't want to talk about it,' she said.

'Have you asked him?'

'Trust me. He doesn't want to talk about it. That's his catch-phrase.'

TWELVE

George's dawn dreams pin him down by the shoulders and make him watch. He knows he is asleep, and is not frightened by the images as much as the relentless, manipulative way in which they pursue him.

The beetle dream started months ago, with a disgusting scarab crawling along a table. George tried to crush it, bury it. He hated its regal arrogance, its indestructibility – and it seemed more suited to his son's mind. In recent nights, George has seen the beetle morph into a black Honda coupe, which he looks down on as it cuts through the scorched fields and rubble of Blackmoor's outskirts.

He knows the car, he knows the date. He is aware that he sits in the passenger seat next to Daniel Frost, a man he knew for only nine vital hours, the day before his wife died. Abruptly he is inside, looking at Frost in his blue shirt, made bluer by the tinted windscreen. Frost tucks his hair behind his left ear. 'It's true what they say, isn't it, George?' says Frost in his southern accent. 'You never forget.'

George turns on the car radio, but his son's yodelling falsetto floats from the speakers. *'I want to live and I want to love, I want to catch something that I might be ashamed of.'*

George wakes and shouts, 'Vincent.' Across the room, his son stops singing.

And it is not just the dreams. Since he fixed the projector, George has slowly begun to go slack, like fishing wire sailing back to the bank. Anyone can see it, and Vincent is more sensitive than most. With his ability to perceive future trauma, Vincent suspected that the projector would somehow bring trouble. He saw the jowls of his father's shirt wobbling as he worked on the mechanism, and it seemed to Vincent that the thing was sucking his guts out.

Now, each morning, Vincent hears his dad's familiar sounds in the kitchen: the banging cupboards, the stick-peel-slap of his slippers against the laminate and his heels. But the sounds are slower now, quieter. A bigger gap between the peel and the slap. Even his whistling has become fractured. He used to whistle the theme tunes to westerns, but now he makes one or two notes and then stops, as if seeking the remains of the melody behind the toaster, or in the fridge.

Vincent is not the only one to notice his father's weight loss and degeneration. The barman at the Anchor, Church Eaton's best pub, observes the growing sacks beneath George's eyes, and the rest of him getting thinner, as if all the matter is heading for the same place. He watches George fumble his change, and struggle to finish his second pint, choking on the dregs.

Most people, of course, think that the fading aggression of this man, the loss of violence and abruptness, is a straight change from one state to another. A linear development, a metamorphosis. How many individuals in Church Eaton know that George Cartwright's recent blank-faced apathy represents the closing of a circle? Who knows that he is, in fact, regressing?

George himself knows. Soon he and Vincent will see Martin Wagstaff again; he will remember George shrinking away in Blackmoor. The knowledge of a passive father must also be contained somewhere in Vincent's memory, that depository of lost answers.

Vincent actually prefers his dad as an angry old man. He has developed methods for coping with the outbursts, and does not know how to deal with this moping wreck. The last embers of the caustic rage still occasionally glow, and for that the boy feels grateful.

This is the George that Bob Cartwright now meets. This is the house he walks into. Bob, George's middle brother, left Blackmoor soon after the pit closure, and now works at a modern, mechanized pit in Utah. He comes home from the States each spring and spends a few days with each of his siblings. George, Roy and Margie have an uncomfortable relationship, so there is no collective reunion. Bob makes the usual wisecracks (he 'cracks wise' as he now says in his hybrid accent) about travelling thousands of miles to see people who won't even go down the road to see each other, but he knows how it is.

George likes Bob because he feels that they have both broken out of the generational perpetuation of the Blackmoor Cartwrights. They have both made a little money. Bob is much wider than George, and his physical presence is exacerbated by the big coats and boots that he wears. His shoulders are swelled by a life of labour, his stomach bloated with beer, but the muscles creep underneath the fat like the features of a criminal with tights on his head. His hair is receding in a similar fashion to George's, but he wears it long, sweeps it back.

This year George and Bob go 'out on the tiles' in Derby. It proves to be an exhausting evening. George has been told that it is now possible to have a civilized night in the city, but they go to all the wrong pubs – the places where the industrial spirit of week-end oblivion still lingers. They are surrounded by luminous shirts, cheap pinstripe trousers, snaffled shoes, fighting, vomiting and indecent exposure.

'Jeez, George, I thought Blackmoor was bad. We can't go some-where with seats, have a coffee? We're too old for this.'

They end up drinking bottled lager in a quiet place on the Wardwick with a glass front so they can see the grisly end of the night outside. 'So, little Vince is gonna be tall,' Bob says.

George sighs at the banal observation. 'We're all tall. What's your point?'

'I don't know, George. I go to Margie's house and Roy's, and people are close.'

'Well, Roy's got a three-bed terrace and 158 kids, they're bound to be fucking close.'

'George, the only time you and Vince are in the same room is when you're sleeping, which is fucked up by the way.'

'It int. It's for a good reason.'

'What, you think he's going to chuck himself out the window if he sleeps upstairs?'

Silence from George.

'Bloody hell, man. What you gonna do when he brings a girl back to shag, sleep on your front?'

'It's my affair, Bob.'

'Fucking will be if she gets in the wrong bed. You've got to bond with the kid, George.'

'You're such a septic these days, Bob. Fucking *bond*? There were a time when bond meant . . . Araldite to you. Epoxy resin.'

'Huh. Dad used to call it "poxy resin". You remember? "Where's poxy resin, youth?" he used to say.'

'No doubt about it: he were fucking thick.'

'Dad used to spend time with us, George.'

'Oh aye. I particularly enjoyed our games of football, as fondly remembered by me broken bastard legs.'

'But he was there. Yeah, sometimes he dished it out, and it might have been cramped in the house, but do you remember how . . . safe you felt? I go in your house and it's like an office or a hotel.'

'You reckon it's the furniture?'

'Fuck you.'

'Okay. What should I do then?'

'I don't know. Me and Simon go to the ball game. The match. Just the local college football, but it's what he likes.'

'Okay. I'll go to the *ball game* with him.'

'Christ. Do something he enjoys.'

George nods, holds up his hands in surrender. 'Tell you what, I'm famished. Let's get a kebab.'

Bob, rolling back across decades, continents, destroyed villages, finds the accent of his late father. 'I'm not ayin' any a that fuggin' wog-snap, youth. Do us a chip cob.'

George shakes his head, unwilling to be amused, even by the accuracy of the impression. Especially by its accuracy. 'Daft twat,' he says.

For the next few days after Bob's departure, George attempts no bonding exercises. At 9.15 p.m. one Friday night George kills a fly with a rolled-up newspaper. At 9.45, Vincent skewers the corpse with a cocktail stick and winds it into a spider's web outside the bedroom window. This is the closest they come to a conversation. But the light is working on George. If he looks at a bright window and then closes his eyes, the silhouette of an empty vase morphs until it is her face or a giant green hand.

For his first attempt at bonding, George simply employs twenty-eight surrogate fathers in the form of tropical fish. 'Your Uncle Bob suggested it. I won't be looking after them mind, so it's up to you to take them for a walk and all that.'

Vincent does not smile. Even the thought of harming these astonishing creatures is enough to make him angry. He immediately names the red-finned shark Fergal. The Siamese fighting fish is like blood in the water as he flares up, asserting his dominance. Vincent calls him Red. There are guppies (which remind Vincent of the fluffy pencil ends used by some of the girls in his class) and tiger barbs, clown loaches and neon tetras. 'Dad, these are amazing,' he says.

George laughs. 'I remember this time when your Auntie Margie's fancy man won her a couple a goldfish at Goose Fair. She stood the bowl on the kitchen worktop and me and your Uncle Bob used to stand on chairs, get whisks and forks and really whirl the water up. We'd have them spinning at a right rate a knots.'

Vincent eyes his father suspiciously.

Over the next few weeks it is Vincent who inhabits the kitchen, spending his evenings in only the light of the fish tank. The blue glow reminds him of the globe lamp in Leila's tent, and sitting before it seems to prolong his time with her.

Of course, Vincent loves the fish too. Their appearance borders on the implausible. He cannot believe that something so thin as a tiger barb, with such perfect pearly orange and black stripes, can live in the same world as the spotty boy whose reflection sometimes springs from the tank glass. Occasionally Red approaches the glass and displays his battle dress, the beard-like drifts of crimson flesh. Vincent laughs at his silent rage – the turned-down mouth and exophthalmic gaze. He wonders for a moment if Red can see the water that surrounds him.

After this beautiful gift, Vincent is willing to call it quits. But George is still plagued by the thought of the projector – the flickering spectres in his peripheral vision; the squares of light expanding on the wall tell him that his work is not yet done. Unfortunately, he has exhausted his imagination pertaining to 'bonding ideas', so he takes Vincent to the Anchor. He says it is time to make a man of his son, but in reality he just needs a drink.

The Anchor is very different from Blackmoor's Red Lion. The bar is L-shaped and divided into two sections. A large dining area serves the growing number of affluent families in the village, while the horizontal stroke of the L is used as a small snug bar for the older locals, mainly those men who claim to remember Church Eaton's industrial past when the Anchor played host to canal workers. The place has orange, green and red coloured windows, and flashing fruit machines, so that it seems to be stuck in a perpetual post-Christmas depression. When the Cartwrights arrive in the snug, the bar manager looks at them with some concern. 'You'll have to sit in the family area, sir, if the boy is coming in.'

George takes two stools and places them right on the edge of the snug, at the corner of the L. 'The usual please,' he says.

'Which is . . .?' says the bar manager with an apologetic wince.

'Pedigree, no nozzle.'

'Flat bitter. And for you, young man?'

'I'll just have a lemonade. On the rocks.'

The bar manager laughs and George grunts. Behind them the older locals are talking. One voice, in particular, rises through the noise. Martin Wagstaff. Vincent knows Mr Wagstaff from the village. He wears overalls and keeps pigeons. It soon becomes clear to Vincent that his father knows him too. A look of rigid panic sets on George's face, as Wagstaff describes his continued virility.

'I were in bath other day, I gave it a bit a tattle, and it were like a gander's neck, youth.'

George stares straight ahead at the ragged teddy bear behind the bar, whose name has not been guessed for charity. 'Is that . . .? That's Waggy,' says George.

'Mr Wagstaff, yeah. He lives on Barley Crescent. One of the council houses,' Vincent confirms.

Something occurs to George, makes him smile. 'Christ, I never thought he'd move somewhere like this. Obviously not as staunch as he claimed.'

'Do you know him?' Vincent asks.

'Knew him. He lived in Blackmoor before it was demolished. That place is going to follow me to my grave.'

Vincent thinks about Leila and the project. This would be a good opportunity to speak to someone more forthcoming about Blackmoor. But he has selfish motives in mind. 'Did he know my mum?'

George remains silent, wrestling with the possessiveness of *my mum*.

'Are we going to say hello to him, Dad?' says Vincent.

'No. Be quiet.'

But George lets his shoulders sag. He drains his pint, turns on the stool and faces Wagstaff. The old man squints, his eyes like old copper coins in the bottom of a wrinkled, scuffed leather purse. George looks suddenly tired, and Wagstaff's usually menacing beam is uncertain.

Eventually Wagstaff calculates that he has safety in numbers, even if they are all pensioners. He raises his glass. 'Eh up. It's fucking Cartwright.'

George stands and walks briskly towards the toilets. Vincent watches him disappear past the dessert display. The old men continue to talk. 'You know him, do you?' one of them says to Wagstaff.

'Aye. I were down pit with his fayther.'

'He was a bit of a nutcase when he first turned up here. Shouting at folk all time, and he crashed into a garden up Vicarage Road. He's not right in the head. Like all you bloody miners.'

Wagstaff lets forth a cackle. 'George Cartwright? A hard man? He's never been down pit in his life, for one thing. The lads in Blackmoor – if there were still such a place – would piss laughing at what you've just said. Youth's a fucking fairy. And his missus—'

'Steady on, Waggy. That's his nipper at the bar.'

'Aye,' says Wagstaff, quieter. 'I'll say another thing and all. George Cartwright tried to kill me the one time.'

'I thought you said he were a pansy.'

'He were. I were sixty-odd and I still beat him.'

They fall silent, and Vincent continues to drink. His father does not return, and after fifteen minutes, Vincent goes to the toilet. George is not there, but Vincent needs to piss anyway. Wagstaff hobbles in, unzips his overalls and hunches up to the next urinal.

'Hello. I'm Vincent.'

'Eh up,' Wagstaff says. Vincent notices that it takes him a long time to piss, and even then it is just a dribble. 'Want to hear a dotty song?' says the old man as Vincent washes his hands.

Vincent does not know what a 'dotty song' is. 'Don't know. Yep.'

> *There once was a man named McCourt*
> *Whose prick were incredibly short*
> *To make up for loss*
> *He had balls like a 'oss*
> *And he never came less than a quart.'*

Wagstaff laughs loud. The limerick seems to help him overcome his stage fright too, for he is now urinating freely. Vincent does not laugh, but regards Wagstaff in the mirror. He wonders if Leila will let him put the limerick in their project.

'You arna laughing, youth,' says Wagstaff, tucking himself back into the overalls. He is a little irritated that his joke has not hit the mark.

'What's an oss?' asks Vincent.

'A gee-gee, you know. A 'oss.'

'A horse?'

'Aye.'

'And what's a quart?'

Wagstaff struggles to keep his temper. 'About this much,' he says, describing a large container with his hands, and bracing himself for the next, the most difficult, question.

'That's a lot of spunk,' says Vincent. Wagstaff cackles.

Back at the bar, Wagstaff buys the drinks, and talks about Vincent's granddad, and mining. Vincent does not like Wagstaff. He seems rotten in some way, and is difficult to understand.

'Toilet? Well, what do you think spade were for? You had to go in corner like a cat and wipe up wi' a bit a sharp dot,' Wagstaff says.

After a while, Vincent changes the subject. 'You must have known my mum, then,' he says.

'Aye.' It seems that Wagstaff does not want to talk about her either. 'Where's your fayther?'

'Up there,' says Vincent. He points to the CCTV monitor above the bar. The camera is trained on the car park, where George can be seen, ultrasound grey, leaning against the dwarf wall, shivering, as if in wait for obstructive cyclists.

Thirteen

As promised, Michael Jenkins visited number five Slack Lane. When Beth came to the door, he was standing back by the flower basin (just frosty soil and dormant bulbs), looking up at the roof, his head craned back so far she could see the livid rash beneath the scarf. 'I hope this doesn't sound impolite, but how come your house is so much bigger than the ones over there?' he asked.

'How come you've got such a flash suit?' she replied.

He smiled (his suit was quite modest, in need of a press). She told him that Slack Lane had originally housed the schoolmaster and colliery deputies, then later the union officials and the administrators they called the 'pen-top men'. She invited him in. Beth still struggled to find a balance between keeping her home clean and assuring everyone she was not insane, so the place contained pockets of contrived untidiness: a neat pile of salt on a clean work surface, a single cushion in the middle of a room. She carried Vincent upstairs to put him down for a nap and explained the three-storey layout as she went. George was at work. In the back bedroom on the top floor, Michael looked out on the muddy field.

'So why are you doing all this then?' Beth asked. 'You after revenge on the Tories? Power to the people and all that.'

Michael smiled at the overwhelming complexity of the question. 'It's my job, for a start. Yes, there have been injustices, and I don't think we should forget people just because they're not in the news. But actually, there is a real situation here, right now, and I don't think people realize how bad it could be,' he said.

'What do you mean?'

'The gases. We've done our research, and if there *is* a large methane leak from the pit, and it ignites, it could blow this place off the map.'

'Another explosion? Like Polly's house?'

'Well, we *think* that was methane. A small burp. It's certainly a worry. We're not so concerned about the monoxide and dioxide, the stuff that killed poor Mr Chambers in his pub.'

'Mick Chambers?'

'Yes. People here seem to think he died of liver failure for some reason, but the coroner was quite clear it was asphyxiation. Poisoned by bad air. It all points to blackdamp. But like I say, if you detect it quickly enough, you can just open a window. It's not a major problem. But Enid Alsop *definitely* found methane in her fireplace, there's no doubting that. Luckily for her and everyone within a five-mile radius, it was just the tiniest amount. If we get enough of that stuff, we're talking A-bomb.'

'Oh please. What a bloody drama.'

'I'm serious. The place will be a graveyard. A lot of people dead. And it's perfectly plausible. From what we can tell, the water has been building underground for the last year and pushing the gases towards the surface. The pressure has also knocked down some of the walls between the Blackmoor mine and the next one. That means that British Coal's lauded pumping station could be in the wrong place anyway. I wouldn't want to say any of this in the meetings, of course, because it would scare everyone to death.'

'That's exactly what you have to do to get people's attention here.'

Beth looked at his face. It was long and thin, with a turned-down mouth. A lion's face. He turned away to the window. Beth regarded her son and tried not to panic about the gases, tried to regulate her feelings. 'Gotta watch those endorphins,' the nurse had said. She placed Vincent on the spare bed, now so often used by her husband.

'Look at those holes,' said Michael.

Beth froze, wondering if this was a trick. Maybe Michael was a spy from the ward, come to test her. 'What holes?' she said coyly.

'Those five in the field.'

'You can see the holes?'

'Of course I can, they're massive. Why would I not be able to see them?'

Beth relaxed a little. 'No reason. I've got bad eyesight, that's all. Judge everyone by me own rubbish standards. So . . . what are they?'

'Boreholes. About 180 feet deep. They contain testing apparatus, to measure gas levels underground.' Michael shook his head. 'British Coal are bastards. People's lives are on the line and their CEO is prancing around on a bloody golf course. They've accepted no moral responsibility for what they've done to these communities.'

'*Rather,*' said Beth.

Michael allowed the worried expression to slide away. He laughed.

'You're one of those people, Mr Jenkins, where I can't tell what came first: the passion or the cause.'

Michael was disarmed by her directness. 'As long as they're both present, it doesn't really matter does it?'

'Oh, there's always some *cause*, int there? We're never lacking problems to sort out. Passion? That's another matter.'

Michael looked at the baby, and then at Beth. 'In the village they tell me you don't like company, Beth.'

'Not so. I don't mind a natter, just like the next woman. I've been poorly, that's all. My husband . . .'

'They have plenty to say about your husband.'

'Yeah, George is a loner. But so what? I've seen everything that's happened to him since he was a kid, and trust me it's no surprise the way he's turned out. You'd have been just the same if you'd lived here.'

'My great-grandfather was a miner in South Wales.'

'Oh aye? And where did *you* live?'

Michael conceded without an answer, and Beth continued. 'All anyone ever talks about in this village is pride. *You've* been here five minutes, and you've already started. People are always banging on about "being a man", being strong, having pride in the village. Well, what if the village is crushing you? What if you're not *strong*? What if you're not *a man* in the way they mean it? What if your wife . . . What are you supposed to do then?'

Michael suddenly saw the contradictions in this woman, her need for contact and her enforced insularity, her social conscience and her individualism. The figure of George grew in his imagination.

'What would *you* do, Mr Jenkins?'

'I don't know.'

'You'd use the strengths you had, i.e. your brain, and you'd get a decent job and look after your family, like my George.'

'Yes. Of course I didn't mean to be rude about your husband. I was just—'

'Repeating what they said down the village? I know. You want to watch out for that,' said Beth, but she smiled. 'It's nice to have fancy ideas, Mr Jenkins, it really is, but in the end you do for your own. It's all about the folk nearest to you. That's always your reason.'

Michael put Beth's advice into action, and the results were encouraging. He formed a 'Compensation Committee', appointed Mrs Hargreaves as Chair, and demonized British Coal. He had a mining safety engineer write a report on pit gases, and read the warning to the Committee. 'You should be alert to difficulty igniting fires or cookers, dizziness, headaches. The gases stay low to the ground, so look for babies experiencing distress when crawling, and the sudden, unexplained deaths of pets.'

This held the attention of the Blackmoorians long enough for Michael to make reference to the iniquities of the past. The faces of old union leaders glowered behind him from the Miners' Welfare Club wall. 'British Coal don't want to hear about your problems, and the government isn't listening, for the same reason it *illegally* closed the Blackmoor pit – because it is engaged in a revenge plot against the coal industry and against you. Maggie might have gone, but it's the same old story. They will not be happy until your thriving community is broken and gutted. But we will not allow that to happen.'

Michael was exhilarated. In Blackmoor he got to cover all the things he cared about. He told his wife that this was the reason he went into politics, and on some level he believed that.

In Blackmoor, people talked about it over their fences, and down the alleyways. When they discussed the permutations of possible court settlements, they used the word 'we' to denote the Blackmoor claim. How many years since they had done that?

Beth occasionally heard them talking from her bedroom. She would lie on her bed with Vincent (growing fast as winter faded) and wait for her husband's headlights to sweep across the ceiling. The sound of the car door opening and closing and his cough. The ticks of the cooling engine, the keys in his pocket. She asked herself if she still loved all this, and she did. In the evening, before he went to the pub, she would sit and talk with him and be amazed that he could go missing every morning and then miraculously return, unchanged at teatime.

And what did that back window hold for George? What drew *him* there to think? The fact that Beth was changing her clothes in their bedroom, and he needed to be out of the way. His discipline was awesome, terrible, for somewhere within him he was desperate for her. Yet he could avoid the hazard of her nakedness without even imagining it. The mantra that protected him from his desires was so deeply buried as to be physical, a reflex.

George stared beyond the holes, the muddy field, the mountainous blue slack heaps, to the unmanageable and treacherous valley beyond. The landscape was so open he could see the shadow of the clouds creeping over the ground. The last light. The abrasive plates of limestone hills appeared to shift before his eyes. In summer, he knew this view would be taken over by giant squares of rapeseed, so luminous in their yellowness that they had to be radioactive. Blots from a highlighter pen. Amazing. The place was unstoppable, merciless, and it filled him with a humbling wonder. George was one of the only people in the village unsurprised to hear that Blackmoor could kill them all with one spark, one breath of gas from the ground. What do *people* matter, and what can they do?

He went into the bedroom when he knew Beth was decent, and for once he shared his thoughts with her. 'Tell you what, you look outside and you just think, this place is billions of years old. Those trees. They're going to be here when I've disintegrated, and maybe in a hundred million years or whatever, they'll be a seam of coal ready for some twat to set another bloody village on. We've been here for, what, a century? It's bugger all. Just a graze. Like a kid scratching around in the mud. We don't mean anything to it.'

Beth was frustrated by the amount of time she had stalled in her underwear, waiting for him to come in. 'How can you say that?' she said. 'Look at the way we've been treated. Decisions have been made about our future—'

'Whose future?'

'By people who think they're Gods. Who don't have any moral consideration for the . . .'

George raised his eyebrows as she tailed off. Another surfacing of the argumentative spirit that had possessed his wife during the strike. 'Look at the way the people in this village have treated *you*,' he said. 'Are they any better? Do you want to know what they say about you down the pub?'

'I already know, George,' Beth said quietly.

'Do you want to hear what they say?'

'No. I know what they say.'

'Well, then, how can you give a shit about them?'

'Because I know how it feels to disappear.'

And at night, if he gave her the honour of his company, she had to watch him twist away in the bedsheets, not even turning the light on now to examine her. But in the morning, the cycle of hope began again. She pretended to sleep and watched him dress. Then, when he had left the house, she sneaked to the window to see him get in his car, and listened until she could no longer hear the engine. And then she sat for hours, watching the jackdaws fight it out for Blackmoor's scrap and glitter, and waiting for him to come home.

FOURTEEN

On 7 April 1991, Michael Jenkins attended an important meeting at the Blackmoor Miners' Welfare Club. He was ready for it. As he got out of his car, he saw Beth, hair still Labrador short, rocking her baby in the doorway. He greeted her with a nod. When he entered the room with his brown leather satchel, the other committee members fell silent. Michael knew this was not a mark of respect. They had been talking about him, expressing their doubts. He had expected such a backlash. After a tough start, the campaign had gathered momentum, and astute speeches on unity and the 'enemy without' had touched the villagers, but legal matters of this sort took time and represented something of a gamble. So Michael knew they would get nervous. It had started the previous week when Steve Grimshaw had asked, 'What are *you* going to do if this doesn't work out? Where will *you* go?'

Michael had assured them he was here for the long haul, that he would not abandon them, as so many others had. Today he prepared for more of the same. His wife had warned him that he tended to overestimate people, that he expected Blackmoor to be a brotherhood of pure socialists when, in fact, they were just like everyone else – out for what they could get.

The hall smelled of smoke and stale beer, onions, the musky undertone of urine. The turnout was small so they confined themselves to a long table near the dance floor and stage. Mrs Hargreaves opened the meeting by voicing her concerns about legal action. Would an out-of-court settlement not be better?

'Well, it's not just about the money, of course, Mrs Hargreaves. It's about bringing British Coal to account. And anyway, out of every pit in the UK, we *can't* be the only one with this problem. Our challenge may prove very important in the scheme of things.'

Michael remained calm, but Mrs Hargreaves was unsatisfied. 'My husband often worked in conjunction with solicitors, Mr Jenkins, during his time at the Union. Legal aid and all that. I do know something about the stacks of money and time and nous you need to see someone as big as British Coal in court.'

'I know, I know.'

'It takes more than a bit a enthusiasm and a sermon on the bloody mount,' she said.

Michael nodded, rode the jibe. 'Mrs Hargreaves is right. It is going to be hard work.'

'You couldn't prove that Polly Grimshaw's house weren't just a faulty boiler, could you?' continued Mrs Hargreaves. 'And it could a been landfill gas, like that bungalow what blew up in Loscoe in 1986.'

Elbows squeaked on the table, the listeners perking up, engaged.

'Are you really fussy about *which* gas is causing your houses to explode?' said Michael.

'They will be in court.'

'Yes, but Mrs Alsop's fireplace clearly—'

'And you said that Mick Chambers died of blackdamp, but any miner knows that carbon dioxide is heavier than air. It stays on pit floor.'

'He was in the cellar. Okay, perhaps blackdamp is a vague term. With Mr Chambers, we are talking about the kind of atmosphere created by an underground explosion. This could be a combination of several gases. His cellar was underground and poorly ventilated.'

'But listen, Michael. We can't actually prove that there's a methane threat, can we? Nobody's monitor has gone off, has it?'

A mumble of endorsement, a few chairs pulled closer to the table across the bare red carpet. Mrs Hargreaves pushed her point home. 'How can we take them to court with no proof?'

The others waited for Michael's response with an air of victory. His friends and colleagues had always told him he was too sensitive, took defeat too personally. But these people were defeating themselves! He had not expected this new level of objection. He looked to Beth, who turned her head to the side and smiled. He wanted to ask her what was going on.

'So what you're all saying is that *there is no problem*? That the village is *safe*? Wow. I expected some doubts about our chances of winning, but I never thought you'd question the actual *existence* of the threat. Not after what happened at Christmas. I mean you were evacuated, for God's sake.'

'We need evidence,' said Mrs Hargreaves. 'Evi-*dunce*.'

Michael paused, his mouth open a little. After a moment he held up his hands. His deep voice rose in pitch. 'No, in fact, you're quite right, Mrs Hargreaves. Forget the fact that you were marched out of your homes in the middle of the night four months ago, in the same way people were evacuated from the cities when they were about to be *bombed* during the war. Forget that British Coal, a company that has left you to rot, were so alarmed by the situation that they saw fit to dump a bloody pumping station on the place. No. No we can't prove there's any danger.'

Michael stood, and gripped the back of his chair, dug his fingers into the plastic cover. He laughed. 'In fact, I think it might be a hoax. Yes, that's it. It's a *hoax* by British Coal. Everyone knows there's a big seam running right under the village. Untapped millions. You boys have been talking about it for years. "They never should have shut the pit," you said. "There's still coal down there." That's what you said, wasn't it, Mr Wagstaff?'

Wagstaff made a dismissive noise, damned if he'd be used to support this upstart outsider. But Michael was into his stride now. 'And what's stopping them getting at the coal, Mrs Hargreaves? You are. You and your houses, sitting there in the way of all that profit. How annoying. So they are fabricating gas leaks in order to scare you out of your homes.'

Now that the facetious sarcasm of the speech was revealed, Mrs Hargreaves shook her head angrily. Some of the others began to smirk and Beth chuckled openly. Something occurred to Michael on hearing her laugh. 'Have you seen the land behind Beth Cartwright's house? Beth, tell them.'

All eyes went to the end of the table, where Beth wiped her son's mouth. She looked up at Michael and said, 'Holes.'

'That field is full of holes,' said Michael.

'We've seen the bloody holes,' said Mrs Hargreaves. 'That's so as they can test for gas.'

'But maybe they aren't testing for gas,' said Michael. 'Maybe they're digging for coal. Prospecting. A couple more scares, another exploding cooker, and you lot will be running for the hills. They'll be in there after you, picking up the little black pieces. Maybe they're sending in flatulent cows at night to boost the methane reading. Maybe you're right. There's no *gas*, Mrs Hargreaves – it's Tory halitosis.'

His joke, born out of frustration, got a bigger laugh than he expected. Even Wagstaff chortled (the humour wasn't too far, after all, from his own coarse jokes). The others laughed at Mrs Hargreaves, who had been made to look foolish, and at Michael himself, who had clearly lost his rag. The laughter calmed everyone down for a while. A little trivial banter was what they needed at such a stressful time. But the significant consequences of Michael's wit were not felt until some time after the meeting.

His public deference to Beth Cartwright did not amount to much. Even after science had explained away the curse, the villagers still saw Beth as someone to be avoided. They were already suspicious of Michael's opening day routine with Sarah Browne, and reasoned that he preyed on 'weak women'.

'Gooing for the young mothers, eh?' Wagstaff hissed later, in the Red Lion. 'The dirty bastard.'

While he was at it, Wagstaff could not resist the opportunity to adapt Jenkins's speech for George. 'Eh up, Cartwright, when did that Jenkins youth get to see the view from your bedroom window?'

'Probably when he was nailing my missus, wasn't it?' said George, without looking up from his pint. He knew Beth was a faithful woman.

In fact, Michael's exasperated conspiracy theory made a much more important impression several days later in the boardroom of British Coal. While the coal company did not employ the level of espionage used during the strike of 1984, they certainly had their informants in the village, and somehow, between Michael's mouth and the ears of the Regional Director, the ironic tone of the speech was lost, and British Coal panicked. Of course, they had no intention of driving the residents from the village. They did not kill Mick Chambers, and they did not create the blue flames in Enid Alsop's fireplace. However, during their investigation into the (very real) methane problem (for which they were certainly liable), British Coal had indeed discovered an untapped black vein on land adjacent to the village. Michael's outburst confused the Regional Director, who believed that information about the potential of the site had been leaked. Were any such notions to reach the press, the public image of the company would be further damaged, and any ensuing court case would be doubly difficult. He referred the problem to HQ and, together with their public relations team, British Coal launched an audacious plan to save face and turn the situation back in their favour.

It started four days after Michael's retort, with a fax to Mrs Hargreaves at the Miners' Welfare Club. Therein, British Coal dismissed any rumoured accusations of wrongdoing, but following their 'findings' on land behind Slack Lane, they were preparing a settlement plan for the residents of Blackmoor.

Now Michael and the villagers took their turn to be baffled. They spent a long time pondering the phrases in that strange memo, especially the term 'settlement'. Did it mean compensation for the gas leaks, as in 'out-of-court settlement'? Or had British Coal decided to purchase land on the borders of the village.

Nobody even dreamed, of course, that they meant *re*settlement.

Her mind was occupied, and she could barely decide if this was a good thing. The debate from the Miners' Welfare Club filled her head, the image of Mrs Hargreaves's fat white fist and pointing digits, and Michael at the edge of exhaustion, his shoulders shrugging and then slouched. Sometimes she found herself contributing to these remembered debates, aloud, in her kitchen. 'Exactly,' she might say. 'That's exactly the point.' Nothing strange in it; just what anyone does when they are absorbed in something they care about.

But Beth was afraid of such daydreaming. She would become suddenly aware of her surroundings: steam somersaulting from the sink, a baking tray scraped of its coating and slathered with the pink ooze from the wire wool, her old grazes glistening around the knuckles, her husband watching her from the dark of the hall, her baby gurgling on the kitchen table, the smell of Milton, the desire to be held rushing up the inside of her like a hand, the underground world blasting and burning and quaking. Without turning around she would quickly undo the scene in smooth movements, as if reversing time, pulling the wire wool from the sink, placing the tray back in the oven, stepping backwards and picking up her baby, rocking him until her husband was apparently satisfied enough to walk away.

She looked at Vincent, and felt a stirring of trouble. Something about the shape of his mouth . . . for a second she thought she was having a relapse, but then she realized what the feeling was. She carried the boy into the front room, and, with one hand, skilfully extracted the photograph from her needle wallet. A man smiling, before a racing green car. Her father, with his thin pale lips. Just the same.

Staring now at Vincent she felt truly aware that her father was a real person somewhere, dead or alive. She had thought – guiltily hoped – that the death of her mother a few years back might have brought him out, with apologies or otherwise. But no. And she could not go looking for him now, not in her state. He would be sixty-one. She wondered if he was laughing somewhere, stretching those lips into a smile the way Vincent had just learned to.

FIFTEEN

George had asked her once about the 'eye thing', as she came to call it. They were fifteen.

'Why do you look sideways like that?'

'Stops my eyes from moving. So I can see. Doctor says it's called a zero point.'

'Doesn't it bother you? The eye thing?'

'Well, I think about it all the time. Especially when I'm nervous or talking to new people.'

'Not so many new folk around here,' he said.

She smiled. 'No. Anyway, I don't think I'd ever like to be completely still.'

He had liked that answer.

She had gone on to tell him of her first day at school. The teacher had done birthdays. Each child took a paper cake and fixed it to the appropriate date on a giant calendar. It was 1961 so there was no 29 February. When Beth mentioned the missing number, the teacher took some cruel pleasure in announcing to the class, 'Beth doesn't have a birthday.'

That evening she had cried to her mother. 'Nobody can help when they're born,' her mother had said. 'Or where.'

He looks outside at his Church Eaton garden now, his son kneeling on the top level, setting morsels of raw turkey in the grass in an attempt to lure a barn owl he has seen in the adjacent field. The redundant washing tree, barnacled with rust, fingers of grass reaching up the pole, creaks one inch in a circle that will take a year to complete. He imagines her there, draped with damp linen.

Behind the pavilion he had said, all garrulous bravado, 'I'm gonna get out of here.'

'How?' she had asked.

'Don't know. I expect I'll design warships or become an actor,' he had said, with droll resignation. 'Nah. Numbers. I'm going to go to college, get me a teaching certificate or sommat. For maths.'

He said it spontaneously, to impress her. He had never considered such a possibility, and didn't really believe his words.

'There is an easier way,' she said.

'Oh aye? What's that?'

'Bus,' she had said, and set off for the main road to catch the 10.48 to Derby.

He should have taken her away from that place. It would have been easy.

Animals that die that spring:

All of Vincent's tropical fish.

A squirrel, messily, under the wheels of Mr Downing's 4x4.

Countless and untold young rabbits, in the jaws of the fox.

A generation of slugs, despite a young man's best efforts.

'If they made a film of your life, Vincey, they couldn't do that bit at the end where they say, "No animals were harmed in the making of this movie." How did your fish die?'

'Weirdly and suspiciously. One morning I woke up and Fergal had a big hole through his belly. A perfect circle. I could see the wall on the other side of the tank through this hole.'

'Did the *Betta* bite him?'

'Red? I thought it might have been, to start off with. He can be feisty. But the next day, *he* had the same thing. This mad hole.'

'Sounds like a fungal infection. I'll ask Mum later.'

'Whatever it was, Fergal swam about for a couple a days and then just dropped to the bottom. Found Red lying by the plastic castle the day after.'

'Contagious.'

'Yeah, even the tetras got it. A little pinhole in their neon strips. The bits of food floated straight through it.'

Leila does her one-syllable laugh.

'It's not funny. I reckon Dad did it. I keep having this dream about him drinking a pint of beer with all the fish in it.'

'Absolutely melodramatic. Vincent, how could he have killed them? Ha? With what? A hole-punch?'

'I told you what he said about whisking his sister's goldfish, didn't I?'

'Look, death is natural. It's scientific. Everything dies, even humans. What would crows do without roadkill?'

'Hole-punching a fish is not natural.'

'Sometimes you say sentences I never expected to hear in my whole life.'

She tells him that throughout the seasons you can watch a puddle fill, freeze, thaw, turn to sticky mud and then dry out. You can watch the floor of the quarry go from dusty yellow to treacle brown, with the skin tones of autumn's slick leaves in between. This is what she loves – to watch the stories unfold there.

Vincent stands on the trunk of the fallen tree and looks up at Piano, the buzzard. Leila is on the sandstone bridge swinging her feet over the edge. She has binoculars. If they both make the mewing noise they can get Piano and her young to drop lower to investigate.

Leila hears the sound of something hitting the quarry floor. When she looks down, Vincent is no longer standing on the log. 'Vincent?'

''M'okay,' he shouts. ''M'all right.'

Leila descends, arrives alongside him as he gets to his feet. 'Have you been doing Mum's exercises?'

'Yes. I'm getting a bit better.'

'And have you been working on the project?'

'Kind of.'

'Lame. Did you at least ask your dad about living in the village?'

'He doesn't want to talk about it.'

And neither, in fact, does Vincent. The whole subject makes

him feel queasy, and he is starting to agree with his father: let sleeping villages lie. Besides, it seems like such a waste to spend his time with Leila trawling over books. Leila, on the other hand, has done a great deal of research on the internet. They now know about methane, about the first evacuation. When Vincent told her about old Blackmoorian Martin Wagstaff's residence in Church Eaton, Leila gave him a severe reprimand for not taking advantage of the opportunity to gain more information.

'Seeing as you've been so rubbish,' she says, 'I've decided to arrange an interview with this Martin Wagstaff myself.'

'I wouldn't. He's a bit weird.'

Leila's eyes widen, she has her mother's sensitivity on this point. 'I don't need looking after. You're the one who can't stand up. *And* the one who gets bullied.'

Vincent laughs, but not at her jibe. He laughs because Leila is positioned between two trees in the background, which appear to be protruding from either side of her head like antlers. He thinks she would make a good deer – the combination of aggression and long eyelashes.

'Do they bother you?' she asks.

'What?'

'David Sulley and all that. At school.'

'Used to it,' says Vincent, playing the hardy loner.

'They say some fairly mean stuff.'

'It doesn't feel mean. You have to be bothered about someone for them to really get to you. Some of the stuff you say is meaner.'

Leila fails to note the very well hidden compliment.

*

They go back to the tent and wait for the badgers. Leila cooks chicken soup on the Calor stove. Vincent runs a finger over his rough beard of spots. His father had *told* him it was too early to shave, that he should wait until he was fifteen like a normal lad, but Vincent thought the hair above his thick lips looked vulgar. Days after that first shave he had every kind of spot in his acne blush: the swollen bee-sting red ones, the painful ones that stay under the skin, the volcanic white ones (his least favourite because of their similarity to foaming slugs when they burst), and the blackheads that cover his nose. He is not averse to the blackheads because they recall Leila's dark freckles. But he has not shaved his strawberry cheeks since that first time, afraid now that he will bleed to death.

'Dad says that my face looks like someone set it on fire and put it out with a pit boot,' he says.

'And you said he wasn't inventive. Here, I bought these for you. Lie back.'

She opens a tub of medicated face pads and climbs over him so that she has a knee each side of his ribs. Her skirt stretches taut and she hitches it slightly. Vincent feels his erection straining against his pants.

Leila reads from the tub. 'The rough side – here – is for opening the pores and getting rid of surface impurities. The smooth side – look – is for a deep penetrating cleanse.'

'Right.'

'I'm supposed to start with your T-zone.'

She begins at his left temple and swipes the pad across his forehead lightly, as though stroking in the sky wash of a watercolour. Then she runs it down his nose, over his filtrum, his lips, his chin.

'Smells like hospitals,' he says.

'Does a bit. As if being spotty wasn't bad enough, now you hum like A&E.'

'Oi. That's cruel.'

'I like the smell of hospitals. Right. That was the rough side. Are you ready for your . . . deep penetrating cleanse?'

'S'pose. Yep.'

The smooth side stings and makes his eyes water so that he has to close them. Leila pushes back his hair to keep it out of the way. She runs the pad from ear to ear, pressing hard now so that the antibacterial fluid seeps out and bubbles. Vincent's face is a glistening crimson and the spots look angry, derisive. Occasionally he takes a sharp breath through his teeth.

'How does it feel?' Leila asks. 'Do you feel clean?'

'It stings. Now it tingles. It feels hot and cold at the same time.'

He opens his eyes and looks at her. Her hair is bunched on top of her head. Behind her, the skin of the tent is the same colour as a finger held up to a light bulb, as sun coming through hands that cover a face. Leila shuffles off him inexpertly, frowns when her knee catches the bump in his trousers. When he sits up, Vincent's hair remains in a startled quiff.

Later, while they work on the project, Mrs Downing brings out a bottle of cherryade, some glasses and Mars bars. Leila hands back her Mars bar, because, she says, she does not want to go into a diabetic coma. Mrs Downing greets Vincent as a 'fellow remnant of a lost civilization'.

'Are you sure your father doesn't mind you staying out this late?' she asks.

'He'll sleep better without my snoring.'

Mrs Downing looks at her daughter, who waves away the strangeness of the comment.

Leila reads from a book. '"Between 1985 and 1995, the Derbyshire Coalfield lost 50,000 industrial jobs."'

Vincent looks at her intently. 'Can I have some of that pop?' he says.

Leila reaches into her sleeping bag, pulls out half a bottle of vodka and the plastic drinking flask from a bicycle. She simultaneously pours vodka and cherryade into the bike flask, replaces the lid, needlessly shakes it and sucks from the teat. 'Bottoms up, Mr Cartwright,' she says, handing him the flask.

'Everything smells of medicine tonight,' he says, and drinks.

When Vincent has gone, Leila takes out her project diary and writes.

When I think of Blackmoor, I used to think of old-fashioned waist-coats and chimney sweeps, but I know it wasn't like that now. It was more like rubbish telly from the 80s that makes you feel sad on Sundays. It's weird but I also think of it as having two levels, like a cross-section in biology. Or like the underworld that Vincent's always going on about. There's the level on top with all the people, and they're really still and don't do anything, and then there's the level below where there's rolling clouds of fire, and burning water, and blackdamp which I imagine like blue mist. And at certain points, where there's a crack in the ground, the mist and fire seep up on to the top level, and one of the still people falls down. Did

that happen to Vincent's mum? Maybe I'll ask this Mr Wagstaff. I
wonder what it was like there. I bet everyone was scared and it's
weird to think Vincent was there, that he breathed in the bad air a
few years ago. I wonder how frightened he was, but he says he can't
remember.

Sixteen

In May 1991, a huge white marquee appeared on Blackmoor Rec. The formerly strict and prohibitive parish councillors did not even enquire after its purpose. The time had been when Mrs Hargreaves would have dashed to remove children with golf balls or firecrackers from that patch of grass, lest a senior resident's dog be injured. Now the guardians of Blackmoor had all but surrendered control of their village. Mrs Hargreaves was so tired from all the meetings with Michael Jenkins, and his energetic insistence on legal action, that she could not have cared less about a stupid marquee. Most of the residents gloomily assumed that another highly dangerous leak had been discovered, and that the marquee was some kind of atmospheric protection tent, its thin fabric the last defence against a fiery death.

A few days after its arrival, British Coal called a meeting at the marquee. They invited every resident. Generations of Sheps, Bettsys, Jackos and Grets attended. Five minutes before the meeting commenced, Michael sat sweating in the muggy atmosphere.

Because of the numbers, extra chairs had been brought in from the primary school, and Michael's knees rose above his waist.

Outside, a cloud slid away from the setting sun and the marquee glowed yellow. For a moment Michael saw Beth's stooped silhouette suddenly defined on the canvas, a shadow puppet stepping over a support rope. The dark shape was scooped away by the closing fist of more cloud cover. She came in (Michael watched the heads turn, the conversations lower, in much the same way as they did when *he* entered a room) and sat next to him, stretching her legs out before her. 'What are they up to now, do you think?' she asked him.

'God only knows,' Michael said. 'Where's George?'

'At home with Vincent.'

The British Coal representative, Jim Balshaw, was tall and bald, with a pink peeling head. He looked like a rubber-ended pencil. He set up a projector and a giant screen at the front of the tent. After his casual greetings, he switched tone. His language became measured and premeditated, almost legalese.

'We at British Coal and British Coal Opencast understand the security concerns of residents relating to noxious and inflammable emissions. We were quick and thorough in our bid to ascertain the nature of the problem, and we have concluded that there may, indeed, be cause for action.

'While this is so, we can't possibly be held responsible for gases occurring naturally underground, and we feel sure that the courts would conclude the same.'

Michael laughed hysterically, and some of the others turned to scowl at him. Jim Balshaw also looked in his direction and nodded succinctly, as if to acknowledge that he had located the class troublemaker. He continued. 'Listen, we're all on the same side here. Most of us. And we believe that by working together we can find a solution that not only ensures the safety of you and your families, but improves your lives considerably too.

'We have, as you may have gathered, discovered a seam of coal behind Slack Lane.'

At this news, *nobody* turned to Michael. In fact, there was a visible stiffening of neck muscles to prevent it. No one likes a told-you-so.

'Now this was an inadvertent find, an unexpected interruption to the conscientious safety investigations of our team. But that's not to say that it necessarily has to be a problem. At British Coal, we always try to turn obstacles into—'

'Get t' point,' said Wagstaff. His outburst received a censorious *sshhh* from Mrs Hargreaves, but even she agreed with the sentiment.

'Okay, sir, I'll do just that. British Coal propose to demolish the current, potentially unsafe village, and excise the coal in the adjacent land by means of opencast mining over a ten-year period.'

He said it with a serene smile, as if he did not anticipate the clamour and cursing that almost drowned the end of his sentence. He calmly adjusted the projector while he waited for the audience to settle. Michael knew from this reaction that Balshaw had something up his sleeve. Otherwise he would be running for the exit.

An illustrated plan of a housing estate appeared on the big screen. 'Thank you,' Balshaw said when they quietened. 'Behind me is an impression of the brand new 30 million pound replacement village that we plan to construct on a site just two miles from here. It has a pub, a community centre, a sports ground and a woodland area. The money generated by the opencast mine will fund the new village – New Blackmoor, if you like – and each of you will move, free of charge, from old terraced properties worth £30,000 and dropping, to £60,000 detached new-builds with indoor toilets, fitted kitchens and bathrooms. You will leave behind a situation of anxiety and danger, for somewhere beautiful, and you'll receive a £30,000 windfall to go with it.'

A replacement village. Gasps overcame the profanities. In the quiet, Balshaw clicked his remote and projected floor plans of the spacious new homes. 'No need for coal shoots here, I'm happy to say, with gas central heating as standard.'

As Balshaw expounded the virtues of the new village, Beth picked daisies from around her ankles to make a chain. Her nails bit into the stems and sap foamed. She turned to look at Michael but his eyes were tightly shut. She could feel the nature of the silence in the marquee. People were scared to breathe in case the visions on the big screen disappeared. She wondered if it were possible to move Blackmoor in such a way. She wondered if the idea of the place was rooted in the ground somehow. Wouldn't they just dissolve?

Balshaw came to the end of his speech. On the screen behind him, two words: 'EVERYBODY WINS'. 'Obviously if we're going to do this, we need to move quickly. The sooner you and your families are away from the threat, the better.' They were given ten days to decide. The marquee would remain for that time and the residents were to return to vote.

The crowd stood hastily, eager to celebrate their good fortune. Beth saw couples discreetly holding hands, something of a rarity in Blackmoor. Tom Betts began to clap, but Wagstaff smacked him around the head. Michael and Beth remained seated as the others left. Michael had his hands over his eyes. 'What will they do?' he asked Beth, although he already knew.

Beth held her daisy chain up against the length of the crowd filing out of the marquee. 'They'll go to the pub. And then they'll accept.'

Meetings naturally ensued. At the Miners' Welfare Club later that week, the residents voiced their almost unanimous favour for the move. 'We've lived in fear for long enough,' said Polly Grimshaw. 'The way I felt in that tent, bloody hell, I realized I hadn't been happy for so long. I'd got so used to feeling bad and frit, that I didn't even notice it any more.'

Mrs Hargreaves turned to Michael, who had thus far been quiet. 'Mr Jenkins, I can see you chomping at the bit. Why don't you tell us about your theory that British Coal pumped happy gas into the marquee? Or is the new village a hologram?'

Cruel, sarcastic laughter. Michael scratched at the raised white hives on his neck. He spoke quietly. 'You *must* realize that it's a scam. Surely. Four million tonnes of coal they're going to mine. That's six hundred million pounds. They are spending *five per cent* on your new village. We had them. They were backs to the wall, and facing huge compensation payouts, facing justice. Now they're going to make a massive profit. How is that fair? They are smashing your village into the ground and getting paid for it.'

'*We're* getting paid for it, you mean,' said Sarah Browne. 'I feel like I've won the pools.'

Michael heard a few grunts of assent. The people supported Sarah Browne now, it appeared. He had succeeded, at least, in that.

'It's short term, Sarah,' Michael said. 'Step back and look at this in sequence. The government closed down the pit, put every-one here out of work and said there was no coal. Now British Coal has come in, with a new method, and they're taking it all for themselves.'

Steve Grimshaw reacted to this. 'But they're going to need workers at the opencast site, aren't they? Quarter a the folk in this village are unemployed. This'll make jobs.'

Michael shook his head. He was too frustrated to see the frag-ile look of hope on Steve Grimshaw's face. 'They won't employ *you*, Steve. They've got specialist people, trained for the job. You don't have the skills.'

Polly Grimshaw stood out of her chair. 'Shut up, you. Don't you say he's got no skills. He's ten times the man you are.'

'I didn't mean it like that, Polly. I didn't . . . You've been neg-lected, all of you.'

Beth held her boy to her bright green sweater; her lip twitched as she looked at Michael and he knew it was useless.

'Look,' he said. 'Go if you like. Blackmoor's been here for over a hundred years, but by all means move to your new village, if you want. All you have to do is forget your principles.'

'You can afford principles, Michael,' said Mrs Hargreaves. 'All *you* have to do is come here and pick up your pay cheque. *Your* house hasn't been reduced to worthless scrap. *You* don't have worry about your kid's school blowing up, do you? You said yourself that the place was dangerous. And even if we did get compensation, where would we go? We can't all move out.'

'You wouldn't need to move out. They'd have to secure the area.'

'Most of us have lived here all our lives. We don't know anything else but Blackmoor.'

'Exactly. That's exactly what I'm saying. You have to fight for that.'

'Shut up, prick,' muttered Wagstaff.

Michael turned slowly, to look at Wagstaff's stubbly face, his slack mouth. 'I beg your pardon?'

'A say keep your trap shut for five minutes. Everyone's sick a your pissing and moaning.'

'*Moaning*? I've been working myself into the ground for you.'

'Bugger off back to where you came from.'

Michael looked at Mrs Hargreaves, who stared out of the window. The others around the room kept their heads down. The porcelain click of snooker balls came from the other room. Michael began to laugh under his breath. He left the room, and Beth lifted her baby and followed him.

'That's it, duck,' said Wagstaff. 'You go and give him some comforting.'

Beth stopped, turned around, and smiled at Wagstaff. 'Martin!' she said, high-pitched, as though she was greeting him after a long absence. Her smile faded, and she lowered her voice. 'Martin, I think that your life has been a terrible, terrible waste. I know you're sterile, and that must torment you, but, really, I think it's a blessing. I really do. When you die, you'll be wiped out and forgotten for ever.'

Wagstaff was, for once, speechless. He frowned, unaccustomed to hurt. When he looked at the others around the table, nobody would return his gaze, only Beth with her sidelong glance.

She caught up with Michael outside and asked if they could

take a walk together. When he consented, she ushered him down a slim footpath concealed by hawthorn. 'Living here, where everyone can see you, you learn ways to get a bit of privacy,' she said. They emerged on to the disused loop track. The grass on the railway cutting had overgrown, and up ahead, where the banks were highest, stood a giant pile of household rubbish. The place had become an illegal tip.

'I can't believe they're going to accept it,' he said.

'What will you do?' asked Beth.

Michael opened his top button, and craned his neck like a cat, scratching. 'I'll fight them,' he said.

Beth laughed.

'What?' Michael said.

'Well, it's just that when you came here, you had the intention of helping folk. Now you're talking about fighting them.'

'What should I do? This is wrong. What's happening here is wrong.'

'I just think you've done your job. You've pulled folk together, and you've forced the coal boys into compensating us. I know people don't seem grateful at the minute.'

'I'm not doing it for adulation.'

'They'll eventually realize how important you were in all of this.'

'You think I should stand down? Let them vote yes?'

'I think you should let people have what they want.'

'They don't know what to want.'

Beth frowned and Vincent moaned. 'I think that's just patronizing, Michael.'

Michael rolled his eyes. 'God. You people.'

'Don't give me that "you people" rubbish, either. We're not a different species. It's not a bloody zoo.'

'I'm sorry.'

'Look at this place.' Beth pointed to the weeds constricting the train tracks and curling up into the bank. A few pink sweetbriars glowed oddly in the tangle. Beth stroked one, as you would stroke a dog's chin. 'This is where the signal box used to be. There used to be a yellow box, and a little garden with roses and forget-me-nots.' And there, by her feet, the alarming blueness of the small flowers, still. Beth kicked away at the cage of thorny weeds and nettles. 'When we used to go to Skegness as kids, we used to wave at the signalman as we went past. And you could look back and see the pink of these roses for a good distance down the track. Not me, like. I couldn't see five yards. The other kids could see the roses. "Still see 'um," they'd say, right the way to bloody Lincoln.' Beth smiled at the memory. 'Look at the place now. It's a hellhole.'

Some of the lighter items from the rubbish dump had drifted down and caught in the bushes. 'Michael, everything here is disused or used up or burnt out. Would a new start really be that bad? It'll be *nice* for people. New carpets, new bedrooms. Nothing nice has happened here for such a long time.'

Michael walked on moodily, eyeing the dark stripe of the seam which outcropped on the railway cutting, above the garbage mountain.

Beth broke the silence. 'You're not going to take any notice anyway, are you? You're going to carry on fighting your own little battle. I can tell.'

Michael smiled at her. He often mistook people's exasperation for a bewildered respect for his tenacity. Beth looked down. 'My eyes are going, aren't they?'

'I didn't notice. Wasn't looking.'

'They go when I'm tired or nervous.'

'Which are you?'

'Tired. You know in the Middle Ages they'd have taken one look at these eyes and burnt me at the stake. Not easy for albinos in those days.'

'Well, in the nineteenth century they'd have praised your pallor.'

'Blackmoor in the 1990s is a compromise I suppose.'

They laughed. 'I think it's very charming,' said Jenkins.

'Yeah. Would be if I could see anything.'

'Most of my job involves trying to figure out what people are thinking and feeling. With you I know when you're nervous from what your eyes are doing.'

'I'm just tired.'

'Okay, tired. In any case, that kind of transparency is very refreshing.'

Beth pulled up the sleeve of her green sweater. 'I *am* transparent. Look at these veins. George used to say that when I stood in front of the sun he could see my guts.'

Michael sighed. 'Will *you* be going to "New Blackmoor"?'

'We'll have to ask George, won't we, treasure?' she said, kissing Vincent.

'You'll have to ask George,' said Michael.

Beth led the way over the bank and towards the disputed territory behind her house. 'It's a bit like a bible story all a this, intit?' said Beth.

'What, Sodom and Gomorrah?'

'I don't know which *bit*. It's just got that feel, hasn't it? The land is at stake. I suppose the gases would be a plague, or something.'

'If it was a parable, you know what would happen, don't you? If the people are greedy and vote for the nice new detached houses, they'll probably burn in hell,' Michael said, and they both laughed.

'Who do you think you are: Jesus?' said Beth.

'Thou shalt not have an indoor toilet.'

George watched from the upstairs back window as they climbed the stile into the field. The boreholes were now enclosed by metal construction fences, and surrounded by hazard signs, so Beth and Michael Jenkins had to take a circuitous route. The sight of them confused George. A faint firing of Blackmoor male pride forced him towards jealousy, but that kind of jealousy had a sexual element and he could not complain, because of his abstinence. Maybe this bloke was doing him a favour. But it *did* hurt and George did not like pain. He had always seen himself as a different breed to the other men in Blackmoor. They were tough, he was clever; they had antiquated views, he was enlightened. But this Jenkins made him realize that he was just a watery alternative. Jenkins was a better version of what George tried to be.

A smudge of white paint remained on the windowpane from Beth's overenthusiastic home improvements. The slants of brush fibres had created a blot that looked like a face half in shadow. George remembered Beth saying that, as the depression set in, everything appeared to have a face. The washing machine was the worst, she said, with its shocked mouth bellowing 'no'. Now George was seeing faces.

Michael and Beth reached the back gate and George slid behind the curtain, peered around. His son reached out for Michael. The three of them looked like a happy family. Maybe I should just bugger off and leave them to it, thought George. And with a few more such phrases, George managed to replace the self-effacing jealousy with indignation.

That evening he appeared in the kitchen doorway while she washed the pots again. The water had been poured into the sink straight from the kettle, and Beth had rested her hands in the freezer compartment for a good five minutes before. Looking for that painful contrast. 'Listen,' said George. 'I want you to stop seeing Michael Jenkins.'

Beth let a plate float to the bottom of the sink. Steam rose into her face, along with the smell of apple-fresh washing-up liquid. 'Why?' she said without turning.

'Because I've asked you.'

'I'd like to have a reason.'

'Because it embarrasses me when I hear the lads talk about you carrying on.'

'The lads,' Beth whispered to herself.

'What?'

'I want a reason from *you*, George. Does it make you angry?'

'When people come up to me in the pub, and . . .'

'Never mind that. Does the thought of him . . . the thought of him and me. Does it wind you up?'

George tried to think of the right answer, tried to work out what Beth wanted him to say. He remembered what Waggy had said about Jenkins and the view from the window. He tried to think of his wife with Jenkins, but he could not even imagine Beth having sex any more. Eventually he gave up. 'Look, Beth, go and see him if you have to. Just don't take the boy, okay?'

He tried to walk away but Beth turned and called out. 'I won't see him, George.'

She grabbed at his wrist, and he felt the scalded slimy hand on his. 'There's nothing between me and him, George. You know that, don't you?'

George hesitated. 'Yes.'

'I've never kissed him or touched him or slept with him. I would never sleep with anyone apart from you.'

George despised the way she switched to this infantile register when talking about the fundamentals. All this never-ever business. Her hand slid from his arm and on to his belt. He slapped it away, and she put it back. He squeezed her fingers tightly, twisted them until she winced.

'Please, Beth, not now.'

SEVENTEEN

Wagstaff and his wife Joan had become anxious about conception two years after they married, in their late teens. Sex was never a pleasure for Joan, and the longer she went without getting pregnant, the more punishing the act became. She loved Martin for a few years, but by her mid-twenties, she did no longer. He said there must be something wrong with her, told his friends she was barren.

Two days after her twenty-eighth birthday, Joan went to the doctor, partly out of her own desire for a baby, and partly because she wanted to win the argument. The doctor said she was perfectly fertile, and that her husband should make an appointment. She had won the argument, but the prize from Martin was a bloody mouth and a forceful attempt to prove the doctor wrong.

'There's note wrong with me. You're a liar and so's that doctor. You speak a word a this and you'll wish you hadn't,' said Wagstaff.

Joan smoothed down her dress and crawled backwards, keeping her eyes on him. 'Where are you going?' he said. When she got out of the bedroom door she turned and ran downstairs, out into the yard. It was midnight, and quiet. She could hear him coming, so she ducked into the coal shed and wedged the door shut with a breeze block. That cool smell of coal, the warmth of the sun trapped in there somewhere, like a pearl. Her eyes adjusted gradually to the shimmer of black mounds. A few moments later, she heard him pacing around outside. She was one step ahead of his thoughts but powerless to make the advantage count. He began to shout her name and then stopped, wary of the nosy neighbours. Then he walked towards the shed. Quiet for a moment. He booted the door and she screamed. He got close to the wood so that she could see flashes of him in the gaps between the panels. 'You don't want to make one more noise,' he whispered.

Then he began to kick the shed on all sides, almost rhythmically. He did not speak, just kept kicking. She hated the pauses most, because she did not know where the next strike would land. The blows made slight dents where the wood had weakened, so Joan clambered into the middle, sat against the landslide of coal. Her foot nudged something on the ground. She picked up a cold, sharp object. She recognized it as the old trowel that Martin and Harry Cartwright had found down the pit. She held it like a knife and waited. He continued to kick until someone came to their window in one of the houses on the terrace. 'It's all rate. Lav's blocked. That's all,' she heard her husband say. After one last kick, he walked down the right of way and out into the street.

Joan waited in the shed for a long time, until she felt that the darkness in there was somehow radiating from herself. She felt better. She knew, quite suddenly, that if Martin had broken down the door, she would have slashed him with the antiquated tool. The next time she saw him, and every time after that, she would pick out the exact spot under the eye where the jagged blade would have sliced. She would imagine the wound with precision and quality.

Eventually she opened the shed door and stepped outside. She looked down the terraced row. One of the lights was still on in a window: a concerned neighbour. She coughed, and the light went out.

As the octogenarian Martin Wagstaff stands now, in his Church Eaton garden, the place where Joan would have stabbed him is scribbled over with wrinkles. Leila appreciates the accuracy of Vincent's description of the old man. ('First, make a fist. Now, look at your fist from the thumb side. The thumb is his sticking-out jaw, and those two creases in your index finger are his squinty eyes.') Wagstaff stares up at his pigeons, but Leila stares at him. He wears those blue overalls – not the overalls of a miner, but of a shower gel operative, the job he took at one of the factories after the pit closed.

Leila has rolled up her skirt, because she has seen women do this in films when they want information. The man at the local studies library recently gave her an article called 'Why Did the Village Cross the Road?', so she knows all about New Blackmoor. Her Dictaphone is rolling in the inside pocket of her blazer.

The pigeons loop around the primary school clock tower for the fourth time. Leila is suspicious of them. As they spread into race formation they look like a dark arm sweeping a table of dominoes. Too human, too controlled.

'The first village, the proper Blackmoor, were a great place. I could start at first house and go rate through and tell you all folk that lived there. Everybody helped everybody, and they were all friendly because they were all miners, see.'

'So you weren't very happy when they wanted to knock it down?'

'I were dead against it from start. I never wanted to goo to new village.'

'But wasn't it dangerous in old Blackmoor? What if the gas caught fire?'

'Oh aye. Every day you were in fear a your life.'

'So you didn't want to stay, but you didn't want to go?'

Wagstaff looks up at the pigeons and sneers. He scratches himself through his pocket. Leila asks another question. 'Why didn't you like New Blackmoor?'

'It were a maze for a start. One a these new estates. All streets looked same, and when you turned a corner you ended up going in a cirtle.'

'A what, sorry?'

'A cirtle. A cirtle. All those dead ends.'

'Oh. A *circle*.'

'It made you look a tit. And we were used to terrace and all. Being close to one another. In a de-tached house, it's like you're miles from anyone. Just me and the bloody wife, may she rot for all times.'

'Did your wife pass away?' asks Leila, pleased with her adult euphemism.

'I wouldn't bloody know. I look in obits every week, but she never has the decency to turn up, the stubborn bitch.'

'She didn't move with you to Church Eaton?'

'She booted me out of me own home what I'd worked for forty year. Having to shit in corner like a cat, and . . . The minute we make the money on the brand new house, she kicks me out.'

The returning pigeons make sarcastic applause, just above his head. 'If I'd a known, I wouldn't a worked a day. I'd a gone long-term sick with whitefinger or lung like every fucker else.'

Leila bends to her blazer pocket. 'Foul language,' she whispers.

'You what?'

'Nothing.'

Little does Wagstaff know that he is, in fact, long-term sick right now. The tumour which will kill him is currently doing two things he has never been able to do: self-replicate and self-nourish. Wagstaff cannot cook. 'What are you then?' he asks Leila.

'Year eight.'

'No, I mean what *are* you? You're not quite a blackie, are you?'

Leila ignores the question. She crinkles her nose at the stink from the pigeon shed, and carefully turns off the Dictaphone. 'You knew George Cartwright, didn't you? What was he like?'

'Pansy. Lives here now, dun't he?'

'Yes.'

'Know him, do you?'

'Not really.'

'I fuggin' told him that night. I says to him, "Your fayther would be ashamed a you." Then I clouted him. He were a twat. No wonder his wife topped hersen.'

'Topped? What's "topped"? Did you know his wife?'

'White Witch? I don't like talking about her. She were evil, bad luck. The way she died, people say it were an accident, or that it were young lad's fault, but you don't die in one fuggin' second, do you? You build up to it. Takes ages.'

'The young lad? You mean Vincent?'

Wagstaff waves his hand dismissively. 'Told you, I don't like talking about her. We're a superstitious lot. But it were probably George's fault more than anyone. It's same as a say: you don't die in one second.'

Eighteen

The first eager voters arrived at the marquee before breakfast. Michael, as a non-resident, had to stay outside. Enid Alsop approached him, tugged on his shirt cuff as a child might. 'I'm with you, Mr Jenkins.'

'Thanks, Mrs Alsop.'

'Even if no bugger else is. Me and my Alfred bought that house when we were twenty-two, and we bought it to die in.' She hobbled slowly towards the road, on two sticks now. Michael wondered if there was anywhere else in the world where people considered their own death when purchasing their first property.

Wagstaff and the Grimshaws ignored him as they entered, talking already about their new houses. Even Michael, the great optimist, was under no illusions about which way the vote would go.

More of a mystery to him was the whereabouts of Beth

Cartwright. Her presence would have been a comfort at this time, for she allowed him to be miserable. In fact, his failure was so necessary to the success of their friendship that sometimes Michael found himself craving defeat. A dangerous loop. He decided to walk to Slack Lane.

Beth did not answer the door. When Michael knocked for the third time, Mrs Hargreaves across the road went to her front-room window to see what all the fuss was about. She wore her black and white Jackie Kennedy coat, ready to leave for the Rec. Under the net curtain she could see Michael, the white and burgundy frills of lobelia from the flower basin against his grey suit. Nothing unusual about Michael Jenkins knocking on doors, the bloody nuisance. *Certainly* nothing unusual about him calling on Beth Cartwright during working hours. The exceptional element of the scene was the fact that – as Mrs Hargreaves now saw – Beth stood at the top front window of her house, half-obscured by the curtain, looking down on her visitor. And she made no move to answer the door.

Michael sighed, scratched his neck and took a few steps backwards. He stumbled over the flower basin, and ended up with his hands in the dirt. As he cleaned his fingers with a handkerchief, and berated himself for his clumsiness, Michael looked up at the house and saw her. Beth made no movement from the top window as their eyes met. Michael waved once and when that was not reciprocated, he made a motion to wave again, but aborted it, suddenly perceiving a final change in things. He stared for a little longer, and Beth stared back, her head turning very slightly to the side. Michael moved slowly away, nodding.

Beth's word to her husband would not be tested by Michael Jenkins again. He returned to his comfortable home, as the residents said he would. They had defeated him.

Blackmoor accepted the proposal. British Coal said the residents would move to the new village in November 1992, eighteen months later. A scale plan of New Blackmoor lay over the snooker table in the Miners' Welfare Club. The pink and orange houses made it look like a tray of seafood hors d'oeuvres. After meeting with the architects and planners, each family wrote their name above a particular plot number. For two months that summer, happiness radiated from the snooker table. People greeted their 'neighbours-to-be' with great enthusiasm, and those who had recently been assigned a plot wore the bashful smiles of newly-weds. They were happy in the sheepish, hesitant manner of those who find notes spewing from a cash machine. For once, the people of Blackmoor felt lucky. They almost forgot about the threat hanging over them.

They did not miss Michael Jenkins. Originally, the residents concluded that he had left because of defeat at the polling station, but Mrs Hargreaves soon provided an alternative reason. She gave a fairy-tale edge to the scene she had witnessed from her front-room window, describing the White Witch, icy at the top of her tower, and Michael the broken-hearted mortal beneath. She said that Michael had left because he was lovesick.

In March you could see how the shadow of the house fell blue in the smoky garden. See how Beth's hair (growing slowly back) took on the sorrowful colour. In that light she looked like stone. Indeed, her stance also gave her the appearance of a statue: she stood on one leg as though caught in motion. In the realms of the shadow, Vincent lay in a pram waving his orange mittens.

Beth chewed with a languorous rhythm. Her left foot became hot on the lawn, so she changed standing legs, arched her head back like a jazz trumpeter straining for the note, and spat shards of crushed cashew nuts in a high loop on to the grass. Within seconds, wagtails began to fly into the tree beyond the fence, like tiny thrown pebbles. Then they swooped down on to the hot grass – one or two at first, then many – bouncing back into the tree with their prize. Steam rose from the ground beneath Beth's foot.

This was the scene that greeted drunken George as he slipped around the back of his house. He sniggered, and Beth turned to greet him, gave thanks that he was happy-drunk this evening. As if to emphasize his unusual mood, George lifted the cine camera and began to film Vincent in the pram. Beth joined them. Sometimes, she had noticed, George could drink just enough to turn him into that boy she had known, with all his brashness and gangly cheek. What rare combination of elements did it take to effect this change? Since her illness, Beth often pondered the minuscule chemical reactions responsible for behaviour. The tiny random meetings of energies and their enormous consequences.

Vincent gurned at his mother. The wonder of his rapid growth brought attention to her own atrophy. So Beth reached down, evading his basic grasp, and removed the mittens.

And yes, he saw his hands, noticed them for the first time. Beth laughed. George fixed the lens on Vincent, one eye closed tight.

Beth absently dropped the mittens on to the grass.

George directed the cine camera at Beth. 'Poor little bugger probably thought he was orange,' he said.

Beth did not answer. The cine camera had no microphone, and she knew that any words would be lost or misconstrued in the future. George lowered the machine and its clicking slowly subsided, to be replaced by the noise of birds in the neighbouring field. Vincent hooked his fingers together with glee, and Beth shook her head. 'He's starting to recognize himself. That's how it bloody starts.'

'How what starts?'

'It's terrifying,' Beth said.

She went inside. George stood for a moment and then bent over her single footprint in the grass. Blades strained to rise against the memory of her pressure and a crescent of cashew slept in the steaming bay of her big toe.

Enid Alsop did not die in the house she had bought for that purpose. The gardener at the Parish Church found her small body stretched across her husband's grave one morning, her sticks discarded. He was not the first graveyard gardener to find a body. Sometimes blood seeps from the wrists into the soil, sometimes vomit from the mouth. Enid was pale and dry.

Although she did not have many close living friends, Enid held a position of respect in the village and the funeral was well attended. Beth Cartwright, who had worked briefly with Enid at the Miners' Welfare Club, wore a man's bowler hat she had converted with flowers and feathers. People noticed how typical it was these days to see her without her husband. Tom Betts wore his only tie, which, unfortunately, was of a bright mustard and maroon design.

'God loves you and therefore trouble comes to your house?' said the minister. 'At first, these things make no sense to us.'

Tom appeared to find some horror in those words, for his eyes widened and he walked quickly away, beginning to run as he reached the lychgate. Whispers shivered through the crowd, and as they watched him go they detected a sharp sulphurous odour.

In the low mist of the morning, it took them a while to recognize that several thin spires of smoke were winding out of the graves by the eastern flank of the church. Blasphemy ensued, and Mrs Hargreaves gripped her husband's arthritic hands so hard that he cried out. A hissing emanated from the earth, grew louder. They assumed this sound to be connected to the smoke, but it was, in fact, the mass movement of soil. Twenty feet from the gathering, a green gravestone cocked to a crooked angle, and a dip appeared in the land, like a sudden shadow. Two tiles, guttermoss and green water slid from the roof of the crude apse, which shuddered, releasing a handful of dust.

Over the protests of the group, the minister appealed for calm. 'Please don't panic. It's not an earthquake. Let's take a short walk to the Rec and finish the service there. This has happened before. It's just subsidence.'

Beth Cartwright's shoulders were seen to drop as she directed her slanting gaze to the newly contoured earth, which was still moving, bubbling and steaming like a baking pie. She cried openly for Enid Alsop, and for her mother, whose grave was among those affected. In the cool wind the smoke curved towards Beth, who held out her hand, sobbed and moved on, a few paces behind the others, the jade of a magpie's feather flashing in her hat.

Nineteen

The local studies library is down an alley, behind a row of chain pubs in town. Already, late on a Friday afternoon, the rumble and screech of karaoke reaches through the open windows. In the library, Leila can smell beefy sweat, bananas and old paper. Vincent had offered to come along, but he said it with a sigh, and she does not appreciate token gestures. Sometimes she doubts his commitment to the project.

She scrolls through microfiche images of the *North Derbyshire Herald*, and finds a few dense and boring articles on Blackmoor. A melodramatic man named Michael Jenkins is often quoted. Leila's concentration wanes. She finds the 'photo-stories' more amusing: a boy with his prize cow, a couple who take a motorcycle tour for their honeymoon. The fashion sense of 1990s Derbyshire was bizarre. Leila grimaces at the cardigans, shellsuits, tight white jeans and big basketball boots. Haircuts like Davy Crockett hats.

Her mother is shopping, and will not be back to collect her for another half-hour. Leila looks down at a small note she has made

at the base of her exercise book. *26.06.92. Elizabeth (long for Beth??)*
Cartwright. She scrolls along, her fingers moving like she is
unscrewing a bottle. By the time she finds the article, crunched
into a marginal corner, her mouth is dry.

> A Blackmoor woman jumped to her death
> from the second-floor window of her house
> last Thursday.
>   Witnesses believe that Elizabeth Cart-
> wright, 36, of Slack Lane, had watched
> her young son fall from the same window
> moments before. The boy, a toddler, had land-
> ed safely in a flower basin below the house.

Leila reads it twice and then laughs out loud. One syllable. Ha. The
library assistant looks her way and she regains her composure.

Leila calculates the dates. *He* is the toddler. It's him. She feels
the buzz of discovery. The musty library, the ancient microfiche
machine – it is like a film.

By the time the talc-sweetness of her mother's scent invades the
stale atmosphere, Leila is twitching with excitement. She prints
the page on to A4, and then photocopies the article into the centre
of a blank sheet. Her mother pays.

'What is it, Leila?'

'Nothing much. Just homework. For my little project.'

That night she lies awake and wonders why Vincent has not told
her how his mother died. Could it be that he is *ashamed*? He was
only two when it happened. In her mind he changes, he grows.

She conjures his curling hair as if for the first time, and perceives the stringy strength of those long limbs. He has become a man for her now. He has a secret, a past, a burden – characteristics so often lacking in boys her age.

Every time she closes her eyes she feels like she is falling. She sees reality torn like a membrane by her flailing hands, a gloopy blur of bricks passing her eyes. She stirs. What if he doesn't know?

As the seasons torque the quarry and garden, so their bodies are changed by the elements within them. Even in these few months Leila has filled out through the hips and her shoulders have rounded. The sun has enriched her brown skin but lightened her hair a shade. Vincent is broader and leaner, stretched beyond her in height. He has grown his dark-blond hair to cover his spots, and weighty curls frame his face.

After school on Monday she cannot think of anything to say. They lie outside the tent and listen to the sound of the place: the crows and wasps, the sandstone diggers on the other side of the quarry. Her heart beats to the dissonant rhythm of the bell-ringing practice at the village church. 'Have you remembered anything else about Blackmoor yet? You know, since we started the project.'

'Nope.'

'What about stuff to do with your mum?'

Vincent looks at her quizzically. 'Are you a psychologist or whatever, now?'

Her cheeks flush. 'No. Just wondered.'

Vincent sees that she is upset. 'Sorry.' He thinks for a moment. 'Sometimes I kind of know what it might be like if she was in the next room.' He offers this information like a guess at the answer to a factual question. Leila keeps quiet for a while, looking up at Wood Edge.

'It's big, isn't it, my house?' she says.

'Your arse?'

'No. The house. My house.'

Vincent shakes his head and smiles. 'Yep. 'S bigger than mine. Congratulations.'

'Do you reckon you'd die if you fell off the roof?'

Vincent looks blank. 'Listen, if you're bored we could go down the village, get some ice creams or something.'

He does not know.

He doesn't know, and in a way that's worse, because she has to tell him, doesn't she? Usually, in a situation like this, Leila would savour the revelation as an opportunity to observe human behaviour. This is clinical Leila Downing, a scientist, a girl who chooses her acquaintances on the basis of academic merit. But on this occasion she is taking things seriously. For perhaps the first time in her life, she is faced with a moral dilemma.

Wednesday is her allocated evening with her father. They spend it typically: he gets very drunk, makes omelettes, tells her that her feet smell and washes them in the bidet (she really loves this, although she knows she is getting too old). At the end of the night, he tells stories she has heard many times, about his great friends whom he no longer sees. He makes modifications to incriminate her mother where once he lauded her. When his repertoire is exhausted, she asks his advice.

'Dad, is it wrong, when you know something really important, not to tell someone?'

Mr Downing's sense of moral outrage is at its peak at 11 p.m., and he tells her it most certainly is wrong. He uses the family swimming pool as an example, how her mother drained it without his permission. 'Imagine if you didn't tell someone there was no water in it, and they were about to dive in. And you didn't tell them. Well, they'd be killed. Bosh. Like that. Bosh.'

'Is it worse than a straight lie?'

'Well, you can't get much worse than cracking your head open on the bottom of a pool. Can you? If you want to know about lies, ask your mother.'

'How's your father?' her mother always asks sternly on Thursday evenings. On old TV programmes, 'How's your father' means sex, and Leila finds it amusing that her mother should say something that means 'sex' in such a brusque manner.

'He's fine. He was asking after you.'

'I'll bet.'

Leila thinks of Vincent again, feels that sensation of falling. Is it better not to know? She thinks of her own parents, failing to tell her about their separation. Withholding information can be as hurtful as a lie. She puts this to her mother, who sighs. 'We just wanted you to feel normal I suppose.'

'Mum. We live in a castle. Lots of kids at school have divorced parents. None of them live in a castle.'

A desire for normality, she realizes, is no excuse. She has to tell him.

Meanwhile, Vincent is falling in love. Leila has avoided him for two days and this has hastened an inevitable process. He misses her. He goes back over their recent conversations, looking for a fault. Was she stern when they last spoke? No. If anything she was less aggressive than usual. Perhaps she is letting him down gently.

Yesterday night he climbed up through JEM woods to see that the tent was still an unlit dull cherry red.

At home, Vincent surrounds himself with Leila substitutes. He has scraps of paper with her handwriting on, and he buys the brand of lip balm she uses. His most valued substitute is the tape recording of the Wagstaff interview. The part when she whispers, 'Foul language' has almost warped from rewinding. That is her little message to him, proof that she considered him in his absence.

The tape is old, and after the interview with Wagstaff, Vincent finds some recordings Leila made as a little girl. At one point, she creeps to The Stables, pretending to be on a mission to extort money from 'evil baron Mr D'. She whispers a commentary on to the tape as she climbs the stairs, and then asks her father for seventy-five pence. Vincent listens to her tiny feet crunch back across the hard-core drive. She shouts, 'Go, go, go. They're on our tail!' He regrets that he did not know her then. He thinks they would have been great friends.

After this 'mission', the young Leila obviously ran out of ideas, so she just left the tape recording while she did some colouring-in and sang 'The Anchor Song' by Björk in a slightly Welsh accent. Vincent leaves the tape playing as he changes out of his school uniform. He feels paternal towards the child, and the nylon scratch of her felt-tip pen is reassuring. When the tape ends he turns it over and plays the interview again.

*

Through the wall, in the living room, George wakes to a distant female voice. For a moment he thinks of her, sees the purple blotch of her cine-film shape on his eyelid again. The voice comes from his and Vincent's room. The radio, probably. George has been asleep on the big leather sofa, reclining in the position of someone who has been hit by a truck. He often naps in the early evening now, to compensate for the sleep he loses to Vincent's singing.

He looks down at his thighs and sees that he has lost more weight. He considers this a good thing, for had his body not touched Beth, just like the furniture? Not as much, perhaps.

It is mid-June now. On Saturday, the annual event known as 'Concert in the Park' will be held on the banks of the Derwent. It is a mini-proms with an orchestra and fireworks. The Tories and the pikeys unite for that one evening under the flag of St George, with their smoked salmon or their sausage rolls. George hates it. Last year he listened to 8,000 people sing 'Land of Hope and Glory' while he watched a drunk, pregnant fourteen-year-old pissing in the reeds. Depressing. The glut of red-cross flags brought back memories too, of his meeting with Daniel Frost. But it gives him a bonding idea – they don't come often, and he feels more and more compelled to act upon them.

A couple of hours later Vincent hears his father call from the dark garden. When he looks out of the window, he sees George lying belly-down on the bottom plateau of grass, his face pressed into the ground. For a moment, Vincent thinks his father has suffered a heart attack, but then he sees the flaming splint in the out-stretched hand. When the firework is lit, George stands and walks away. The banger hisses back towards the house and explodes not far from the roof, causing Vincent to duck and the sloping garden to turn silver. A second of false daylight. Milky cobwebs of smoke descend on George, who beckons Vincent. Vincent sighs, turns off the Dictaphone and goes outside.

George waves a large rocket called 'Megaton' in Vincent's face. 'Saving this one for last. It cost fifteen quid.' Vincent is surprised by his father's enthusiasm, exhibited by the rather dramatic prostrate position he assumes to light the fireworks, and the way his mouth falls involuntarily open when he looks up at the scattering light. Then Vincent remembers reading that incendiaries were banned in Blackmoor after the first evacuation. No bonfires. Vincent feels smug that he knows this, that he can work back to the motives of his father's present behaviour. Everything he knows, he knows because of Leila.

After a few more bangers Vincent tires of the strain on his neck, and looks over the village. Through the dark woodland, he can make out the haze of the floodlights that point up at the castle. He remembers Leila chipping away at the stone of one of the turrets with a steel ruler, removing the greeny-grey coating of 150 years of weather to reveal bright yellow brick beneath. 'There's a big clean castle hiding under here. I'm not sure I want to see it yet, but it's nice to know it's there,' she had said. He wonders if she can hear the fireworks now, in the tent. Maybe she feels guilty about neglecting him. Perhaps she misses him. Maybe not.

'Dad, I've got a bit of a problem,' he says. (Who else can he talk to?)

'Woman, is it?' George says, laughing.

'Yes, actually.'

'What? You're bloody twelve.'

'I'm thirteen.'

George angrily picks up a small firework and storms over to where the other wasted shells lie strewn. He kneels on the grass, about to light the banger in the same aggressive way, but his shoulders drop and he puts a hand to his forehead. 'What's the trouble?' he says.

'I just need to let her know – you know – what I think of her.'

George shakes his head. 'Women only rub their eyes in the morning because they've got no balls to scratch.'

'What?'

'Something your granddad used to say.'

'Right. What does it mean?'

'Buggered if I know. He was a bit of an idiot to be honest. Have you tried talking to her, this girl?'

'We talk all the time, but only about other stuff.'

'What other stuff?'

'You know. Badgers and birds and stuff.'

'Yes, well, I was never one for the chat either. Your mother always.' He stops, thinks about the shoeboxes filled with journals. 'You're good at writing though, aren't you? I've still got that poem you wrote about setting fire to the church.'

'Have you? Dad, I was seven.'

'I'm not saying you should send her *that*. Write her a letter or something. Explain yourself.'

Vincent looks puzzled. It is a good idea. They stand in unbalanced silence for a moment. 'Right. Megaton,' says George.

The rocket is red and black, and has its own super-long wick, but George still lights it lying down. Vincent checks the sky for owls and birds. He imagines Piano, rocket-speared through the neck, falling to the ground and exploding before his eyes.

They watch the sparkle crawl along the wick, and the rocket tremble with power. It wobbles into the night with barely a whistle. George and Vincent stare at the sky. After a few moments Vincent forgets what he is looking for. No bang, no lights, nothing. He stumbles.

'Where the bloody hell is it?' George asks.

Vincent begins to snigger.

'What you laughing at?'

'Well,' says Vincent.

George walks purposefully around the garden, searching the heavens. 'Fifteen fucking quid,' he says.

'You wouldn't want it to *explode* if you paid fifteen quid for it, would you? That's just a waste,' says Vincent.

George combs the grass for red or black debris. Then he looks up, points at the sky. 'There. Look. What was that? That was it, surely. I saw white.'

Vincent strolls over as the clouds part. 'That's the moon,' he says.

It takes him a long time to form the letters of her name.

Dear Leila,

You've been avoiding me lately, which is fine. Actually, it's not fine, it actually sucks, as you say (you do, sometimes).

I probably shouldn't say this, but my dad told me to write this letter, which is probably the best thing he's ever done. I feel better already (except I can already imagine you saying 'Point?').

Vincent writes the letter in the blue light of the fishless fish tank. He wonders sometimes why there aren't perfect circles of fish-flesh floating among the weeds. He looks at the model castle, leaning in the shingle, and he imagines what Wood Edge would be like underwater. His overactive imagination, he is alarmed to find, has no mercy on his favourites.

Well, the point is I've been listening to the tape you sent me and thinking about you a lot and I've decided I'm completely obsessed with you. (I think you probably just slapped yourself on the head. I heard it from here.) Along with a load of other things, I love the way you half come from an exotic country. When I said that thing about you looking weird I meant it in a good way. I think they should get everyone from Egypt and everyone from England and get them together for a mass orgy. (You probably think that's sick and perverted.)

You might think this is freakish, but once I watched you in the quarry from behind those pine trees when you didn't know I was there. You were pulling weeds out of the cracks in the rock and I felt so peaceful just watching you I could have stayed there for all eternity. I wasn't perving.

It's weird because I really like talking to you but sometimes I'd just like to look at you for ages without you knowing. When you cleaned my face with those pads, things happened to me. I can't write them here because Dad said don't ever sign your name on a letter that you wouldn't be happy with everyone in the world reading it. I'll tell you another time, but I think it's good.

You are the one person I think about when they're not around. It's been killing me this last few days not seeing you.

There are a few lines in his rough draft that he is not so sure about. He thinks *'I don't know where my own arms are half the time but I could find you in a four-acre wood in the dark'* might be a bit cheesy. Leila has a low cheese tolerance. He leaves it out.

This is not a token gesture. I've got a real actual feeling in my stomach like indigestion and it only goes down when you're there. Can you remember when you first showed me Piano? If you fancy someone else, please just say and I'll honourably leave you alone.

Regards,

Vincent G. Cartwright (I'm not ashamed to sign this, despite what you might think of it.)

PS: I want to kiss you.

Vincent scribbles out the postscript but leaves enough of it showing so that she can still read it.

TWENTY

Beth took Vincent down the hawthorn alley and on to the loop track, sunk almost beyond visibility now. She wore a red kagoul, and pulled the hood up, despite the dry conditions, perhaps to hide the stark white straggles of her hair. Vincent was walking now, and he toddled about, tugging his reins taut. They lingered by the old signal box where Beth had once stopped with Michael Jenkins, and she talked for some time about her childhood. Vincent failed to comprehend most of this, but he seemed to enjoy the story about when the train was delayed because of wallabies on the track at Wirksworth. They had escaped from a local animal enclosure and bred in the woods. Beth tried to explain the incongruity of the creatures to her son. 'Oh aye. They're like kangaroos. It was a regular thing at one time, wallabies on the track. They must have been bloody freezing.'

She used her sharp sewing scissors to cut a few sweetbriars from the mesh of nettles and weeds. The dump by the loop track had grown. It stank in the warmth of late March and threatened to smell worse when the summer came. Beth fished out a faded cider bottle label from the bush and wrapped the sweetbriar stems in it.

Three teenage boys gathered down by the dump. With their damaged olfactory nerves, the solvent-abusers were the only ones who could stand the stench. They all looked the same, with red moustaches and watery eyes. From that distance, Beth could only make out their postures. One sat hugging his knees, another lay on his back, and the third stood, struggling to get out of his red football shirt. After removing the shirt, this last boy walked over to piss in the long grass of the bank. She would have to walk another fifty yards towards them to reach the entrance to the field behind Slack Lane, but she was not scared. Beth was accustomed to her own power to disturb. She walked on.

'Eh up, it's Red Riding Hood,' said the urinating youth, amused by her unseasonable dress.

'You've got me wrong, kid,' said Beth. 'I'm the wolf.'

The other boys had taken hold of the football shirt, a Nottingham Forest replica, and set fire to it. The third boy now noticed this and ran back towards them, trying to fasten his jeans at the same time. 'You twats. That were twenty quid.'

One of the arsonists held up the burning shirt, laughing wildly. The flames quickly consumed the nylon and rose towards his fingers. With a squeal he launched the shirt, which dropped on to a rucksack. As the shirtless boy attacked his friends, the flames passed on to the fabric of the bag, which contained several canisters of lighter gas and industrial fixative. It exploded once, and all turned to watch, including Beth and her boy, who gave a hiccup of shock. Then it exploded twice more, bigger bangs this time. Beth pulled Vincent into the long grass and shielded him with her kagoul. The world was red to him, moons of sunlight and fire floating beyond the fabric, the apple scent of briars.

The rucksack popped again and hurtled through the air in a flaming ball. It rolled up against the base of the rubbish tip. Several more bottles of lighter gas ignited in quick succession and the rucksack spun with each bang. The two arsonists sprinted away from the blasts, towards the bank on the opposite side of the tracks, seeing God-knows-what in the haze of their hallucinations. The topless boy, however, stepped slowly away and then sat on the tracks, his eyes moving from Beth to the fire and back. Together, they watched the fire hatch from the bag and climb through the rubbish. The flames gnawed at newspaper and nappies, twisted the shape of food packaging and groped at a car seat. A crisp packet took flight, sucked into the fiery haze. It was already too dangerous to approach the regular entrance, so Beth took Vincent in her arms and scrambled over the bank into the field behind Slack Lane, leaving the topless boy to his spectacle, and the sweetbriars in the grass.

When she arrived at the back gate George had arranged the frame and wheels of a child's bicycle on the lawn. He stood above the disparate parts. 'Bought the frame off Steve Grimshaw,' he said. 'He's already selling his stuff. He says to me, "It's like a shit, youth: get rid on it early and you won't be carrying it around all day." Bloody imbecile.'

Beth struggled to regain her breath. 'George, have you seen?' she said, lowering Vincent on to the turf, and pointing towards the smoke on the other side of the field.

George raised his eyes. 'Oh aye. Same as you say, woman: somebody's always burning.'

He went back to his toolbox. Beth began to lose her temper. It was his weary sneer, his lack of concern. The place was *on fire*. She remained silent for a few moments. 'The kid can't hug a bike, George.'

George did not even look up. 'And a hug won't get him anywhere. The lad's got any sense he'll ride a million miles from here the minute he can reach the pedals.'

Beth did not even bother with the well-worn retort. She had given up.

Within an hour, the flames reached the top of the rubbish pile. From this position they flirted with the exposed outcrop of the coal seam, that gorgeous glinting swathe. Coal smoke, its thick yellow-grey once so comforting, now caused panic among the villagers. The fire service could not prevent the ignition of the seam, and there was nothing anyone could do then. The energy had transferred, and was burrowing underground along the stripe of coal, where it could not be reached. The fire would burn, above and below the surface, for two months in a village where people were scared to even smoke a cigarette.

They believed that their luck had turned bad. Sarah Browne called it 'The Countdown'. Talking to Tom Betts outside the Post Office, she looked across at the plume of black. 'It's just a question a which comes first: my new house or big bang.'

'Aye,' said Tom. 'No good building a swanky new village if all that's moving in is burnt corpses.'

That night, Beth saw the moonlight expose distinct jaundiced bodies of smoke, which crept across the village. She saw a fleck of flame spat from her own garden evaporate in the dark. And she saw the Jacksons down the road, loading their car with possessions, unable to bear the threat. They would not be the last family to leave early.

Floodlight bled into every home as the fire service tried to keep the superficial blaze under control. And when the fire-fighters retired for the night, it was the erratic pulse of firelight that entered the bedrooms of the residents. It threw shadows on their beds. The words of Jim Balshaw, once considered glorious, now haunted them. *'The current, potentially unsafe village . . . a situation of anxiety and danger . . . The sooner you and your families are away from the threat, the better.'*

After their lucky streak, the residents saw the loop track as a sparkling fuse, a bright reminder of the real reason they had to move: the gases.

A week later, a private company called JJR Mining bought the majority share in British Coal, and took over the Blackmoor relocation project. A new map appeared in the Miners' Welfare Club, with no community centre, no woodland area and no sports ground. No names stood above the houses, and the moving date was set back six months. A long time to wait with a threat hanging over.

At 3 a.m. one April morning, a bulldozer knocked down Blackmoor Parish Church. Parishioners had noted a fine dust falling on their shoulders as they prayed, and that the bell tower had a slight lean. The church decided it was better to set up a Portakabin on the Rec rather than have the place fall down around their ears. On seeing the blackened shrubs and rubble in the smoking churchyard, many regular churchgoers in Blackmoor felt that damnation was upon them. Those who could moved in with family elsewhere.

Throughout April and May, Blackmoor became an ugly place to wait. Tom Betts was regularly turned away with his lawnmower. 'What's point?' the women said from their kitchen windows. There was more fear than smugness in that phrase now.

In the land of stepscrubbers and houseprouds, the neglected grass wound around the unsold items from the garden sales. People just left the junk outside. If someone wanted a stained pisspot or a typewriter with no 'e', then they could take it. What did it matter? When the demolition men moved in, it would all go the same way as the walls and drainpipes and old sash windows. Doors rotted, gates dropped, damp climbed up sheds like a sleeping lover. The job-lot pebble-dash facades on Pit Lane, long past their guarantee, crumbled to reveal old bricks beneath. Everyone had been caught in the excitement of the move. Now they were all packed up with nowhere to go.

George worked on the bike when he was drunk. He could have easily afforded a brand new junior bicycle, but this was a sentimental act. The alcohol brought no clarity, but rather a state of confusion necessary to see the unlikely mess of feelings he had for his small family. It was a miracle to him that he could love his son so much when the boy had brought such misfortune on the house, made his wife untouchable. As he worked in the shed he remembered Beth's nocturnal obsessions during her illness, remembered finding her in the front room at 4 a.m., cleaning silver. The pink streaks of polish, the strong wiry shoulders and delicate waist of her pale back. 'You only need a little bit a polish,' she had said, 'to make it shine. Like Gran used to say, "On like thunder, off like lightning."'

As George oiled the joints of the frame he thought of these words. He did not know what to do with Beth, or the boy. The bicycle was something saved – love put aside for a later date. With a bicycle he could show his son that there was reason in the world. You press the pedals and the cog winds the chain which turns the wheel. The eternal, simple routes that power takes.

Beth could hardly rest in the bath. The water felt like a gritty silt against her skin, but she opened her eyes to find it steaming and clean. Sweat found its way into her mouth. The increasing disrepair of the village disturbed Beth more than most. A gaping tilted fridge, abandoned on the mini-roundabout, haunted her thoughts like a ghoul. Even as she lay back against the cold porcelain, she could hear another roof tile slide towards the gutter. The tiles moved in minute increments and Beth heard every one. It sounded to her like a patient thief was very slowly breaking into the house from above.

She hoped that George had stopped working on that bloody push-bike. It was too cold for Vincent to be standing out in the shed. There were too many tools lying around.

As she stood slowly into the bathroom mist, she felt the blood drop through her limbs in a mass. Through the two windows the night turned navy blue. Two blue eyes and a tap spout for a nose. A noise interrupted this thought: a rhythmic creaking from the bedroom. Beth had often dreamed that George took a lover. A short woman with dark skin. The bedsprings (*definitely* bedsprings) continued to creak, and Beth left the bathroom, walked towards the noise in a state of weird excitement. Outside on the landing, the air cooled the water on her skin and pimples rose. By the time she reached the room, an enormous anger had taken hold of her. How could he – with someone else – when he had not touched her for so long? She flung the door open to find Vincent bouncing on the bed. His face had turned pink and his eyes rolled up in his head from exhaustion or delight. He flapped his arms against his thighs with each leap. Beth sighed at her own stupidity, and scooped Vincent up with one arm. It shocked him for he had not heard her approach. She felt his legs kick out for the mattress. 'You're a little rascal, aren't you?'

'I bounce,' he said.

'No. You mustn't. If you go too high you'll fly right out of the house.'

Beth thought of the roof tiles parting to let him through.

'I bounce,' said Vincent.

TWENTY-ONE

'I'm not ayin' any a that fuggin' wog-snap, youth,' said Bob in perfect mimicry of their father. 'Do us a chip cob.'

Only George had bought a kebab at the end of their night 'on the tiles'. Bob complained because he could not get falafel. They flagged down a taxi. George placed his meal on his left thigh and picked at the aromatic meat and onions. 'Your dinner looks like a leg wound, George,' said Bob.

'Aye,' said George, drunk and suddenly beyond hunger.

'You getting any action then? Got yourself a woman?'

'Stop trying to solve my fucking life, Bob, it's making me jumpy.' For several minutes George looked out of the window at the teary grease-streaks of passing lights. 'I've blamed him, you know,' he said.

Bob was confused, a little drunk himself. 'Who?'

'Vincent.'

Silence for a moment. 'Fucking hell. You told him that to his face? Please tell me you didn't.'

'Course not. I told him she got ill, that he wasn't involved. But I've treated him in a way that . . . I've treated him as if it were his fault. I convinced myself it *was*. If he hadn't a been born, she wouldn't a got ill. If he hadn't a fallen, she wouldn't a jumped. But what about me? What did I do?'

'You're not guilty,' said Bob. 'No one is. It were an accident.'

'Not quite, pal. Not quite. You know I drove her to it.'

'Now don't talk shite, George. Every fucker blames themsen when something like that happens. Anyway, Beth were always a bit . . . you know.'

'I didn't touch her for two years.'

'Well, I can't remember the last time me and Susan . . . it doesn't mean oat. She was probably grateful. You're an ugly bastard after all.'

'It must a been like a prison. I didn't love her properly, Bob.'

'People don't die of that.'

'Don't they? There were other things and all.'

'George, you're pissed.'

'Something happened the day before. In the kitchen. We were with this guy from work. Fucking blue shirt on. She looked at me and something happened. Sommat snapped in her brain. I saw it happen in me own kitchen, Bob. I saw it happen on her face. It were me.'

George cannot bring himself to say the name of the man in the blue shirt. He cannot bring himself to say Frost.

Twenty-two

Blackmoor, 17 June 1992.

A black Honda pulled into the EM Water Centre car park. Behind the green-tinted windscreen sat a man in a perfectly ironed pale blue shirt. Baby blue, you could call it. He pushed a strand of his damp black hair behind his ear and folded his sunglasses. He shivered in the air conditioning. The engine hummed through his fingers as he folded a pile of handouts into his leather case. He took out the keys, closed the door and walked across the car park in solid, athletic strides. As he stepped into the main corridor his figure darkened and the shadows of the structure enveloped him. The heels of his shoes clicked as he walked.

By 4.30 p.m., that man, Daniel Frost, lay on the floor of the EM Water conference room, his arms contorted at strange angles, his legs wide open. George Cartwright stood above him, swearing under his breath.

The two men were performing an exercise as part of Frost's

training course, 'Inducting and Instructing'. There had been an odd number in the group, so George had had to pair with the lecturer. George's task was to tell the prostrate Frost how to rise to his feet, without recourse to general phrases. It supposedly taught the site managers about clear instruction and the dangers of 'assumed knowledge'. After five minutes of following George's commands, however, Frost now looked as though he had crashed through the ceiling and died on the carpet. The other site managers also attempted the exercise, with varying degrees of success.

'Right. Time up,' said Frost in his southern accent. He stood, and George looked surprised, as if he had become convinced that Frost really couldn't co-ordinate himself.

'Mike, I'm sure I heard you tell Alan there to "get on his knees,"' said Frost.

The group of managers laughed, apart from Mike Sadler, a Nottingham site boss. Wit came easy to Frost. He knew his routine, knew how to get people to like him. He was in control. '"Get on your knees" is a vague phrase, non-specific. You're assuming that Alan knows what it means. Now maybe that's because you've met his missus, but it's no excuse. Just because *you* understand something, it doesn't necessarily follow that everyone else does.

'I've had plenty of time to think about this exercise, so I know what I'm doing. George, on your back.'

Frost gestured to the ground, and George lay down. 'Right, George. I want you to think about the heel of your right shoe. Now bring that heel up towards your arse, so your knee is bent, and points to the ceiling.'

George did so.

'Good. Now do the same with the other one.'

When George's knees were up, Frost sat on a chair in front and kept eye contact through George's legs. The comic element of this process was not lost on the other managers, especially Mike Sadler, who was keen to reverse his own humiliation. But George seemed not to hear the sniggering and whispered wisecracks. He responded carefully and promptly to Frost's voice.

'Now, turn your palms over so they're on the carpet. Keeping your left elbow on the ground, push it in the direction of your colleagues until it is bent to a right angle. Spot on.'

One arm, and then the other, slid across the carpet. In a series of smooth, symmetrical movements, George rose to his feet. It felt like the first really physical thing he had done for a year. He enjoyed the lack of responsibility in those few minutes of submission, and for a moment he just stood, dumb, facing Frost, awaiting further instructions. Mike Sadler broke the silence with a poor imitation of a cockney accent. 'Right, George. Go down the shops and get me twenty Benson.'

Laughter all around. Frost smiled, cracked the trance. George went back to his seat. 'Ladies and gentlemen, Debbie McGee,' said Mike Sadler.

'Fuck off, Mike, you fucking red scab,' said George. More laughter, and eventually George joined in. He looked like he had woken from a good, long sleep. At that point, there seemed no reason not to laugh.

After the session Frost asked George where the nearest pub was.

'The Goose. Left out the exit, left again.'

'I wouldn't mind some company. You got anything to get home for?'

'I could murder a pint, youth.'

And what did George have to be home for? In his garden, in Blackmoor, his wife kneeled at the fence above a tin of creosote. Her brush dripped on to a leaf. She carefully watched the paint find the veins. She had rolled her sleeves halfway up her forearms and the white shirt was already covered with drops of the dull orange shade described by the manufacturers as 'Cedar'. Earlier she had wiped the sweat from her face, and a dash of creosote had caught the top of her jawbone and dried on a strand of her white hair, which she now kept modestly short.

Beth had managed to paint only ten panels in the four hours she had been working. She had placed three open tins around the garden (the panels she painted were not necessarily adjacent). The wood seemed to drink the paint.

Her son sat cross-legged on the grass behind her, holding a piece of string. His mother had attached the string to a plant cane that propped up one side of a cardboard box filled with viewing holes. A trail of bread led to the entrance. A bird trap. Vincent, like his mother, sat completely still and silent. The only time he had moved all afternoon was to choke a fit of sneezes. As for birds, a sparrow had landed behind him at around three o'clock. Since then, nothing.

Beth shuffled around on the grass. 'Shall we go to the shops?' she said. 'Get some lollies?'

'Lollies,' Vincent whispered. They left the garden. Daddy

would be home soon, for his customary hour before going to the pub, and he would want his tea.

George would have called the Goose a 'yuppie pub', but it was really just a Harvester. He drank three pints of Pedigree, while Frost supped a Guinness. 'So. I bet you're away a lot, aren't you? With the job,' George said.

'Yeah. You have to travel. Most people pity you for it.'

'I don't. It must be nice to move around. Free hotels, free meals. Girl in every port.'

'Yeah. Something like that.'

George hardly ever drank outside Blackmoor, and he enjoyed it. He felt like a man on a foreign holiday, soothed by the green light coming through the coloured glass. Although he avoided the subject of his home life, the change of venue loosened his tongue. He talked at length about Frost's 'standing-up' exercise.

'I'm not being queer or anything, but it was really relaxing. I felt like I'd had an hour's kip.'

'I suppose it's a bit like yoga in that way. It can be very calming to just concentrate on something simple and do it right.'

'That's it. That's exactly it. Don't tell anybody this, but I can hardly walk properly these days.'

Frost's chin dimpled and began to shake. He had taken off his tie and opened his shirt. George could see his collarbones, where they almost met in the middle. 'What do you mean you can't walk?'

'Straight up. I trip over the pavement four times a fucking day. It's preoccupation I suppose.'

Preoccupation. The word was almost a transgression. He could not have said such things in the Blackmoor Miners' Welfare Club. Frost began to laugh. 'Surely, George, I don't have to follow you everywhere, telling you how to walk.'

'No.'

A grey-haired man in overalls entered the bar. George looked alarmed for a moment, and then, when the man turned around, he relaxed.

'Are you okay, mate?' said Frost, still smiling.

'Fine,' George said. 'Just thinking about home.'

'Oh. Did you want to go back?' Frost said, standing.

'No,' said George. He sounded desperate, but Frost did not hear. George followed him to the bar.

As Frost paid the tab (on expenses) George asked for a double whisky. 'One for the road, eh George?' said the barman.

George looked confused. He didn't know the barman, and had visited the Goose maybe three times. The rules of reality began to slip from his grasp. 'How did he know my name?' George whispered to Frost. Frost placed his thumb on George's chest pocket and peeled away the name sticker, still there from the training session. He did it so fast that George didn't even flinch. Frost folded the sticker so that it read 'orge' and returned it to the owner. 'There you go, mate. In case you forget who you are.'

Back at the EM Water Centre car park, George mumbled his goodbyes and walked towards his car. 'Where do you think you're going?' Frost said.

''Ome,' said George.

'You can't *drive*. You're arseholed, mate. You'll be dead before you get out the gates.'

'Be right,' said George. 'Done it before.'

'Look. As your corporate training guru, I cannot allow you to set such a poor example to impressionable members of the team.'

George frowned, and then jumped as Frost activated the central locking on the Honda behind him. 'Get in.'

George did as he was told. On the car stereo, a foreign woman sang about her home – a noiseless watery place, and as they cut through the scorched fields on the outskirts of Blackmoor, George had a sudden urge to drown.

As they approached the village Frost hit the brakes. George shot forward, and wondered for a moment if some sort of force field had been erected around Blackmoor. 'Bloody hell,' said Frost. The dry tarmac in front of the car was divided by three black gashes, each of them emitting a slow sheet of opaque smoke. The largest rent was ten yards long and frayed with lumps of dislodged stone.

'They weren't there this morning,' said George. 'You'll have to drive around them.'

Frost did so with care.

The scarab car raced into the village, and lodged in the recesses of George's mind. He could see the dark blot of smoke rising from the loop track and hoped Frost had not noticed. George wondered for a moment if this might be the day when the village finally relented, was swallowed by the fire. As they passed the boarded-up shops, and the shaggy grasses by the roadside, the scattered hubcaps and gutted VCRs, George glanced at Frost. He felt embarrassed about the state of the place, but he wanted Frost to see it, wanted him to understand.

When they arrived at his house, George had a sudden insight into how the evening would unfold without Frost. His drunkenness would soon wear off and become misery. He would be unable to face the Red Lion after talking to this man. Cartwright the closet townie. It had always been this way. 'I'll leave you to it then, mate,' Frost said, offering his hand.

George did not take it. He looked out of the window, pretended not to recognize the place, tried to imagine what it would be like to be *just passing through*. A St George flag hung from a neighbour's window. The football, of course. Suddenly the things George secretly hated became his best friends. 'Hey, are you watching the match? England, Sweden. You can't watch it in a fucking hotel, it's not same. It's not the same.'

'I don't really—'

'Tell you what, our Beth'll do us some chips or something, then we'll go down the Miners' Welfare. They've got a telly in there.'

Frost hesitated. 'Okay,' he said.

'Great.'

George could not open the door. Frost attempted to guide him through the process, in much the same way as he had in the training session. 'You have to pull the lever. No. The one next to your left index finger. Pull. No.'

George gave up. 'This is what it's like all the time now. I can't do the simplest things. I feel like I'm going backwards.'

Frost got out of the car. 'Here. Just get out my side.'

George crawled across the seats like a child. His trousers rode up above his calf. His ambition, he realized, had become to avoid humiliation. It was a pointless endeavour in the company of his fellow Blackmoorians (they had seen him ridiculed on so many occasions) and now it seemed that he had failed in front of his new acquaintance. Within half an hour. He looked flushed and angry as he straightened up on the road. But then he smiled. He saw the unique potential of this evening. This could be his turn to laugh.

He tried to appear natural entering the house through the front door, although he had not done so since they'd had the kitchen fitted six years ago. Once in the house, George noticed the angles of the early evening light in the hall, the way they expanded after spilling through the gaps in the front-room door. He could see the dust. No matter how hard she scrubbed, Beth could never get rid of it. How many times had he told her, 'In a house, cleaning is just moving dust around'? The submerged green colour of the carpet at this time of day reminded him of what light looks like under clear water.

'Nice pad,' said Frost.

'Let's put kettle on,' said George.

The kitchen was frighteningly clean, with its sinister stacks of glasses, the regimented handles of pots and the stench of bleach. The one sign of habitation lay on the table: a large sheet of paper with the word 'Co-op' daubed in creosote. George held the paper and nodded, as though it were an official document. Then he turned it over and placed it face down on the table. He looked at Frost. What a novelty to see a man like him in such proximity to the old green glasses and the mug tree and the spice rack that had been there for a million years. Frost did not know the history of the objects in front of him, and in a way, they almost shed that history in his presence.

'Somebody keeps this place properly clean,' said Frost.

'Let's go in the garden. I'll show you my little project.'

George's heart rate increased. He had only mentioned the 'project' – his son's bicycle – to avoid talking about the obsessive cleanliness of his wife, but now he felt bashful. 'It's not finished or oat. Or anything,' he said as he opened the back door.

From the garden the cloud of smoke from the loop track could not be avoided, and neither could the stench of coal and rubbish, the heat in the air. The menace of it. George saw Frost squint, but thankfully he did not ask any questions.

There was, however, no escaping Beth's original touches in the garden. At least her neurotic hygiene in the house had (to the untrained eye) removed her trace. Out there, a branch stuck up from one of the half-empty paint tins, and the fence panels were randomly painted to give the appearance of a smashed piano. George's expression did not show alarm or fear or concern or sadness. The lips pursed, the tufty eyebrows dipped, and the eyes searched for something inoffensive to settle on. He looked ashamed.

Frost bent down to study Vincent's bird trap. He frowned. 'George, this grass is . . . *warm*.'

'No it isn't,' said George. He looked at his son's box and string, welcomed the opportunity to talk about something else. 'That's my lad,' he said.

'He's going to be a huntsman?'

'A poacher, probably. Look. I've been building him a bike for when he's older. I could have bought him one, a course, but, you know.'

George took the bicycle from the shed. Apart from some minor cosmetic work, it now lacked only brakes. George held it up for

Frost, who nodded, his chin dimpling. 'It's dead light,' George said.

'You built it yourself?'

'Aye. It's not finished though, same as a say.'

George peeled one of the original decorative stickers from the crossbar and let it coil on the grass. He sat down on the seat and both men sniggered at the creak of the frame as it took George's weight. He pushed himself forward and put his feet on the pedals so that his knees came up to his chest. As the bike weaved, George shouted 'yee-ha', and a crow barked, departing from the tree in the field over the fence.

Frost laughed, showing for the first time a discoloured molar. 'It's true what they say, isn't it, George? You never, ever forget.'

'Bang on. No instructions needed for this one, boss.'

George looked over Frost's shoulder, and saw Beth in the kitchen window. He saw her frown, saw the splashes of orangey paint on her white shirt, and thought for a moment that they were lacerations. He still remembered her scrubbing a chopping board until her fingers bled. George reached for brakes he had only imagined, and had to put his feet down to stop the bike from freewheeling into the fence.

And what did Beth see from the oblique angle of her tilted stare, through those washed-out quivering eyes? An idiot on a child's bike? A circus clown? Initially, she felt wary, for Beth was a woman ever alert to the toe-tip creep of daytime hallucinations. When she had established the reality of the vision, Beth felt sad for her husband – sad for the way his face had changed when he saw her at the window. He had been 'showing off', she realized. His mother had chastised him for that so many times when they were young. It was also dizzying to see a new human form in the garden. The Cartwrights simply did not have visitors since she had rebuffed Michael Jenkins. And for Beth, the famous Blackmoor community spirit had vanished sometime around 1985.

The man in the garden followed George's guilty gaze back to the kitchen window and squinted with an uncertain smile. His long shadow ate into the last patch of light on the lawn.

In the kitchen, George tried to sober up with some strong tea. He let the heat condense on his face. As soon as they vacated the garden, Vincent toddled out to keep watch over his trap.

'Has he been out there all day?' George asked.

'About five hours. He keeps telling the birds he'll let them go. "I tromise," he says to em.'

Frost laughed. George and Beth turned towards him, curious. 'Seems like a great kid,' said Frost. He did not stare at Beth's eyes, even though they shook rapidly.

'Have you not got any yourself, Mr Frost?' said Beth.

'No. I'm not really into kids,' said Frost.

'Bloody good job and all. We don't like pervs around here,' said George.

'Jesus, George,' said Beth. She turned back to Frost. 'George doesn't want any more children.'

'Beth. Daniel doesn't want to hear the bloody life story.'

'*You* don't want to hear it,' said Beth.

She put her hands together and pushed them between her thighs as she leaned towards Frost. You could hear the whip of her skin across the denim. 'People say that the problem with this place is that there isn't any privacy, Mr Frost, but that's just not true. It goes the other way. Most folk here are more blind than me, and deaf an' all with it. Did you know that Blackmoor is basically a disaster zone? It could explode at any minute.'

'Sorry?' said Frost.

George cut in. 'It's all right, Daniel. It may be some months before we're consumed by hellfire.'

'Hellfire is right,' said Beth.

She seemed poised to continue but became distracted by a small stain on the table. She frowned and muttered an apology. George decided to attempt an explanation. 'You see, the thing about people here is, they let everything wind them up. That Tom Betts. You only have to look at him and he flies off at handle. That's what keeps them here. Petty concerns.'

'What about you?' asked Beth. She meant, of course, *what keeps you here?*

'Me? I don't get wound up. Whatever it is that snaps in them, doesn't snap in me.' He looked at Frost with satisfaction.

'You just let it all go?' said Beth. 'Let it all wash over you?'

'I just let it go. Nothing's worth losing your rag over.'

'Nothing.'

Beth stole a sideways glance at Frost. After a few moments of silence, the visitor stood and walked towards the sink to rinse his mug.

'I'll do that,' said George. He tried to intercept Frost and they collided. George might have fallen, but Frost caught him by the arm. The two men stared at each other. George felt the hand on his elbow.

Beth had witnessed the little accident, and it intrigued her, that much became clear as George freed himself and looked at his wife. She smirked and gazed at the floor.

'What now?' said George. He had not meant to say 'now'. He tried to cover his mistake with a smile but Beth was not looking. The two men anxiously regarded her, expecting another strange outburst. 'Beth. Seriously. What's wrong?'

The wry smile remained. 'Nothing. It's just. That's the first time in fourteen years that George has offered to wash a cup.'

Frost laughed, and George exhaled with relief. Fourteen years. George did not try to read the tone of her comment. He was a little too drunk, a little too tired to care.

Frost and George moved into the front room and raided the liquor cabinet. George felt like a teenager before a night out, drinking at home to save money on the town. Most of the bottles had not been touched for a long time, and a sticky residue covered the threads. George took a few (regrettable) swigs of Malibu, and the taste reminded him of his wife's lips. He passed the bottle to Frost, who sniffed the liquid and then backed away. 'No thanks, mate. Not really my cuppa tea.'

George knew what they would think of Frost in the Miners' Welfare Club. He could hardly wait to see how offended they would be by his long hair and southern accent. He would nudge Frost and they would laugh together. The whole thing gave him a delicious sense of rebellion. He wanted Frost to help him mock his own life.

As Frost parked the Honda next to an abandoned pram, George marvelled at how sober his new friend seemed (in fact, Frost had drunk only four, well-spaced units of alcohol all day). 'Welcome to the Blackmoor Miners' Welfare Club. A Miners' Welfare with no miners in it,' George said, in a disdainful voice, giving no reason as to why he returned to the place so very often.

As they got to the entrance, George heard Wagstaff's rasping cough, and he hesitated, unsure. The smell of piss and disinfectant cubes came through the open toilet window. George liked Frost. He was an intelligent, peaceful man, who had been spontaneously friendly. They would tear him apart. George half-turned back towards the car, but Frost walked past him on the blind side and went into the lounge. As Frost disappeared through the door, George heard an animal din, and glass smashing. He rushed in, half-believing that Frost had been immediately attacked. He got there just in time to see a replay of David Platt's early goal on the TV. 'Cartwright, you cunt. You've missed first goal.'

The men from the Miners' Welfare Club were not usually so animated, but they soon sank back into their habitual misery. They all gradually became uncomfortable about having been so open in front of a stranger. 'Lads. This is Daniel Frost. A colleague from work. Daniel, the lads.'

'Hi, how's it going?' said Frost.

A low murmur of welcome, maybe one hello. Frost's chin dimpled. George looked at Wagstaff, in his overalls, stroking his trout-coloured stubble and staring at the TV with rigid intensity. George laughed to himself.

'Right, George, I'll get the drinks in. You guys okay for beers?' said Frost.

Another grumble of assent. Wagstaff shook his head. Anyone

could see that the mere presence of Frost had already begun to ruin his evening. Bitter old fool, thought George.

Gary Lineker appeared on screen. If England failed to win, this would be his last international game. He had forty-eight goals for his country, one short of Bobby Charlton's record.

The members had arranged their chairs in a semicircle around the TV, so George pulled a couple of high stools out behind them. Brian Chambers, son of the late Mick Chambers, manned the bar. He had closed the Red Lion in exchange for a cut of the Miners' Welfare Club profits. He used the football as an excuse not to look at Frost. George stiffened when he heard the order. 'Pint of bitter for George, and I'll have a Jack and Coke, please.'

A couple of the lads turned around to look at George as if *he'd* said the words.

'*Jack and Coke*?' said Brian.

'Yeah. Jack Daniels. Bourbon?'

'We haven't got no Coke.'

'You got lemonade?'

'Yes.'

'Jack Daniels and lemonade then, please.'

'Haven't got no Jack Daniels.'

'Yes you have. It's in the optic on the far left. Just over your shoulder there.'

George almost laughed, but the sober part of him realized that this could become a serious situation. He hoped that Frost would not ask for a slice of lemon. As Brian Chambers poured the pint, George turned to look at Frost's reflection in the bar mirror. The lecturer tucked an errant strand of hair behind his ear and smiled.

With Frost there, George saw the club with a new vision. He

could see the *need* behind this manly fiction. Wagstaff, reduced now to the professional position of Shower Gel Operative at one of the factories off the motorway, was so tense with fear and arthritis that he appeared to shake, and as Brian shovelled ice noisily into a glass, some of the younger lads looked as though they might cry. With dazzling clarity, George witnessed every mental stage of each man's strategy for coping with the stranger. They pulled together, communicated with a language of darting looks. Tom Betts even *shifted his chair closer* to Wagstaff's. Men who had been ready to kill each other over the uncut borders of a shared garden, or their daughter's prominence on the carnival float, suddenly stood united. The whole club solidified against the alien presence. The men literally slowed their movements, like atoms in a freezing liquid.

Martin Dahlin, Sweden's mixed race centre forward, shot wide from close range. "'Allo my darlin',' said Steve Grimshaw, running his hand over the orange bristles of his hair.

Wagstaff shook his head. 'How can he be fuckin' Swedish,' he said. 'He doesn't know whether he's black or white.'

As the match continued, George and Frost resumed their own conversation. Frost spoke about the body language course he taught. 'That's probably my favourite. I had a letter off a guy the other day, saying that he'd managed to bed six women in two months, and he thought it was all down to the course. It wasn't quite what I intended, but it's a pay-off, I suppose.'

'You teach people how to get women? Wasn't it a business course?' asked George.

'It *was* a business course. But these things help in all situations,' Frost said, becoming interested in his own train of thought. 'You can do a lot before you even open your mouth. Making eye contact is important of course, but just pointing your shoes at someone can make all the difference. Women have told me that the grooming thing really works too.'

'What, like brushing their hair?' George said. He saw Steve Grimshaw lean back in his seat, listening in.

'Well, I would advise them to use an actual brush *before* they went out, George, yes. But when a woman adjusts her hair with her hands, she uses the muscles that lift her breasts.' Frost pushed his own hair back to demonstrate.

'It doesn't work with you,' said George.

'No. My tits look better when my arms are down,' said Frost. Steve Grimshaw laughed. Wagstaff swore under his breath and raised the volume on the TV.

Grimshaw turned his chair around. 'What about chatting up? I'm all right looking at them, and if I already know them I can talk. It's just first line, like.'

'Shut up, Grim, else I'll tell your fucking missus,' said Tom Betts.

'Fuck off,' said Steve Grimshaw. 'There's note wrong wi' talking to 'em.' He gestured that Frost should continue.

'Well, it says in the book they gave us that you shouldn't try to say anything clever. No jokes, and definitely none of that "Your eyes are like sequins" bullshit. You should just introduce yourself in a polite and friendly manner. It actually says you should imagine he or she is a cousin you haven't seen for a while, but I don't really go with that.'

'Be about right around here. We've got a bit of a reputation for liking us cousins,' said George. Steve Grimshaw laughed.

'Stop fucking yapping, Grim. The match is on, youth. You're like a fucking woman,' said Wagstaff.

Tom Betts was wound tight. Anyone could tell from the way he smoothed his hair back every few minutes until it was lank with grease. Everything was falling apart for Tom. He could almost feel the grass growing beneath his feet, and yet nobody wanted their lawn doing; England were playing shit, practically begging to be beaten; he had only enough money to get to that excruciating, empty stage of drunkenness; Grim had told him to fuck off, and George Cartwright – well – George fucking Cartwright had walked in with this gleaming ponce and introduced him to 'the lads'. It had riled Tom that Cartwright had called them 'the lads' when he hardly ever had the decency to say hello to them. And he knew that Beth was at home, probably sewing those little T-shirts and wondering why her husband would rather watch David Batty and Neil Webb with a bunch of jobless wasters than spend time with her. No wonder she was tapped.

In the second half Sweden equalized through Eriksson, and Graham Taylor replaced Lineker with Alan Smith. Lineker walked towards the camera, shaking his head. He removed the armband.

'England's saviour in Poznań will not be their saviour in Stockholm.'

George smiled at the thought of this man, with his hairless legs and short shorts, as the country's saviour. Everything seemed ridiculous to him. He was carefree. He did not think, for example, of his wife's face in the kitchen, the way she bit into her lip. He did not think of the three tins of creosote that now stood, under cover of darkness, like goblins in his garden.

'What's Taylor doing?' said Tom Betts.

'It's right. Lineker's a fairy. Big lad'll come on and knock 'em about a bit,' said Wagstaff.

Nobody seemed to share Wagstaff's opinion. The other men just watched nervously. With seven minutes remaining, Tomas Brolin, who looked younger than George's infant son, neatly knocked England out of the tournament. The papers would call him the Baby-Faced Assassin. 'Lock-in, Bri, drown us sorrows,' said Grimshaw.

Time ticked on. The eighteenth of June arrived.

On the middle floor of the tall, thin terraced house, Vincent slept in his cot. He was getting too big for it now, and had to curl up. The index finger of his right hand lay on his cheek, covered with snot. He had picked his nose on 17 June, but fallen asleep before he had a chance to transport the goods to his mouth. Vincent had refrained from picking his nose for a good while, since his mother's gentle but urgent lecture on dirtiness. The pungent images of filth – transmitted as much by Beth's garish facial expressions as by any exotic language – had been an effective deterrent until tonight, when a summer cold had made the pickings too easy to resist. His blocked sinuses also caused his mouth to fall open, allowing him to breathe. As a result of the dry summer air, his tongue stuck to the inside of his lower gum.

He woke suddenly, choking and unable to swallow. With his last reserves of energy, Vincent scaled the bars of his cot (a recently acquired skill) and crawled to the door. He lay down when he reached the hall and screamed that word which had been his first word. The one they would make him forget.

On the top floor Beth leaned towards where her husband should have been, but his stubborn bulk was not there to meet her so she rolled on to his side of the bed. Her face hit the pillow and the sensation of falling jolted her awake. She looked at the clock hands: tomorrow. She stayed on George's side, the dent of her own body beside her in the mattress.

Beth's mind was changing pace and shape. She could feel it pressing against her skull. In fact, beyond the pitiful fuzz of the sleeping tablets and her usual medication, Beth could feel everything, from the half-digested toast in her stomach to the fading pressure of the elastic from her socks, which she had removed hours before. She could feel the soft ache in her breasts, the onset of menstruation.

Purple blotches of light gathered on her vision, morphed. Over by the door she could see the man who had been in her kitchen that afternoon. He stood still, with his back to her. The man shrunk, swung around, became Michael Jenkins. She panicked, called out, and then realized her eyes were still shut. She opened them and felt a crushing weight of unfocussed doom.

The man had touched her husband, gripped his arm. She had craved such deliberate physical contact for so long. For an hour that afternoon, the garrulous, arrogant, ambitious young George had been in her house, somehow found again by Frost. The boy who had talked about a different place, who had said, *I've got you*, behind the pavilion on the Rec. It had been so nice to see him.

Fuck him, she thought. He was as bad as Martin Wagstaff. Fuck Michael Jenkins, too. Fuck them all.

Beth realized she was crying – loud sobs. She felt herself losing control. She wanted her husband. The light of a passing car made the curtains light up like a dreadful blank face. 'No,' she said. 'You're just tired. I'm just tired.'

As she turned over, fumes rose from the creosote-covered shirt she still wore (why change? For whom?). She stank of wood, dirt and solvents.

She slipped between zones of sleep.

For a moment she thought it was her own crying she could hear again. She was glad to wake, to give full range to her frustration. But her eyes were dry. Vincent. She went down to the middle floor, where Vincent kneeled, coughing, and calling her. His lips were swollen and ridged with white marks. 'Come on then,' she said, and picked him up. In the bathroom she filled the toothbrush cup with water, and gave it to him. She loved Vincent like this – half-struck by sleep, distressed in the serious manner of an adult. She ran her hand under the hot tap and then the cold, and stroked his hair across his head. 'My little man, aren't you? Eh?'

Vincent did not answer, but Beth was content to watch the xylophone ripple of his throat as he drank. Two streams of water ran from the edges of his mouth and twined at the chin. 'Not too quickly, though,' she said, taking the cup away from him. He reached after it with both hands.

George looked over Frost's shoulder at the line of sports photographs on the wall. His father dominated the fifties teams. It seemed extraordinary that a man could reproduce a pose (arms folded, sleeves rolled up, left eyebrow raised) so precisely over so many years. Moving along the decades, George appeared in the football team of 1973, on the back row, looking away from the camera. He watched the prints drift into colour. His shoulders broadened and his hair got shorter, and then he vanished in 1983. His gaze moved from 1984 to 1983 and back again (he could hardly help it, his pissed vision swayed uncontrollably). He found his own disappearance oddly satisfying, and perhaps this was the seed of a tiny epiphany: if he enjoyed his erasure from the team photos, maybe he really would enjoy leaving Blackmoor altogether, maybe it was just as simple as his wife said. He would return to this thought in his own time. Too late, in other words.

The news showed the purple-lit streets of Stockholm. A group of men chased another group of men, with riot police in between. In the dark, their flags looked identical. George turned to Frost (who had sat, straight-backed, on a stool for four-and-a-half hours) to check his reaction to the footage. But Frost did not watch the TV; he stared at George. It was an enervating stare. It had the blankness of a mirror. One thing George did not like to look at was himself. Say something, he thought, anything. He turned back to the TV screen.

'Wankers. We lost. Big deal. Why don't they just go home?' said George.

'You don't care about anything,' said Tom Betts. Tom was so angry that he could not raise his voice, and so nobody heard him. Wagstaff, however, was thinking along the same lines, and never had trouble making himself audible. 'Why don't *you* go home,

Cartwright, if you don't think it's important?' the old man said, stroking his swollen knuckles.

'Important? *Important*? What's important to you, Waggy? Eh? Sitting in here, fucking . . . fucking . . .'

'Look at you. You're pissed as a cunt,' said Wagstaff. A couple of the other lads turned around. George had a moment of clarity.

'What does that actually mean? Pissed as a cunt. Can a vagina get drunk, Wag? I suppose it would have to be to let you anywhere near it.'

Frost sat still on his stool, looking at his shoes. Wagstaff grimaced, almost smiled. 'Jesus, Cartwright. What a mess. If your old man could see you now.'

'If my old man could see me now, he'd say just what he said when he was alive: fuck all. You're all afraid. You can't talk, you can't even look at each other you're so frightened. King fucking Harold was exactly the same.'

'You can shut that up.' Wagstaff stood, perhaps expecting someone to hold him back. Nobody did, so he came towards George. 'Your fayther stood on picket when he were over fifty to fight for—'

'To fight for what?' said George. 'For the right to do a job that made him miserable. That crippled him. You know it killed him in the end. Do you really think he liked it down there?'

'No. I know he didn't like it, because he *told* me. He did it for you, you ungrateful little bastard. He did it to keep you alive. I bet he wished he'd never bothered.'

This response silenced George. The argument had been proceeding perfectly, Wagstaff coming in with the old picket story. George had checked to see that Frost was listening. He had relished the prospect of ridiculing the old man later. He had expected Wagstaff to follow on with his *Socialist Worker* speech, the old 'thirty year, man and boy' line. But George was not ready to hear that his father had hated the pit, although it seemed so obvious now. The way Wagstaff said it made it sound true, personal, and George did not think of his father in these terms.

Everyone in the club waited for George's reply. He should have just admitted that he had nothing left to say. Instead, he continued with the argument he had expected to have. It was a sorry sound, the hesitation in his voice, the defeat.

'Don't give me all that community bollocks. The village fucking people. The only time you get together is to hate someone else. You can't even . . . fucking hell. You've ignored this bloke tonight, just because he's from out of town.' George pointed to Frost, and everyone looked.

'Generations of racist inbred wankers telling their kids to drop out of school and break their backs to make sure they don't do anything worthwhile. It's impossible to fucking leave the place.'

It was a self-justifying speech. An excuse.

Wagstaff moved forward again, but did not encroach beyond Frost, who remained seated between them. 'Get out, George, and take your sweet boy with you. God knows you haven't touched your nutcase wife in years.'

It was a throwaway line, a generic insult to the manhood, and Wagstaff turned back to his drink, expecting no response (he did not know he had just uttered the most penetrating words of his long life). George felt Blackmoor's web of whispers descend on him again, and he could not take it. He jumped up from his stool, stepped across Frost and took hold of Wagstaff around the neck.

Wagstaff elbowed him in the ribs and George took one hand away, began digging at the older man's kidneys. Steve Grimshaw tried to intervene, but George kicked him, and tightened his grip on the neck. Wagstaff's strength began to fade, his skin turned red and his veins protruded, George could feel them throbbing under his fingers. He felt angry, but lucid. The man they used to call soft as shit, he thought. Frost came forward, but Grimshaw restrained him temporarily.

Tom Betts stood from his small stool and watched the struggle for a few seconds. Then, with a barely perceptible nod of decision, he stepped forward and punched George in the face. From George's perspective the blow seemed to come from over Wagstaff's shoulder, and the shock floored him. It was a powerful but inaccurate strike, catching him just above the eye and causing as much damage to Betts's knuckles. Tom Betts did not care. He advanced on George and watched him writhe on the carpet. 'You don't deserve. You don't deserve,' said Tom Betts. Then his shoulders dropped and he became quiet. It would occur to him in the glory of the early hours that his punch might have changed Beth's life for the better, that the serene sensation he felt was a result of having liberated her. By the end of the week he saw it for what it really was: another split second of selfish pleasure.

George's mind replayed Frost's instructions on how to stand from earlier in the day, and he almost smirked. Frost freed himself easily from Grimshaw's grasp, helped George to his feet and sent him towards the exit with a strong shove. Frost followed and Grimshaw marched after them. Frost turned to face the pursuer, who stopped abruptly. Wagstaff's hoarse gasps filled the silence, and Tom Betts remained standing, pacified. 'Don't fucking come in here again, Cartwright,' said Grimshaw, over Frost's shoulder. 'Jesus. That's a bloody pensioner you've just tried to kill.'

As they stepped out into the night, George turned and tried to get back in, but Frost barred the entrance. Frost had a strong grip, and George gave up. He kicked a bin in the car park instead. Frost calmly watched him exhaust himself. When his anger had all but faded, George looked up at the sky. 'It's dark,' he said. They had entered the club five hours ago in soft sunlight. This sign of passing time soothed George's temper slightly, or at least made him feel insignificant.

'What a waste of fucking time,' George said, placing his hands on the wall of the club, as if he could somehow push it away.

'Come on, mate,' said Frost. 'You're about ready, aren't you?'

'Yep.'

The lights of the Honda flashed their welcome. The engine yawned, and George looked out on Blackmoor, which seemed to tumble and disintegrate, swallowed by the motion of the car and his drunkenness.

'God. What was I doing?'

'Well, I don't know about the strangling bit, but it sounded like you had something to say.'

'Talk, talk, talk. I'm nowhere. No one. No . . . don't listen to me, I'm—'

'What you *are*, it seems, is pissed as a cunt,' said Frost. George laughed for a long time and then stopped.

'I don't know why people would be like that,' he said.

'Don't you?' said Frost, looking out on the gutted shops, slack heaps and hollow works outside the car. George cursed aimlessly, and then directed his attention to the less troublesome lights and dials on the dashboard. The clock said 01.23, and George's drink-drowned brain found sympathy in the simple procession of numerical order.

'Back again,' said Frost as they pulled up outside George's narrow house. 'You seem to have recovered quite quickly from your little breakdown anyway.'

'Habit,' said George. He stared up at his section of stone and glass. Even full of drink, he could see every bruise in every brick.

'Well, mate, thanks for this evening. I've got a feeling I won't forget it,' said Frost.

'Yeah right. I bet it was a pleasure, sitting in that dump watching me get rat-arsed.'

Frost just smiled and looked down the road. George followed his gaze, but could not see past the nasturtiums and lobelia in the flower basin, unusually exposed by the headlights. 'I suppose you'll be off to wherever it is you go, then?' said George, a hint of bitterness, a little envy in his voice.

'That's right,' said Frost.

George nodded. He pulled at the door lever but it would not open, so he pressed the nearest button. There was a crunching sound. 'No. That's locked it,' said Frost. George dragged his fingers down his face.

'Here. I'll do it.' Frost leaned across George and flicked the handle. The blue shirt pulled tight across his shoulders. George lowered his hand to within an inch of the cotton. Frost lifted himself gracefully so that George's fingers rested upon his back. The door had come open, activating the interior light and letting in some air. Frost raised his face until it was level with George's.

Keeping his hand still, George felt Frost's ribs slide under his palm as he moved. The southerner smiled, tired.

He kissed George.

George felt everything. He felt the thickness of Frost's lips as they tugged on his own, the engine's resonance through the soles of his shoes. He felt Frost's warm breath in his mouth, the dry skin of his own lips softening. What he noticed most was the sheer human silence, the speechlessness. Since 5 p.m. George had tried to avoid silence, tried to fill each second with talk. Nervous, energetic, futile talk. And now there was only breathing, the occasional nylon shift of the seat belts, the engine ticking over. George moved his hand across Frost's back, and then out along the fin of his shoulder blade. Frost took his mouth away but stayed close so that George could not focus on his face. They stayed like that for a while. 'Goodnight, George,' Frost said.

George got out of the car and closed the door. The interior light went out and Frost became a black shape. A few seconds later he became two red dots curving around the corner, and then darkness. George stood for a moment. He felt confused, sorry for himself, and wished for rain, for some dramatic weather. For a fraction of a second, he thought about the people in his house, about how what he had done might affect them. For a moment he thought that he had wrecked his family, but he reasoned sadly that it took more than one night, one kiss, to do that.

Beth heard George come in. He coughed once. She elbowed the bathroom door so that it almost closed, to protect her son from the sight of his father. But Vincent was no longer there. He had freed himself from his mother's embrace and gone to his cot an hour before. A thin sliver of George passed the door. Beth saw it in the mirror.

When she returned to their room, Beth found George sitting on the bed, removing his trousers. This meant he was drunk. He had screwed up his shirt and thrown it on the carpet. Blood stained the cuff. Beth closed her eyes and inhaled. Beer, sweat and a light citric aftershave. She switched off the lamp and tried to crawl over him into bed, but he caught her by the calf and dragged her down. He kissed her, and roughly took hold of her breast, which was tender, but she could not afford to waste an opportunity. As she lowered her fingers down George's stomach he took hold of her wrist. Beth resisted the grip, and when she put her hand on his cock she felt the bee-sting pulse of it, the hot liquid seeping into his underwear.

She took her hand away.

After a minute or so, she tried to get up, not knowing where she would go, but George forced her down on the bed and then rested his head on her shoulder. Beth felt like hitting him, but instead she rubbed his hair, as she had her son's.

'I'm sorry, Beth,' he said.

'What for? I'd really like to hear you say why you're sorry.'

'For being drunk.'

'Is that why? That's not why. That's an excuse.'

George sniffed her shirt. 'You smell of creosote.'

'Where did you go? Tonight. The Welfare?'

'Yep. Yes.'

'With him. With Daniel?'

'Yes.'

'He seemed strange.'

George paused. 'Yes,' he said.

'You seemed to get on well.'

'He was only here for one day.'

Beth waited, her muscles taut. It was unclear what she waited for, but in any case, it was not forthcoming. Soon enough, too soon, George's breathing settled into the despised familiar pattern: the loud exhalation, and the long silence before he breathed again. A thousand deaths. Beth's trapped arm began to tingle under his weight. She grasped a handful of George's damp hair and lifted his head. His eyes remained shut.

On the morning of 18 June, George took his turn to wake alone. It was late, nearly lunchtime, and he tried to concentrate on this, tried to panic about work. He felt sick and hollow.

He hid his soiled shirt in the wardrobe and put on a clean one with yesterday's suit. He could hear Beth rattling around somewhere, but he did not wish to see her just yet.

He found Vincent in the garden, already sitting by his cardboard box. He ruffled the child's hair. 'Mummy'll be down in a bit,' he said. 'I'll sort everything out tonight. I swear.'

The boy did not stir. George found the coiled sticker from the crossbar of Vincent's bike snaking through the grass. The open creosote tins were still in the garden, and the portable radio was on. The news report told of more trouble in Stockholm. The England supporters had flipped a Kurdish kebab stall and stolen the money. The story made George nauseous, and he switched it off, but the programme continued to blare out of a neighbour's radio.

George remembered something. He took the folded badge from

his pocket, opened it up, and read his name. He would sort everything out tonight, he swore. As the sun came out, the shadow of
the house altered before his eyes. He heard his pulse beating in his
head. He went back through the house and emerged from the
front door. On the pavement stood the large concrete basin, six by
three feet. The granite looked like gooseflesh and the soil was dry
like cooked minced meat. Hangovers, thought George. He
thought of his father, imagined him in the Miners' Welfare Club
instead of Wagstaff. His father shouting abuse at him, asking him
outside for a fight in the car park. He thought of the battered shoe
on the mantelpiece.

George spent a few moments looking for his car before he realized that he had left it at the EM Water Centre. He walked to the
bus stop at the end of the street. When he turned to look back at
the house he saw Beth on the roof, lying in the posture of a sun-
bather, her head propped on her hand. She was attached to the
drainpipe by a piece of blue towrope and a karabiner. Fixing the
tiles. The sun hit the gutter, which glowed beneath her. George
thought about going back, if only for Vincent, but he did not.

Through the bus window he saw the Brownes strapping their
belongings to the roof-rack of their car. He saw the steady procession of smoke coming from the loop track, passing across the
sun, darkening the land below.

This place is going to hell, thought George.

Twenty-three

In her brief absence, life has overtaken the tent. The grass, mown to within a yard of the pegs, has already sprouted up through the holes in the groundsheet. She finds a luminous caterpillar, two dead hoverflies, and a patient moth that goes crazy when she switches on the globe lamp. The cleansing pads, without their lid, have dried to a crisp lump. Leila has a pink folder containing the Blackmoor research (including the newspaper cutting), and a bottle of Pernod swiped from her father's house. She mixes the fragrant spirit with Co-op Cola and drinks from the lid of a Thermos flask.

It is the right thing to do, she tells herself.

Later, Vincent approaches Wood Edge under cover of night, with a tin of Scotch broth and his letter, muttering 'Shit or bust, shit or bust' (one of his father's phrases) under his breath. Watch him for a moment. His jeans ride up to his ankles now, and the sleeves of his hoody reveal bony, downy wrists. For a little while longer, he is still the boy who doesn't know.

He has made resolutions. If she turns him down, he will not chase her. More rejection would only sully the good memories. He has the cassette and the lip balm – his Leila substitutes. A fuzzy, sensory re-creation of her is preferable to stern refusals. But when he arrives on the grounds through JEM woods, he sees that the tent is glowing. The reddened light taints the trunk of the cedar next to which he stands. As he looks up into the canopy, the needle-decked platforms of the tree are like thin clouds against the purple night sky. Leila is an orangey shadow inside the tent, hugging her knees with one arm, bringing a cup to her mouth with the other.

'Knock, knock,' says Vincent, awkwardly folding himself into the space. 'Smells like liquorice.'

'Tastes like petrol,' says Leila, offering him the cup, which is by no means her first of the night. He can tell she has been lying down because the imprint from the zip of her sleeping bag snakes down her right cheek. They drink in silence, Vincent wondering whether it was wise to include the line about the orgy, Leila trying to follow the blurry, shifting image of Vincent off to the right. Is this what it is like to fall, she wonders.

'I've brought soup and a letter,' Vincent says.

Leila finds this inordinately funny. 'Oh Vincent. There's one thing that you're never, and that's predictable.'

Vincent notes that the word 'predictable' has picked up a few extra syllables. Leila's bare feet are crossed before her, the baggy trousers discoloured where the hem has dragged beneath the heel. She leans over her lap and takes hold of his thumbs. He guards the pocket containing the letter.

'Vincey. When you know someone really well, you sometimes

have to say difficult things to them. Although in some ways this is no big deal and you might even already know.'

'Go on,' he says, his spirits rising.

'I have this *feeling* about you, which is why—'

'I know. Me too.'

'You *know*?'

'Yep.'

'Well, then, why didn't you just tell me?'

He smiles. 'I never found the right time. I was nervous about what you'd say. You can be harsh sometimes. I wrote a letter about it.'

'But it's okay. It's really no big deal.'

'When did you figure it out?'

'Local studies library.'

'Oh.'

'I found it on the microfiche.'

'Eh?'

'Look.' She fumbles with the folder, takes out the cutting. 'It's a funny word, isn't it? Microfiche. Like tiny fish. Here.'

Vincent takes the piece of paper. Leila has scrawled *North Derbyshire Herald, 26 June 1992* across the top. Vincent is confused. He does not want to talk about the project now. Maybe she has just gone shy, he thinks. 'Leila, it's okay. Look. Read the letter.'

'Not now. Not sure I could. Feeling a bit.'

'Fine. I'll read it. Probably make more sense anyway. You know my handwriting.'

'Vincent, just shush.'

'*Dear Leila. You've been avoiding me lately.* Actually the first paragraph's a bit "bore me". Where shall I start?'

'Vincent, you don't have to, really. Honest to God. Honest to God.'

'Where's a good bit? *When you cleaned my face with those pads, things happened to me* . . . No, I can't read that. It's embarrassing.'

'Vincent.' Leila is laughing now. She's relieved and confused and drunk.

'*You are the one person I think about when they're not around.*'

She leans over, takes him by the shoulders and kisses him. Their teeth bump. Her mouth tastes of Pernod, which reminds him of the woods, of a fire about to go out. Her tongue, however, makes him think of the rough side of an antibacterial cleansing pad, that denim burn. He holds her hair, as he has imagined. It folds in his hand. Then she pulls away, her eyes closed, and crawls past him out of the tent.

He waits with the letter in his hand and the cutting in his lap. She is not a noisy puker, it just sounds like someone turning on a hose. He looks down. His stomach flips when he reads his mother's name, in the same way it flips when he sees Leila, and the way it did when he got caught stealing pencils. Funny, he thinks, that such different scenarios should provoke the same sensation. There can't be many feelings in the world, he decides. Not enough, anyway, for all the things that can happen.

Of course, he does not understand. The words seem dead on the page – a concrete poem in the shape of a breeze block. Then he reads it again, three, four times.

The mother jumping, the boy falling. The boy falling. The date.

After the fifth reading, he covers the paper with his hand. An involuntary, childish reaction. The incremental unravelling of the story's logic seems to Vincent like a clever, delayed joke. And is 'joke' such an inappropriate word? The events do not hurt him (although he is *interested* in them), and at that moment he feels nothing more than a slow-creeping sense of discomfort, exposure.

He folds the piece of paper many times, until it fits into the palm of his hand. Then he ducks out of the tent, leaving his letter behind. It is already a forgotten relic of an old world.

The floodlights from Wood Edge are strained by the undergrowth, and Leila is dappled white, dry-retching on all fours. She knew.

When he gets home his father is in the kitchen, eating. Let us watch them from a distance in their square of yellow light. Vincent sits across from his father with an incredulous smile on his face. He unfolds the cutting in the centre of the table. It lies between them. See its edges slowly curling up.

They stay like this until the early hours, George – for once and at last – doing most of the talking. At a certain point, around midnight, George spreads his hand and says something to Vincent that changes the nature of the exchange. Watch it register on Vincent's face. The smile has gone, and now he will not look directly at his father, viewing instead George's bulbous, bulge-eyed, chicken-necked reflection in the stainless steel kettle.

It is not long now before Vincent is back outside, walking to the quarry, leaving his father to gaze dumbly at the flashing green digits on the broken cooker clock. The false time, as always, reads 10.53, but to that man, who has been hastily stripped of many of his own delusions, it will seem to spell the word 'lose'.

TWENTY-FOUR

Blackmoor, 18 June 1992.

You can spy on the place from your bird's-eye view. The mid-morning sky is hot, empty, and it is no chore to lose some altitude. Down there on Hardwick Street, Mrs Hargreaves approaches the Post Office, eager to spread the news of the trouble at the Miners' Welfare Club the night before. The rumours are sketchy because of the intoxication and general unreliability of the witnesses, but Mrs Hargreaves has established that good old Martin Wagstaff was involved. Some say he fought one of the younger lads (infighting was not as rare as folk would have you believe), while more sinister reports suggest that the aggressor was an outsider. Astonishing things.

The village is temporarily clouded by a wind-blown trail of smoke. As Blackmoorians collect their milk from the doorstep they look up and frown. Fights and fires – these are the things they tentatively discuss with their neighbours today. The tension increases. George is not the only one to wake with a hangover on the morning of 18 June. The whole village has the shakes.

Soar over the empty Miners' Welfare Club, which seems like a grumpy toad this morning, with its rough facade. When you reach the local authority housing you can see that Tom Betts has his windows open and is listening to the Clash as he fries eggs. He alone seems happy. Look, for example, at Sarah and Trevor Browne, attaching an old roof-rack to their Nissan Bluebird. This morning Sarah had opened the curtains, seen a smoking village, heard the nerve-jangling piano on 'Rock the Casbah', told her husband that enough was enough.

Drift west over the old colliery, the white eyesore of a pumping station, and out to the loop track where the black heart of Blackmoor's current anxiety beats: a pile of ashy garbage and a blazing strip of coal. It is unwise to linger here, for smoke gets in your eyes. Try instead to catch the thin breeze and climb over the bank and the copse and the muddy field with the holes, to Slack Lane. A small boy begins his second day of waiting by a cardboard box. His head bobs for he has not slept well. But hover for a moment on this precarious thermal and your eye will pick out something else, something extraordinary.

A woman on a roof.

The roof is by no means flat, but she lies there quite still and lets her cheek rest on the hot tiles. A piece of coiled towrope and a karabiner on her belt secure her to the drainpipe. It seems that her face has altered over the last few years, as though it has been subject to subtle sustained pressures. Her nose seems to tip slightly while her mouth turns down at the edges, so that, in the moments before she smiles, you think she might cry. The sun emboldens her white shirt, and her short hair is radiant in its lack of colour. George comes out of the front door below and she turns her head to watch him over her shoulder, pretending to be asleep as usual. Through her half-open eyes she sees that he is searching for his car. After a few moments he shakes his head and walks towards the bus stop. By the time he looks back and sees her on top of the house, she has turned away.

When he has gone, Beth takes her hammer and nails and begins work on the roof. The tiles look like sealskin when it rains but when they are dry, like today, they have the colour and texture of beach pebbles. Beth works slowly, and the sun-stiffened creosote on the back of her shirt loosens with sweat. She can fix tiles because she has made it her business to learn. The demolition men might be on their way, the village may be falling apart, but Beth Cartwright's house will be perfect when they knock it down.

At lunchtime she descends and makes a ham sandwich for Vincent, who has caught no birds. They take a walk to the shops. Beth buys potatoes, eggs and marrowfat peas. She goes to the pharmacy to collect her prescribed Haloperidol. The old woman in front of her in the queue asks the pharmacist for a 'packet of diarrhoea'. When it is Beth's turn, the smirking man at the counter observes her shirt. 'Looks like you spilt a bit a paint, love,' he says.

Beth sighs, holds his gaze and scratches at a tiny speck of creosote on her collar. 'All gone?' she asks in a slow drawl.

The pharmacist looks down and retrieves her prescription in silence.

When they approach the loop track, Beth stops, observing the fire. She has watched it change moods. Yesterday the heat fed a pulsing column of purple grey, like bell heather, but this afternoon it is livid and static, a painful golden face. 'Might be a bit hot down there, Vince. We'll have to go back the way we came.'

As soon as Vincent is safely reinstalled at his trap, Beth returns to the roof. There is little left to do, but she needs the elevation, for the world is too vigorous at ground level. Even up here she is simultaneously assaulted by the noise of the mower on the Rec, the syrupy crackle of the fire, the despondent drumbeat of someone climbing their stairs three doors down, a girl saying, 'What's the point?' to her friend, the distant muffle of a megaphone and – always – the thirsty gasp of cars. It is worth noting that most cars on this day are travelling towards the motorway, and a few of them carry a little more weight than usual.

The Brownes come down Slack Lane about mid-afternoon, Sarah telling her husband to wind the window up, never mind how hot it is. She trusts the recirculated air of a baking Bluebird more than the atmosphere of the village in which she resides. The Brownes do not spot Beth, and it is their last chance to do so. In fact, throughout the day, nobody sees her. It makes a strange picture, the occasional pedestrian sauntering past, holding their ice cream away from the nosy bees on the nasturtiums in the flower basin, the tall house with the windows flung open, and Beth above it all, lying so still and long and quiet.

At 4 p.m. she is finally able to slow her thoughts. The smoke helps. As it crosses the sun, the shadows on the tiles are like speech, the soft variations of a whispering mouth. The anger has drained from her now. She continues to think of how George looked, in the kitchen, his eyes furtive and full of mischief for the first time in such a long while. It was like a Scrooge-style visitation. But this image no longer heartens her. The lost George must have been sad to see the man he had become. What must that optimistic youth have thought, standing there surrounded by the beached detritus of his future life? A house not half a mile from where he was born, a mad despised wife, and no friends. Beth blames herself. It seems clear to her that she has halted his progress. That long-haired southerner had changed her husband completely in just *a couple of hours*. Frost had given him the things that she could not: sanity, intelligence, excitement. What had George said last night? 'He was only here for one day.' Beth had felt the loss in those words. She presses her forehead against the sparkling mica of the tiles and cries with the waste of it all.

At half past five she finally descends. She ignores the ladder, pulls the towrope flush against the fixture collar of the drainpipe and abseils down the face of the house. The rope pulls taut when she is a few feet from the ground, so she simply detaches the karabiner from her belt and drops safely to the pavement.

In the rapidly darkening garden Vincent lies on his belly and quietly commentates on his bird-catching game. He has wide brown eyes, curly blond locks and wears a red T-shirt, grey shorts and rubber sandals. He holds the string tightly in his fist.

'Have you caught any birdies yet, Vince?' his mother shouts from the kitchen. The voice shocks Vincent, who spins quickly and accidentally pulls the string. The box drops and the cane bounces towards the boy. Vincent stands and then falls down on the grass. He knows that the game is over because he does not have the dexterity to reset the trap.

'I'm making your favourite. Egg, chips and big peas.'

Vincent watches her through the open window for a while longer and then comes inside. 'Bosna hurts the governor,' he says earnestly in the doorway.

'Yes. Yes I'm sure she does,' says Beth. Vincent walks past her into the front room.

When his mother has been peeling potatoes for a while (Vincent is already smart enough to recognize the sounds), he climbs the two flights of stairs in the long thin house, using his hands to hoist himself up. He goes into his parents' room, and gets on to the bed. The bed is ten inches from the window, and the top of the mattress is just about level with the sill. The window is open, and gives out on to the street. It is not George's favourite window, not the one at the back with the view of the valley. The noises of the village fill the room. Vincent does not recognize the clap of the wicketkeeper's gloves coming from the cricket session on the Rec. It sounds to him like the amplified wingbeat of a giant bird. He is now an experienced bouncer. He can go high, and twist in the air. If he stretches his arms upwards, Vincent can almost touch the ceiling. At the highest point of his jump, he looks sideways and sees the chimneys of the houses below his eye level. He is higher than everything. 'I bounce,' he declares triumphantly.

He smells frying oil, and hears his mother sniffling. This is normal. When she sneezes, it sounds like she is saying, 'No.' A few minutes later, the chips hiss in the pan, and his mother comes to the bottom of the stairs. 'Can I hear bouncing?' she shouts. 'I can hear bouncing. Get down please, Rascal, you'll knock your teggies out.'

Her voice sounds. He cannot really gauge how her voice

sounds. Sad, perhaps. That is how a child would put it. But Vincent cannot relinquish this wild pleasure, so he simply alters his technique, bending his knees so the springs won't squeak. 'I bounce,' he whispers. Through the open window he can smell rotting cherry blossom, dry dust and smoke.

What he loves most is the plateau he finds at the peak of the rise, a moment of stillness in the exchange between ascending and falling. Each time he arrives there, he feels that he can stay suspended in the air for as long as he wants, that this is really just a nook in space that he can crawl into. The open window is so close that he can feel the breeze on his face, so that he could almost be outside, in the sky. The shadows of the furniture extend across the carpet, and Vincent is at peace.

He is so sheltered by his niche in the air that he remains oblivious to the sudden movements on the ground floor. His mother can still hear the bed creaking and she begins to climb the stairs. Vincent is unaware of her approach until she is in the doorway with her hand on her hip like the teapot song.

'What have I *told* you?' she says.

Her appearance shocks him, and he twists in mid-flight, loses his balance. He topples backwards, and falls out of the open window. It is over so quickly that he does not know he has fallen. He is not aware that he is lying in the soil of the flower basin outside his own house. He is cognizant only of a numbness in his right shoulder. His mother always says, by way of a warning, 'You'll take off if you're not careful.' So he concludes that this is what has happened. With his final jump he must have gone through the roof and into another dimension. He stares at the sky, feeling like he has left his insides in the room. The numbness in his shoulder quickly becomes a pain so severe that it almost takes his breath away. He passes out.

Up in the bedroom, Beth's son has gone. Everyone has gone, and the emptiness of the room crushes her like water pressure. The sun has taken hold in the red curtains and given them a wicked glow, a redness that Beth can almost taste, something like desire. The breeze penetrates the wardrobe and her vacant dresses clash within, the hangers rattle.

Suddenly she knows everything. She knows that in the eyes of the villagers she will always be at fault. She is ill, and recognizes the minuscule disconnections in her mind. She understands that this makes her impossible to love. She is aware that from this moment, time will move on, that it will bring grief and then cruelly – when grief is all she has got – will diminish it. She knows that if she were to look out of the window her eyesight would prohibit the clear vision of her dead son.

She crumples at the waist, clutching the folds of her shirt. She lets out a silent gasp and then straightens suddenly, making her decision. Her eyelids droop, and she steps lithely on to the bed. Beth grasps the frame of the window. See the short shudder of her eyes, the giveaway signal of her distress. Trace her veins for the last time, through the pellucid skin.

She pulls herself through, smashes her head on the edge of the flower basin, and lies on the pavement, motionless. The last thing she saw was Vincent, moving.

On the street, the noise of a woman running in slippers. The curses she mutters are so quiet and profane that they almost sound like a prayer. It is Polly Grimshaw. She begins to shout. 'Steve. Steve. Jesus, it's Beth. Call someone. Quick.'

Beth Cartwright is dying before her, perhaps dead already. Beth's face looks no less normal than it usually does, just a little wider. Black blood pulses from the back of her skull in a steady, efficient stream. The blood flows across the pavement and down on to the road, where it follows the camber back to well against the kerb. It soaks into the pores of the stone, beginning already to dry. Polly Grimshaw moves away, coughing violently. Other people come out of their homes and walk briskly over to the scene. They slow down, however, when they realize what has happened. When they identify the dark pool behind Beth, some of them duck, as if avoiding a blow.

Mrs Hargreaves comes out of her front door across the road, and walks unsteadily towards the gathering group. She is shaking her head. 'Where's the little'n?' she says sternly, impatiently. 'Is the little'n okay?'

In the noise and general panic, nobody understands what she means, and they barely look up from tending to Beth, but Mrs Hargreaves saw Vincent fall while she was cleaning her sink. She had been watching his little head, appearing and disappearing in the window as he bounced. The fall was like a smudge on her vision, but she knew what had happened immediately. As she tried to ascertain where he had landed, Beth came down. Mrs Hargreaves, usually a tough woman, is frightened as she reaches the scene. She does not want to find a dead child. It is not long before she sees the boy among the flowers. He is barely conscious, and for a moment she fears the worst, but his feet kick up the soil, as though he is bathing in shallow waters. Mrs

Hargreaves steadies herself on the concrete basin. 'Jesus wept,' she says. When she tries to lift Vincent out, he wakes, screaming with pain, and the group congregated around his mother turn to look.

'I think his arm's brock,' Mrs Hargreaves says.

'Whose arm's broke?' says Polly Grimshaw.

'It's Beth's lad. He fell out the window.'

Polly looks up at the house and then down at Beth. Three slim lines of blood roll out of Beth's mouth, over her cheek and twine near her ear. Vincent continues to roar, and for want of anywhere comfortable to put him, Mrs Hargreaves lays him back in the soil.

Mrs Hargreaves is also the first to notice the burning smell coming from the house. 'Polly. I think the dinner might still be on indoors. See to it,' she says.

'What?' says Polly, turning around to see the smoke. 'Oh bloody hell,' she whispers to herself. Polly stands from her knees and tries to discreetly wipe her hands on the back of her dark skirt. She clops down the little alley by the side of the house.

'Where the bloody hell is George?' shouts Mrs Hargreaves. Then she lowers her voice, and hisses, 'The useless swine.'

He is sitting on a swing. George had gone to the Rec with the intention of lounging on the grass, in peace, and curing his resilient hangover with some more drink. Hair a the dog, as his father used to say. He didn't know there would be a cricket training session. A few of the lads turned to look at him when he came through the gate with his plastic bag, but they soon turned away again. Considering his behaviour the previous evening, he could hardly rest on the grass now. So he moved over to the swings, where he currently sits, hidden from the cricketers by the hump of the play tunnels.

It is one of those days (there are many) when he hates Blackmoor. Every corner of the village resounds with some story of his past. The place is verbal, noisy with the mistakes he has made. He can hear every self-condemning sentence he has ever uttered.

He turns the seat of the swing, twisting the chains at the top. When he looks to his left he can see the overgrown grasses and nettles behind the pavilion, where his wife first touched him. He had put his hand on her back, and felt his knuckles scrape the wall of the building. As he lifts his feet, the swing chains unwind and when he stops again, slightly nauseous, he is facing the tunnels where he took his first drink. The place is inescapable. It does not help that these locations are now soiled by the rather more profound excess of the current generation of Blackmoor youths. Leaflets have been posted through his door about the dangers of discarded needles. He wonders if it will be the same in the new village. Looking at the drug paraphernalia by the tunnels, George considers the move – and what he is going to do about it – for the first time. It will take more than a few new houses to dissolve the problems in Blackmoor. He may not have to confront the same physical reminders every day, but the spirit of the place will endure, if only in the faces of his eternal neighbours. It has been fine to submit to Blackmoor, and feel sorry for himself all these years. He has secretly revelled in the comfort of low expectations. He convinced himself he was stuck there, even when his siblings moved away. It is only when he comes across people like Frost that he feels any twinge of remorse, a tiny insight into an alternative future. But people like Frost never stay for long. He realizes now that he cannot sacrifice the future of his child to that same, spoilt angst. His decision is made: they are done with this place, and they will not move with the others. The name of Cartwright will never appear above a house on the map of New Blackmoor.

As he sips his can of Kestrel Super, he winces. He knows that when he goes home he will have to confront another difficult memory. He will hear the foolish words he said to Daniel Frost, and remember his hand on a different back.

'Bowling, Grimmer,' someone shouts from over the hump. The wicketkeeper claps his gloves. George appreciates the futility of cricket: long bouts of boredom punctuated by moments of intense pain. He supposes that the Blackmoor squad is well equipped to deal with such a cycle, given the nature of life in the village. They must be top of the league, he thinks with a smile.

Calmly, obliviously smiling while his son falls and his wife jumps.

He looks up at the putrid green drainpipes of the pavilion, and listens to someone screaming way off in the village. Always somebody screaming. He reaches down into the plastic bag, and takes out another can of Kestrel Super. A thin veil of smoke from the loop track adds a dusty tincture to the plummeting sun, and George watches the silhouette of a wooden rocking horse nod and nod by the climbing bars.

See his hands shake as he opens the can, see the crescents of dirt beneath the nails, which appear at the end of every day, no matter how clean his work. A group of children come running out of the scout hut behind, ready to make use of the amusements.

They stop and fall quiet when they see him there. They confer, and then decide to move on. See his broad back, as they do. See this 37-year-old man in his suit and loose tie, twisting the chains of a swing while his wife dies on the pavement a quarter of a mile away.

The crowd grows when the ambulance and police arrive. As the paramedics lift Beth from the road, it becomes clear to all that she will not return. The bystanders have been doing their best to comfort Vincent, mainly by surrounding the basin in order to shield him from the sight of his mother. The pain of his injury has sent him delirious, and he occasionally cries out for her, but it is unclear whether he knows the gravity of her condition. The female paramedic drugs him, puts his arm in a splint, and carries him away, dry soil flaking from his limbs. The ambulance leaves with a significant slowness.

The crowd on the road splinters into small groups. Now the victims have departed, the villagers no longer feel obliged to be discreet, and the latecomers try to piece the event together from the confused testimonies of the original group, some of whom have been interviewed by the police. One lot of people think Beth fell with the child in her arms, while other cruel rumours suggest she had another breakdown and threw her son from the window before killing herself. 'She's got that disease, ant she? Where it makes you hate your kids.'

Mrs Hargreaves seems to be in the know. Polly Grimshaw interrogates her when the police have finished. 'It's same as a say to them. The boy were bouncing. He fell first. Then she jumped out,' says Mrs Hargreaves.

'What, she jumped after him? Trying to save him, like?' asks Polly.

'No. No. It were a few seconds after. That window's high up. They're on three floors. She must have thought he were dead and just lost it.'

'You're saying she killed herself?'

'I'm not saying oat.' Mrs Hargreaves becomes defensive. The police were aggressive towards her. One of the officers said she might have damaged the boy by picking him up.

Polly continues her attempts to make sense of events. 'So Beth thought the lad were dead and couldn't take it, eh? Did she not look for him on the ground? To make sure?'

'I don't know,' Mrs Hargreaves says.

'You'd of thought she'd have checked to see if he was okay first though, wouldn't you?' says Polly.

'Well, *I* would of, obviously. She's not quite right though, is she, Beth?'

'No.'

Black smoke continues to rise from the east of the village. The two women lift their heads in that direction. 'This place,' says Mrs Hargreaves. 'This bloody place.'

It is still light. As the women look on, George turns the corner on to Slack Lane, staring at the ground. When he sees the groups outside his house, he stops like a thief. He alters his gait, walks more formally (as if he can hide the smell of strong lager on his breath). Mrs Hargreaves breaks from the crowd and walks towards him, and he tries to look less drunk, less guilty.

TWENTY-FIVE

At 3 a.m. George sits in his kitchen and watches the flashing green digits on the cooker clock. He drags the newspaper cutting across the table and forces himself to read it again. George had never seen this particular report before tonight. Such a strange piece of writing. When Beth died, most of the newspapers had the scruples to omit Vincent from the story completely, or at least the legal awareness to avoid suggesting that Beth had jumped. But the cutting before him seems to revel in the connection. It contains an overt 'twist in the tale' narrative logic. How different things might have been had Vincent found one of the more neutral reports following the coroner's inquest. An open verdict had been returned.

At first Vincent had simply asked questions in his typical wide-eyed, interested manner. Happy, as always, to be learning something new. The questions were not too dissimilar from the ones George himself had asked, all those years ago: can this be true? Did she kill herself? Why? How did she know the fall would kill her? How many metres was it? How many metres does it take?

George tried to fill the silences between questions. He nearly told Vincent about Beth's illness. Mostly, however, he just found elaborate ways to say he didn't know. 'This report. It's *wrong* in a way.'

For years George had suffered his son's imploring, optimistic, infuriating stare, but tonight, after a certain point, the boy refused to meet his eye.

'Why didn't you tell me?' he said.

Here was a question to which George knew all the answers. (If I'd have told you, I'd have had to tell you everything.) 'I didn't tell you because I knew *this* would happen. I didn't want you to have the burden.'

'The what?'

'Everyone always says it's best to know. *Why* is it? Do you feel better now? Eh? What good has it done you?'

'You don't get to ask me questions tonight,' Vincent snapped. 'You must've known I'd find out.'

'Find out what? Your mother—'

'You wouldn't even talk to me about her. You've stolen her off me.'

'I've brought you up. In *her* absence. What difference would it have made?'

Vincent did not respond.

'You can't *grieve*, Vincent. That's my privilege. You were two years old when it happened. You never had something and lost it the way I did.'

This response startled both of them. George knew he was

wrong immediately. A man who spent his life mourning things that never came to pass, he knew that you did not have to own something in order to lose it. He also knew what Vincent did not: that he lost his wife a long time before 18 June 1992. But Vincent just nodded and smiled, as if he saw some truth in the words. He left soon after, walked into the night.

George looks at Beth's full name on the page. It seems miraculous, that combination of letters, that shape. All other words appear to be misspellings of her name. It is like a grapnel in his mind. Elizabeth Cartwright. Who ever called her Elizabeth? After eleven years of avoiding both, he has seen her name and her face in a matter of months.

For the next few weeks their house on the hill is no place to be. The modern home does not have the formality that facilitates anger and regret. At work you can argue in a meeting and then slam your office door, but at home you must fight and then relax in an easy chair. The trivial cruelly intrudes. You storm out of a room and then remember your book, left on the sofa, and you have to creep back in. In these cases, either the trivial wins and the argument dissipates into the comfort of shared space, or the place becomes unnatural, prickly. For a while, Vincent's quiet fury assures that their upside-down home of mismatched furniture is the latter.

Leila visits the house one night after school. George answers the door and keeps her standing on the drive. Her fists are clenched and white creases of skin radiate from the finger joints.

'Can I speak to Vincent please?'

'You Leila?'

'Yes.'

'Then you can't I'm afraid. He doesn't want to see you.'

George does not even know where Vincent is. The girl looks at her feet and speaks under her breath for a while. To George this quiet incantation seems like a very adult gesture. 'What did you just say?' he asks.

'Why is he being like this? It's not like it matters.'

'Look. Why don't you go home? You don't want to stand out on the bloody drive and get upset. It's pointless.'

She glares. Kids always seem to be angry with George these days. He is part of an unlucky generation who have endured the fury of both their parents and their children. 'Go home,' he says.

'Why are you so miserable?' she mutters.

'What?'

'You think all of this has happened to just you, but it hasn't.'

'It's got bugger all to do with *you*, I know that much,' he says, and closes the door.

He takes a piss and thinks of Beth's hair. When George was a child, and felt ill, his mother would hold him by the chin and squint. 'Healthy hair and healthy eyes, that's how you tell. There's note wrong with you, get to school.'

With hair and eyes like Beth's, did she ever really stand a chance? He remembers a time when Vincent was a year old, after his decision to ban physical contact with Beth, but before she shaved her head. Things had already begun to crumble. He woke early and went to the toilet as usual, but his piss sprayed out in five directions, soaking the seat, the floor and his thighs. He clenched his muscles and cursed as the sticky liquid dried cold on his leg hairs.

Protruding from the eye of his penis, he noticed a tiny white hair. At least, it seemed tiny, certainly less than a half an inch. George grasped the hair between the nails of thumb and forefinger and gave a tug. Then another. The hair kept coming. Eventually he had to use the thumb and forefinger of both hands, pulling as he would a minuscule rope. 'Fuck's sake,' he said to himself. The sensation of a single strand of hair sliding through the internal shaft of his penis was certainly new to him.

When the hair came free (and George felt, for just the slightest fraction of a second, a sense of loss) he held it up to the light, where it drifted in the draught, damp, white, unmistakable, and over six inches long. He had been penetrated, he thought. Fucked in the cock. They hadn't had sex for months, so what was she doing to him in his sleep?

And now, looking down at his penis, he remembers that strand of hair, the feeling of it inside him, and he realizes that some things only ever happen to you once.

At weekends, alone in the house, he thinks about the crates of Beth's belongings. 'Cartons', the man from the storage company had called them. George watches his stylish, impersonal Church Eaton property fall apart. The expensive pine wardrobes gather dust just as quickly as the plastic fold-up chairs in the kitchen. Strangely, for a man formerly so obsessed with fixing things, he does not lift a finger to repair the place. As long as the appliances work he remains content.

While George hides away, Beth's cartons lie in a giant

warehouse on the Derbyshire/Nottinghamshire border. He imagines two red wooden crates, fading to pink now, and slightly battered at the edges. The money still comes out of George's account every month. Perhaps, he thinks, his longstanding order has helped the company to invest in a new carton design. Maybe, in 2003, Beth's red cartons are surrounded by swanky plastic green ones that shift ceaselessly as normal living people move in and out of their homes, get on with their lives. Red and green – a bad clash. George imagines the employees joking about 'the ode red'ns', and the boss reminding them that Mr Cartwright's money keeps them in fags and pints.

As the cartons sit there, mid-morning, George walks through the rooms of his house, unshaven, still losing weight, alive. He has tried to forget them. For years he has ignored his bank statement because the name of the company is printed there. This, he realizes now, is pointless because he never actually forgot the name. *Universal Components*. Such a drolly memorable name, at once banal and industrial, but at the same time so vital and poetic. A name which means nothing and, quite literally, everything – the constituents of the world. After she died, it seemed to George that every word and object resonated in this pathetically significant way. He remembers the symbol on the side of the van, the sphere with the studded rings. An atom, or solar system.

George once dreamed that Universal Components went bust, and the men brought the old sofas, and the crap heavy television and the photographs into his new house and arranged them in the rooms. In the dream, her journals lay in piles of three on the stairs, and her clothes hung from the tops of the doors and swung towards his face. But what difference would it make now?

Her journals.

He has nobody to keep her from any longer. She has surfaced. That was her remarkable trait when she lived: just when you thought you had pinned her down with some easy label (blind, witch, housewife, mental patient), just when you supposed you had dissolved her with a name, she would find another way to *be* in that essential, physical way. After she had bathed, George always had to take a hooded mackintosh into the bathroom, because the steam from her bath and her body would collect on the ceiling and precipitate on his head. He remembers sitting on his toilet listening to that daft patter on the hood. And he remembers how scared he was when he ran his hand over that hairy lamp after she had gone.

You cannot ignore someone stumbling through a crusty field in a green cloak, or strapped to the roof of your house. And now she is back, all around him.

George thinks it is strange, after such a lengthy charade of blamelessness, that he should be unable to convince his son that he, George, was at fault. But he once knew someone more eloquent, with a gift for concise expression and a tendency (which often turned his stomach) to talk plainly and explicitly about difficult matters. Who better to tell the story of his inadequacies, her decline, and their small triumphs?

TWENTY-SIX

On the night she died, a rumour circulated in Blackmoor that Beth had perished from inhaling noxious gas. It was a plausible story, especially given the fire by the loop track – it seemed that Blackmoor was finally collapsing into the subterranean pit of fire that had threatened for so long. The idea that Beth had succumbed to blackdamp contributed to the departure of many families during the next few days. But that night had its own quality – one that proved temporary – and most people returned on hearing of the falsehood of the rumour, feeling slightly embarrassed. The peak of panic proved cathartic, and a week later, Blackmoor was calmer than it had been for some time. Her death was just what they needed.

People got used to the fire by the loop track. The fire brigade regularly tended the surface blaze, cropping it like a privet hedge. The fountains of flame in the Blackmoor imagination had finally sprung forth, and they were not so bad after all. The villagers had survived, had they not? Most of them.

Where were the remaining Cartwrights?

In Corfu. George, suddenly furious, had taken his son on holiday, and even missed the cremation service. He got sunburnt on the soles of his feet. The day they returned, George found Mrs Hargreaves kneeling on the pavement outside his house, scrubbing at the bloodstains by the flower basin. 'Get up,' he told her.

'It has to be done, George, it's only right.'

'Right? Did you wait until we got back on purpose?'

'Don't be disgusting.'

He watched her labour for a while, hating her big arse which stuck in the air. Such a fucking pantomime, he thought. Such lies. As it happened, Mrs Hargreaves's best efforts proved inadequate. Pink foam bubbled under the scrubbing brush. She felt harassed by George's menacing surveillance and her inability to shift the blood. She became aware of the nature of the matter she was dealing with, its utter redundancy. She began to cry, and George went inside, slamming the door.

The coal burnt itself out, and the final few months of village life passed off quietly. A new list of Blackmoor 'lasts' had to be drawn because of the delay: the last wedding and the last birth, the last pint and the final meal. And, of course, those more private final acts, both tender and brutal.

The villagers moved over in small groups as soon as five or six houses were ready on the new estate. Black chipboard in the old windows signified departure. The staggered exodus predictably antagonized those who had to wait longest. The security guards were drafted in to keep addicts from squatting.

The last residents marched out of the village on a dull day in

May 1994, to the tinny sound of the colliery band, now firmly established as the musical harbinger of misfortune and defeat. George and Vincent had moved to Church Eaton the night before. Ironically, the local press grouped George with those few old residents who had rejected New Blackmoor on principle. George Cartwright was presented to the world (or the few people still watching) as a guardian of the old Blackmoor identity.

For nearly two months the village lay dormant, inhabited only by those conquering, garbage-nuzzling foxes. One hundred and twelve years of human habitation left sparse signs: untimely clocks, goalposts and targets chalked on to end terraces. Half-finished bicycles. On the third anniversary of Beth Cartwright's death, Slack Lane stood empty, as did the flower basin outside number five.

The demolition commenced – without the envisaged bang – in July. It took three months of intensive labour. The newspapers of the time stated that very few former residents attended the first day of work. One local columnist commented, perhaps with undue acerbity, that they were 'too upset, or too preoccupied with their new houses'. In fact, most felt that they had spent more than enough time pressed against metal fences, watching stone crumble.

For obvious reasons, explosives could not be used, and this apparent inhibition led the demolition contractors to employ a soft approach. Aware of the sensitive political nature of the operation, JJR Mining described the process as 'eco-friendly'.

Blackmoor was carefully *dismantled* in several stages, to 'allow for the recycling of superior materials'. Roof slates and tiles were stripped and stacked, and some of the older buildings were disassembled brick-by-brick. As usual, a commercial motive soon surfaced. The age and quality of the Derbyshire stone was such that it fetched an excellent price in the trade. Four million bricks and 600,000 roof tiles from the Red Lion, the Miners' Welfare Club, the school and the residential properties of Blackmoor now contribute to the authentic veneer of large town houses in suburban Hertfordshire. Michael Jenkins returned to Blackmoor for the first day of demolition, but disappeared from Derbyshire soon after.

New Blackmoor continues to struggle on in much the same way as all isolated industrial villages in a post-industrial age. Most of the country has forgotten that such people exist, and many of the younger residents do their best to forget they exist too. Not long after the move, their parents became disillusioned with their new habitat. The smirking middle-aged Blackmoorians became old wistful ones, who moaned about the self-enveloping design of the place. As Waggy said, the cul-de-sac was an unfamiliar concept to men and women accustomed to the possibility of shortcuts, and they found themselves, especially in the early days, stomping shamefacedly back the way they came. And what was this vague pervading guilt they felt? Would it ever go?

The opencasting is now complete, the coal has been taken and the land sewn up like a belly. The old village has been landscaped, its former state marked by a wooden bench and a plaque.

As the energy crisis looms ever larger, there is talk of a new seam detected under Old Blackmoor, far deeper than any mined by hand or machine. Researchers have proposed that its energy could be captured using 'underground coal gasification'. It is also said that it may be possible to process the coal using gigantic syringes. Such an absurd, dream-like image, vulgar in its irony in a village where heroin addiction was the result of a government's adjudication that its coal stocks had run out.

TWENTY-SEVEN

Vincent is persistently assaulted by the memory of that night at the kitchen table. He had waited many years for his father to talk, and when he finally did, Vincent could hardly bring himself to listen. The sound of that moody, volatile man becoming suddenly emotional struck Vincent as weak and false. It was like cheating.

Reading the cutting had been an overwhelming experience, but not as hurtful as one might imagine. Vincent could hardly make sense of it (how could anyone?). But hearing his father speak had been far more illuminating.

'It wasn't your fault.'

Those words had changed everything because Vincent had never ('never', in the three hours since finding out) considered himself to be at fault. He *wasn't*. He was just a baby, and it was just an accident. With those four words, things began to make horrible sense. He knew then that his father had blamed him. In the kettle, his father's eyes expanded like those of his late *Betta splendens*, only less aggressive, more fearful. The thin spike of the neck seemed poised to puncture the inflated head. Vincent could no longer look him in the face.

'You never had something and lost it the way I did.'

That was better. That was more like the old Dad. Vincent smiled, and left for the quarry.

These days Vincent goes to the quarry alone, and often after dark, when he knows Leila will not be there. The darkness is no matter, for his feet know JEM woods on their own. The quarry is transformed by night. On the rough footpath near the entrance stands a young beech tree with a streetlight embedded in its spread. He had never noticed it by day, but it is beautiful. The orange bulb backlights the leaves, picks out the veins and the bristly male flowers. Soaked webs look like lasers and the branches scrape the corrugated lamp guard. The whole thing is stunning, at its peak, ready to decline. Leila would have shown him that the tree was nothing but a black claw in winter, a ghoulish candelabra. She would have read from her handbook that the beech is short-lived and falls suddenly to pieces after only a couple of hundred years. But Leila is not there. He will not see her, and skips their English lessons.

In the basin of the quarry, the deferred light is not so uplifting. It has a gooey convalescent glow, like the liquid centre of a throat lozenge. It makes the green dust on the fallen tree seem white. The sound of covert shifting, along with other more urgent noises, rises out of the black fathoms of the woods.

Mostly he spends his time standing on the sandstone bridge, trying to imagine the event described in the cutting. When he is alone, and free from the suspicions and accusations of other people, he approaches these fantasies not with sadness, but with something like wonder, awe. Of course, the report was so vague, and he has so many unanswered questions, that the event assumes an open-ended quality. He lives it out in his mind over and over, making tiny alterations to the scene: his clothes, his mother's hairstyle, the height of the drop. He has been forced into an absent-minded research, picking out articles about bridge suicides, the torn shoulder ligaments of those who change their minds but can't hold on. He reads about a drunk who fell from a hotel window and landed safely in a swimming pool, and an old woman who tripped over her shopping bags, fell the five feet of her own body length and died on her kitchen floor.

A few weeks ago he had no concept of what a toddler looked like. A carer's manual described the mobility of a two-year-old: *Has the capacity to climb, but without a full appreciation of danger.* Recently, Vincent saw a toddler in the supermarket and caught himself imagining the child falling from the striplights, calculating the way the limbs would spread and the head would turn. He laughed at himself.

During these times in the quarry, Vincent generally thinks of his mother's death in calm, abstract terms. It is hard to imagine yourself into something like that. But occasionally the realness of the fall possesses him and makes him wretched. Only once, however, has Vincent contemplated jumping from the sandstone bridge. Leila's voice rang in his head. 'Melodramatically predictable,' it said.

At school, his behaviour worsens. The joint project on Blackmoor is, of course, untenable now, so he cobbles together a folder about Houdini, which is branded 'brief, lazy, inadequate and sarcastic in tone'. Vincent chose to point out that most of the situations from which the great man escaped were of his own making. The last line read, *Many of Houdini's admirers said that he could cheat death. They were wrong.*

As his shoulder improves, however, Vincent discovers that he is a surprisingly elegant and laconic footballer. In fact, now that he doesn't fall over all the time, he becomes quickly renowned for his ability to stay on his feet throughout an entire match. He avoids the physical conflict of the game, and often leaves the pitch, even after summer rainstorms, with clean socks. 'His mum says he's not allowed to get his kit dirty,' says one jealous opponent at the end of PE. The comment is followed by sniggering and whispered explanations. Vincent wonders how much they know.

The number of bullies decreases, but those that remain become more determined. Doubtlessly, the fact that he no longer talks about birds, or carries binoculars, or hangs around with Leila the Sphinx (or 'Sphinx-ster') helps his cause, but Vincent finds that personality and conduct count for nothing if you are good at football. The only problem with his talent is that it seems effortless and deliberately antagonizing, designed to embarrass the humble opponent. He is often accused of 'taking the piss'. This is not Vincent's intention, but he is left-footed, and has recently taught himself to stand up again, two factors which give him unpredictable angles of movement. One day he glides past David Sulley, who swings viciously at clean air, and falls over.

Late in the game, Sulley skids into Vincent's calf, running his studs down over the ankle. It is painful, but also irritating because such acts have earned Sulley the reputation of sporting 'hard-man', but Vincent does not see anything particularly courageous about assaulting someone when they are unprepared and defenceless. So, with a certain fascinated premeditation, Vincent stamps down on the prostrate Sulley's right hand. He feels his studs slide off the bony fingers. Sulley gives a pig-squeal, and looks at his hand in utter shock, as if it is attacking him. John Grain, Sulley's best friend, tries to strike Vincent, but his new allies intervene and a ruck ensues.

Vincent backs away from the scrap, cranes his neck to keep eye contact with Grain, who almost cries with hatred. Vincent watches it all with the mild interest of a window-shopper straining to see beyond his own reflection.

When the teacher has separated the fighting boys, and Sulley's index finger has swelled to resemble some obscure coral plant, they leave the pitch. A hundred yards away, a group of girls comes out of one of the science labs, followed by Leila, still wearing her white lab coat. She looks over at Vincent, who bears the upright of the goalposts across his shoulders. He smiles, but she cannot see his face.

As he walks back from school, the sun seems to follow him, flashing in each window he passes. He leaves the road and takes the river path, where the Derwent blinks like a strip of tinfoil, ringlets of cassette tape and polystyrene cartons caught in the brunt. Now that the violence is spent, Vincent feels exhausted.

He enters through the kitchen door, but what he sees makes

him turn around and leave. Wrong house. But it's not. There is no mistaking the Rorschach blot of oil on the drive from his father's car, or the garage door dented from where he kicked it or the number on the front door, which Vincent looks at, just to check. As he stands outside he cannot recall any single unusual detail from his quick glance into the kitchen. There was only a general sense of wrongness. So he enters again and looks around. Wrong. He concentrates on the omission first. The kitchen table has gone, leaving behind four hoof-like dents in the laminate, eight pence in coins and a line of dust, rice grains and vegetable matter by the skirting board.

Crockery and kitchenware lie in the sink and on the work surfaces: a spice rack, a mug tree, a chopping board with an orange stain in the shape of a dog's paw. Vincent can't recall having seen any of it before, and at this point he is bemused in a fairly careless way. He has more pressing matters to concern him than his father's decision to raid a 1970s junk shop.

It is when he bends down to untie his shoes that he gets the shock. He looks up at the window ledge and sees four wine glasses, two with repaired hairline cracks, one chipped at the lip, and one half-smashed so that it looks like a paper crocus. Where the stem meets the bowl, the glass is thicker and green. The sun bulges within this jade tint like a grin, and the colour and the light grip Vincent's heart. They thump inside his head. He does not know why, or how, but that colour is already within him; it has been found. Something is happening.

A thin chalkboard rests against the cupboard. Vincent, feeling weaker by the second, picks it up and sees the limbs of old semi-scrubbed letters. He can make out what looks like one of his father's capital 'Gs', the unnecessary loop hanging down like a chicken jowl. After some staring through the squiggles he deciphers an entire word: 'You'.

He goes through to the top-floor hallway and finds an old cabinet facing the wall, and a box full of black and white photographs on sugar paper mounts in oval frames. 'What?' he says. His voice sounds different, bouncing off the new objects. The acoustics have changed in here. The echo has softened. The photographs are old, formal portraits of men in shoddy three-piece suits standing behind stern seated women. He looks at a few, indifferently. He fails to recognize his infant mother. Vincent has only seen pictures of her as an adult, and is incapable of imagining her at any different age. Even so, the baby in the cumbersome frilly dress is worth a second look. On black and white film she is a radiant blankness emanating from Helen Fisher's plump lap. She is so white she is almost a colour.

When he looks down the small staircase into the living room, he remembers the sofas. It is strange to remember something when you are looking at it. Green corduroy sofas. As he descends, he knows how the cushions will feel under his hand. The sofas look just as out of place in this modern new-build as the big leather monster did, belittled by the high white walls. A table sits between them, marked by a star of white paint.

Over by the window, curtains with the faint design of peacocks are spread like a rug. Vincent can see where his dad ripped the other curtains down, taking some of the white plastic rings from the runner. The peacock curtains are the kind that need a pole.

On the windowsill is a lamp with a bone-coloured canvas

shade. There are claw marks on it, as though someone was hanging on for dear life. Flecks of white dust rise from the lamp and sparkle in the tube of sunlight burrowing into the room. Vincent stands back and watches this busy display of illuminated matter. He sees the dust settle on the banister, this new material already taking root in the house.

Vincent lopes across the room, stands at the French doors and looks down into the garden. The leather sofa lies upturned on the bottom plateau of grass, a sparrow trying to land on one of its swinging metal wheels. Piles of black bin-bags surround it, and in the afternoon sun, the effect is of a tarry pool. Other items formerly of this house have been abandoned. His father's wardrobe rests on its back, a brown shirt lolling from its doors like a tongue. Various gas-lift and flat-pack chairs sit casually, in the formation of a garden party at the end of the night. For the moment, Vincent prefers to stare outside rather than confront the huddle behind him. After all, his most vivid memories are linked to the furniture at the end of the garden. As he stands there now he recalls his father picking the leather flakes from the armrest. He thinks of the time his father fell asleep on the sofa with the French doors open, and Vincent found him in the morning, summer drizzle slanting in against his legs. The back wall had been covered with insects. There must have been a hundred of them, slim diaphanous vials of blue or yellow or green, with clear folded wings.

Let us leave him to his memories for a moment, for soon enough it will be dark, and the houselights will be lit, and Vincent will have the reflections of the room forced upon him by the glass of the French doors. Until then, let us ascend the small staircase, and then descend another to his bedroom. Yes, *his* bedroom now, with one single bed. The shoeboxes are stacked in the corner, by the globe lamp he recently purchased. Soon he will take a sea-green exercise book at random, and read.

This morning, our lawn is smoking . . .

Who can calculate the effect of her words? Vincent will reach no easy conclusion. He will develop a sense of 18 June, the day to which his mother's journals build, as a sort of personal nativity. He will look upon those hours, and the attendant characters, as forging him. But he will also come quite quickly to an impasse: he will be able to conjure stories of a boy in the flowers, knocked out by the fall (as his father suggested), but he will have to admit the possibility, no, the likelihood, that he hadn't been unconscious at all, that he had lain there staring up at the curtains when she stepped through the window. He will have to allow that there exists, somewhere in his memory, the vision of his mother falling to her death. And that misplaced image, he will think, contains the solution to the whole mystery, the secret of her end. He had once known whether she had looked down on him, safe in the flower basin. He had known whether her eyes had been closed or open, if she jumped as a bereaved mother or a miserable woman. If her last second of sight had been her dead son, or his miraculous landing in the flowers. He will never access that memory; it will elude him for ever. That is his loss, and he will come to realize that loss far exhausts blame.

The hours pass, and new shadows fall. In the shoe cupboard, Vincent finds a bulb for the lamp but fails to see an ancient, crumbling, child's slipper. Out in the garden, the spewed contents of their broken home become a dark hulk, and beyond the fence, clusters of orange light prick the blue dusk. When Vincent was a child, he always thought those streetlights were the reason the district was called Amber Valley. He remembers what his father once told him, drunk: if you look really hard, a black hole the size of a postage stamp deepens where the old village used to be. Vincent is old enough to know that is not true.